ADVANCE PRAISE FOR

GOLD
MOUNTAIN

"Ling Fan felt like my indomitable best friend—I was rooting for
her as she faced impossible stakes and truly terrifying villainy.
I loved this book!"

—Karen Bao, author of The Dove Chronicles series

"*Gold Mountain* is the unforgettable tale of Tam Ling Fan: a story
of strength, courage, and resilience that not only brings the past
to vivid, complex life, but has much to say about the present. Set
within the perilous world of nineteenth-century Chinese sojourners
building the Transcontinental Railroad, Ling Fan's journey is
thrilling, engrossing, and moving. I couldn't put it down."

—Kate Racculia, author of *Bellweather Rhapsody*

UNTAIN

BETTY G. YEE

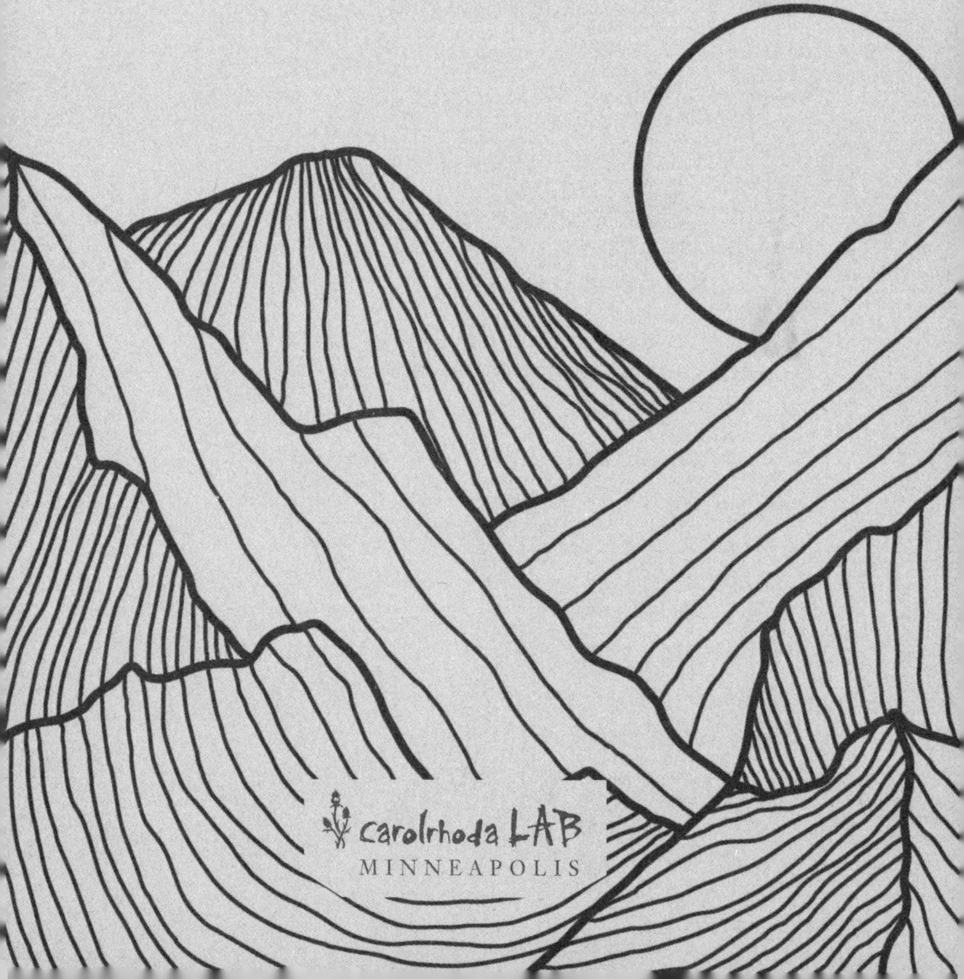

carolrhoda LAB
MINNEAPOLIS

Carolrhoda Lab®
An imprint of Lerner Publishing Group, Inc.
241 First Avenue North
Minneapolis, MN 55401 USA

For reading levels and more information, look up this title at
www.lernerbooks.com.

Image credits: vectortwins/Shutterstock.com (mountains);
aekky/Shutterstock.com (texture).

Main body text set in Janson Text LT Std.
Typeface provided by Adobe Systems.

Library of Congress Cataloging-in-Publication Data

Names: Yee, Betty G., 1966– author.
Title: Gold mountain / by Betty G. Yee.
Description: Minneapolis : Carolrhoda Lab, [2022] | Audience: Ages 11–18. | Audience: Grades 7–9. | Summary: Fifteen-year-old Tam Ling Fan disguises herself as her twin brother, journeys from her village in China to California, and works as a laborer on the Transcontinental Railroad—where she faces danger on multiple fronts—to earn the money her family desperately needs. Includes author's note.
Identifiers: LCCN 2021016023 | ISBN 9781728415826 (lib. bdg.)
Subjects: CYAC: Foreign workers—Fiction. | Chinese—United States—Fiction. | Disguise—Fiction. | Railroads—Fiction. | Sabotage—Fiction. | Central Pacific Railroad Company—Fiction. | Sierra Nevada (Calif. and Nev.)—History—19th century—Fiction.
Classification: LCC PZ7.1.Y436 Go 2022 | DDC [Fic]—dc23

LC record available at https://lccn.loc.gov/2021016023

Manufactured in the United States of America
1-48775-49186-10/7/2021

FOR BAKE QUIN AND SUY KUE.

AND FOR THE UNNAMED WORKERS OF
THE TRANSCONTINENTAL RAILROAD.

CHAPTER 1

They came in the darkness of early morning.

The hammering at the front door echoed through the courtyard and rolled up to the second floor where Tam Ling Fan's family slept. It startled her brother, Jing Fan, awake and made his coughing start up again. Across the hall, Ling Fan pushed her silk quilt aside and thrust her feet into her slippers. She lit a taper from the brazier burning in a corner of her room and stepped into the corridor. Baba passed her, a lantern in his hand.

"Stay here," Baba told her quietly. He was still in his daytime attire, a long gray tunic edged with silk. "Take this." He pressed a piece of folded paper into her hand. She knew without looking that it was the railroad contract. "Keep it safe."

Grotesque shadows flickered along the walls as he descended to the lower level. Ling Fan hurried to the low latticed wall overlooking the courtyard. From there she saw Baba cross to the outer door and unlatch it. The door flew open and four men pushed inside. Two held lanterns suspended from long bamboo handles, while the other two seized Baba's arms.

"How dare you put your hands on the magistrate?" Ling Fan shouted down at them. She made a dash for the staircase, but somebody grabbed her arm. Aunt Fei had slipped out of her room, silent as a gui. Her grip was like a clamp, but her eyes were bright with fear. Ling Fan tried to shake her off.

"Don't!" Aunt Fei hissed, drawing her back into the shadows. Ling Fan couldn't see the men below now, but she could hear them.

"Tam Chung Ha, you are under arrest for conspiring with the outlawed Taiping Rebellion," a tenor voice declared. Ling Fan would've gasped, but her aunt had clapped a hand over her mouth. She knew that voice. It was Ghong Fok, Baba's second in command. What was this nonsense? The rebellion had ended almost three years ago, back in 1864. And her father had had nothing to do with it!

"Is it conspiracy," Baba asked calmly, "to refuse to execute a poor man for stealing rice to feed his family?" There was no fear in his voice.

"It is when that order came from the provincial prefect," Ghong Fok replied. "But you can explain that to him." To the men restraining Baba, he added, "Bring him."

No scuffle, no sounds of struggle. The outer door closed softly, leaving Ling Fan and Aunt Fei alone with the sound of Jing Fan's coughs.

CHAPTER
2

One more. One more would do it.

Ling Fan kept her eyes on the cluster of oranges that hung on the branch just above her head. Gingerly, she took a step onto the slender branch that grew just below, keeping a tight grip on the leaves behind her with one hand while she reached out as far as she could with the other. Her fingertips brushed the fruit; she set it swaying on its stem. She slid her bare foot out farther onto the branch and felt it bow beneath her weight. At the same time, she heard a loud crack. Ling Fan threw herself back against the trunk with a gasp, her heart beating in her throat.

She looked down through the leaves of the tree. The ground was very far way. Ling Fan swallowed and closed her eyes, cursing her plan to steal Widow Chang's oranges.

She wished with all her heart that her twin brother, Jing Fan, were with her now. He was the brave one. The smart one. The strong one. All their lives she had run after him, copying everything he did, but now that he was gone, she knew she had never been anything but his shadow.

"Aiya!" a voice shouted from below. "What are you doing up there? Get out!"

Ling Fan cracked one eye open just enough to see Widow Chang's old manservant glaring up at her from the base of the tree. In one hand he held a lantern to ward off the early-morning darkness, and in the other he clutched a long bamboo pole with two sharp hooks at the end.

"Get out!" he shouted again, thrusting the pole at her as though she were a pesky animal. Ling Fan scrambled from branch to branch, one arm hugging her bundle of oranges close as she dodged the pole's hooks. Finally, she reached a branch that hovered just above the stone wall that surrounded Widow Chang's orchard. She hopped onto the wall and shimmied down awkwardly. Once on the ground, she ran as fast as she could without looking back.

Ling Fan flew down winding dirt paths through the sleeping village of Lo Wai. Past the well, over the little footbridge that crossed the brook, past vegetable gardens and storage sheds. Finally she had to stop because of the stitch in her side. She squatted down and tried to calm her ragged breath enough so she could listen. No sound of running feet behind her. Sweat and panic drained out of her and left her feeling weak with relief.

Ling Fan opened the cloth sack. Seven enormous oranges stared back at her. Eight would have been better. The number eight was auspicious, and Ling Fan felt that she needed all the good fortune she could find. Still, seven was better than none.

She shouldered the sack and continued to the passageway that connected several homes in the village. It was meant to serve as an escape route from attacking bandits, but Ling Fan had often used it to sneak in and out of her house undetected.

The sky lightened as she climbed a set of steps that led to a narrow passageway in the back of her house. Ling Fan ducked into her bedroom as the rooster next door bawled its morning greeting.

The surge of energy from running through the village disappeared. Pearly gray light filtered through the lattice window, revealing her writing table, her chair, and her chest of clothes in the corner. The light made everything look as though she was seeing it underwater. Ling Fan felt like she was underwater too.

Down the hall, something shattered on the floor. Ling Fan ran to the kitchen, where she found Aunt Fei bent over the remains of a broken bowl. Tangerines from Jing Fan's funeral altar had rolled every which way across the floor.

"Aunt Fei!"

"It's all right," Aunt Fei said. Her head was bowed. A wisp of gray-streaked hair had escaped the bun clasped tightly at her neck. Although she was Baba's older sister, Fei was not an old woman. Still, the past two months had worn deep lines into her face. "I knocked over the incense burner, that's all. I'm so clumsy." She stood awkwardly, balancing on her tiny bound feet, clutching the shards of the broken bowl. "What's that?" Aunt Fei pointed with her chin at the sack that Ling Fan still held.

"Oranges. I thought if we gave some to the guards at the prison, they might be more willing to let us see Baba today." She spoke quickly, hoping her aunt wouldn't ask how she had gotten them.

"Aiya!" Aunt Fei *tsk*ed and shook her head dismissively. "Well, you'd better get ready to go. We have to be at the village gate when Farmer Tan comes around with his cart." At least she hadn't thought to wonder where Ling Fan had come by such fine fruit.

Ling Fan retraced her steps down the drafty hall to her room. The heavy scent of incense was everywhere. It hung in every corner of their house, buried itself in her hair, clung to the fibers of her clothing, and followed her whenever she went out into the village. Ling Fan imagined that if ghosts had any scent at all, it would be the thick, sweet odor of incense.

Her brother had never liked the smell. If he was up in heaven now, he'd be waving a fan and holding his nose as the earthly gray-white plumes of smoke brought him his money, his food, and the best wishes of his living family. Ling Fan smiled despite herself. It was easier to think of her brother swatting at smoke than to feel the hole that seemed to be eating her from the inside out.

Jing Fan had been dead for a week. Ling Fan knew that, but she still caught herself listening for his voice or expecting to see him come around a corner. She caught herself saving up bits of news and snippets of gossip to tell him when she saw him next. He had been her best friend; they told each other everything. Now, when there was so much to say, there was nobody to say it to. She felt ready to explode.

Ling Fan sat down at her writing table and stared at her pen and ink set. Ever since they learned how to write, she and her brother would leave messages for each other on scraps of paper. A joke here, a good-natured insult there. She missed finding his notes almost as much as hearing his voice.

The heavy scent of incense made her head ache. She thought of all the scraps of joss paper money the family had burned earlier that week, the sweet smoke carrying it all to Jing Fan in heaven. Aunt Fei had even fashioned tiny pieces of paper clothing for him. If all those things could get to him, couldn't her own words reach him the same way?

She took out her calligraphy pen, a brush made with the finest goat and weasel hair. She mixed some water in the ink and dipped the pen into it. On a scrap of paper, she wrote,

Baba is still in prison. Aunt Fei and I are going to Peng Lu this morning to give him the news about you. What's going to happen now?

She rolled the paper up tightly and thrust it deep into her brazier. The edges of the paper caught the flame, and black smoke started to curl upward. The acrid smoke was nothing like incense, but for the first time in days Ling Fan felt her shoulders relax as she watched it rise, knowing that her brother would receive her news. She wondered what he would say if he could answer.

Perhaps he would remind her that Ghong Fok would never admit Baba was innocent, and that the provincial authorities could keep Baba locked up for the rest of his life. They'd made it clear that Baba would only be freed in exchange for an enormous bribe—tens of thousands of wen. Perhaps Jing Fan would apologize for not being alive to earn that money.

If he hadn't died, he would've been Baba's salvation. He would've gone to America with the railroad contract that Baba had gone to such trouble to get for him, made a fortune in America—the legendary Gold Mountain—and returned with more than enough to secure Baba's release. Instead . . .

"Ling, hurry up!" Fei called.

Ling Fan pulled on a quilted jacket over her loose cotton tunic and trousers. She pushed her feet into a pair of cotton shoes as she replaited her hair. As she hurried from the room, she saw, out of a corner of her eye, a reflection glide across the dusty surface of the mirror by her doorway. Jing, she thought reflexively before the icy shard of memory made her flinch. She turned her face resolutely away.

Looking at herself was still too much like looking at her brother. She would see his strong square jaw, his thick eyebrows over honey-brown eyes. She would see his thin lips that

7

quirked into an easy smile. Looking at herself was like looking at a ghost.

Ling Fan met her aunt in the front courtyard by the little koi pond. Aunt Fei was wearing her heaviest padded jacket, a blue one embroidered with silver cherry blossoms, and had tied a scarf over her hair. Together, they stepped through their compound's outer door and onto the path that wound through the village.

They walked slowly, Ling Fan matching her stride to her aunt's elegant, swaying gait. Years ago, her aunt—like most girls of their class—had undergone the excruciating foot-binding process. Now, walking anywhere on her five-inch feet was an ordeal, but Fei maintained that her Golden Lotuses were worth the agony. They were her greatest source of vanity and the cause of countless arguments with Ling Fan's father. He had insisted his daughter would never be subjected to what he considered a brutal act of mutilation.

As a little girl, Ling Fan had been fascinated by her aunt's tiny feet. She and Jing Fan used to dare each other to steal Fei's embroidered shoes from her bedroom. Ling Fan loved how the beautiful silk shoes were not much bigger than her own small hand, the pointed toes ending just beyond the tip of her middle finger. Her aunt told her romantic tales of how men swooned over women who had the perfect Golden Lotuses, whose gait reminded them of beautiful flowers swaying in the wind. Ling Fan spent hours imitating the elegant swaying stride of women walking on their bound feet.

All that changed the day Ling Fan's cousin Ming started the process. Ling Fan would never forget seven-year-old Ming weeping over the pain and begging her mother to undo the linen cloths that were tightened around her folded feet day after day. Secretly, Ling Fan was glad that her father had forbidden it.

She realized now that in this, as in so many other things, her father thought differently than most of the villagers. Could this be why they hadn't objected to his arrest?

Ling Fan and Aunt Fei passed the Lo family's mud-brick house. The door gaped open, and the single window stared blankly out at them. Two days ago, the Lo family had piled all their possessions into a wheelbarrow and headed deeper into the countryside, trying to flee the illness that had fallen on the village like raiding bandits.

Ling Fan kicked at a large lump of coal, trying to get it to roll down the path. She could feel her aunt's silent disapproval but kept at it anyway. They passed two more houses that stood silent and empty. Normally, the village would be bustling with activity: people scattering grain for chickens, gathering vegetables from their garden, or leading goats or oxen to the nearby stream. Today, Ling Fan counted only a handful of villagers scattered here and there, looking like lost gui in the early-morning fog. One of them was Widow Chang.

Widow Chang's compound was near the center of the village, at the juncture of its three main paths. Nobody entered or left Lo Wai without passing her home, and it was Widow Chang's pleasure to know of everyone's comings and goings and doings. Jing Fan used to say Widow Chang was like a giant spider sitting on her web.

This morning, Widow Chang was sweeping in front of her compound, but when she saw Ling Fan and her aunt coming down the path, she went inside and closed the door. Ling Fan saw her standing at a window, looking out at them as they passed.

Ling Fan held the sack of oranges closer to herself and drew the sleeves of her jacket over her hands. The fabric caught against the half-healed scabs on her knuckles.

A few nights before Jing Fan died, Ling Fan had gone to Widow Chang's to beg for some of the medicinal herbs that grew in her garden. She'd hammered at the door until her knuckles bled, but Widow Chang never answered. Later, the widow was heard telling neighbors that she'd been out tending other sick folk, but Ling Fan remembered seeing the light in the widow's window go out when she started knocking. Losing a few oranges was the least the old woman deserved.

Ling Fan wanted to kick the lump of broken coal at Widow Chang's house, but Aunt Fei gripped her elbow, as though she knew what Ling Fan was thinking, and led her onward.

A year ago, Ling Fan's family had walked through the village like royalty. People were always giving them little presents: a branch of lychee nuts, a bag of apples, a wooden toy bought at the market. But now that Baba had been taken away to Peng Lu Prison, people turned away from their greetings and whispered things that Aunt Fei told Ling Fan not to believe.

For weeks, Ling Fan had perched on the end of her brother's bed, talking late into the night, trying to piece together the truth. They agreed that the accusations against Baba were ridiculous. True, he often disagreed with the emperor's government, but he firmly believed that violence was never an option. "There are other ways to bring about change," he'd always told Ling Fan. "With the right lever, you can move the world."

And it was true that Baba had many unconventional ideas. Letting Ling Fan learn side by side with her brother was one example. Refusing to have her feet bound was another. She'd often heard him arguing with Ghong Fok about the nuances of the emperor's laws. More than once Ghong Fok had stormed out of Baba's study, fuming that Baba was far too lenient with criminals.

It had been Ghong Fok who led the charge against her father. Ling Fan suspected he had tired of arguing with Baba and had decided to simply sweep him aside. He'd succeeded. Nobody had raised a voice or hand to help Baba. She wished she had a dozen pieces of coal to kick at the people who'd turned their backs on her family.

They arrived at the village gate, an ornamental arch guarded by a pair of fierce stone lions. The sun's rays were just turning the layer of early spring clouds a warm peachy glow when Farmer Tan drew up beside them in his oxcart. Ling Fan and her aunt climbed onto the back of the cart and settled down amidst his piles of winter melon, white radishes, and yams. The market was five miles away, along one branch of the Pearl River, just beyond Peng Lu Prison.

Every Thursday for the past month, Ling Fan and her aunt had ridden in Farmer Tan's cart, arriving at the prison just after the sun came up. They stood in a little hall along with a few other ragged visitors waiting for a chance to see a relative or friend. After a while, a guard would come out of an inner room and read a name or two from a list in his hand. The lucky visitors were led deeper into the prison. Everyone else was told to come again the following week.

Last Thursday, Ling Fan had seen a barefoot man press a package into the guard's hand. A moment later, that same man had been ushered in for a visit. Afterward, it was all she could think about. She wondered what had been in the package. Not money—it had been far too large, and the man far too poor. Whatever it was, it gave Ling Fan a ray of hope. There was more than one way to open the door to see Baba. And she was ready to play the game.

The next afternoon she'd spotted the oranges hanging

from a high branch in Widow Chang's orchard. Big beautiful ones, the color of summer dawn. Oranges were scarce this year, and Widow Chang guarded her orchard as carefully as a pile of gold. So Ling Fan had resolved to climb over the wall and steal them.

Now Ling Fan hugged the sack to her chest and made herself breathe as the guard emerged with his list. She had to try. She had to see her father!

She pushed forward and managed to bump the guard's elbow sharply. When he glanced at her, she tipped her sack open just enough to reveal the treasure within. The guard snorted, but a dizzying moment later, he was taking the bundle of oranges and gesturing for Ling Fan and Aunt Fei to move deeper into the prison. Ling Fan's heart leapt.

Once the outer door closed behind them, the guard led them to a smaller room. "Who have you come to see?"

"Tam Chung Ha," Ling Fan said, hating how much her voice wavered.

"Wait here." He stepped out and closed the door. His footsteps echoed down the hall.

Only one chair sat in the room. A window was set high in the wall where pale light peered in, barely pushing back the shadows in the corners. Chipped plaster clung to the walls like half-healed sores. Ling Fan paced from one end of the room to the other, energy coursing through her, making her entire body tingle. She couldn't help grinning in triumph at her aunt. "It worked! My plan worked!"

Aunt Fei grunted. "We were lucky. Besides, it was only a matter of time before it was our turn anyway." She gestured at the chair and said, "Sit down," in the fussy tone she used when she had nothing else to say or do.

Ling Fan shook her head, fighting back a surge of resentment. It had been like this all her life. If her brother had been the one to think of offering oranges to the guard, Aunt Fei would've praised his ingenuity.

Aunt Fei sighed and sank into the chair, wincing at the pain in her feet. Ling Fan hovered near the door, listening to the sounds in the hallway. She tensed every time she heard heavy booted steps, shuffled steps, steps followed by metallic rattles. Worst of all were the steps that sounded like a sack of rice being dragged across the floor.

At last, the door scraped open. Aunt Fei started to get up but sank down again, her hands at her throat as though something was caught there.

Baba had been arrested only two months ago, but the man in the doorway looked ten years older and a foot shorter. Baba had never been a large man, yet he had a way of filling a room. The man in the doorway was shrunken. His clothes clung to his thin, bent body. Strands of iron-gray hair had escaped his queue, straggling around his shoulders like limp snakes framing a gaunt, ashen face. His beard, once so silky and carefully groomed, was now a greasy mass below his chin. Flat black eyes flickered over Aunt Fei, past Ling Fan, then around the room, searching.

The guard pushed him into the room. "Ten minutes," he told them, dragging the door closed again. The gray man fell to the floor.

"Baba!" Ling Fan gasped.

Aunt Fei launched herself at him and plucked at his body. "Help me lift him!"

Ling Fan managed to get him onto the chair. Fei pulled a bottle from an inner pocket of her padded jacket and held it to his lips. He closed his eyes and drank until tea flowed down his chin and into his tangled beard.

"Jing?" His voice sounded harsh and dry. "Where is Jing?"

Aunt Fei burst into tears.

Ling Fan forced the words out. "Baba." Her voice cracked. Tears welled behind her eyes but she willed herself to stay strong for her father's sake. "Jing is dead. The influenza took him a week ago."

The man in the chair seemed to collapse in on himself. His head fell into hands. Something deep in Ling Fan's stomach twisted when a low moan rattled from his throat. It took a moment before she realized he was weeping. She had never seen him cry—not even on that bleak day ten years ago when he told Ling Fan and Jing Fan about their mother's death.

She knelt by his side and took his hands. Her throat was a tight knot, but her eyes were hot and dry as she focused on letting her father know, through her grip, that she was there.

"It seems half the village is sick with the fever," Aunt Fei said, "and the other half has fled to get away from it."

Baba scrubbed his face with his hands and spoke in a dull, flat voice. "What about Old Man Bao? Has he run away?" Old Man Bao was the wealthiest farmer in Lo Wai. His compound walls encircled three buildings as well as a garden. He kept a dozen giant koi in his pond. Ling Fan and her brother used to spend long summer evenings poking at them with sticks while Baba and Old Man Bao smoked pipes and talked, back when the two men were still friendly.

"Not yet," Aunt Fei said. "Though they haven't left their compound or received visitors since the outbreak started. Some people think they have enough food to last half the year."

Baba sat very still. Only his eyes moved, flicking back and

forth as though he were reading an invisible book. Ling Fan had often seen him like this at his worktable back home.

"Do you still have the railroad contract?" he whispered urgently. Ling Fan nodded.

"That wretched thing?" Aunt Fei sniffed. "Of course, but what good is it to us now?"

Ling Fan thought of the contract she had hidden in her brother's room the night Baba was arrested. On one side was one of the ubiquitous handbills that advertised railroad work in America. But on the other side was a handwritten note that bore the stamped seal of Li Hing Gold Mountain, one the most prestigious American trading firms. It promised paid transport to America, a job working for a railroad company, and aid in sending money back to China.

"That contract is the key to everything," Baba insisted. He closed his eyes, taking a deep breath that shook his entire body. When he opened his eyes, he looked at Ling Fan. "Ling, listen to me."

She waited. Thin light from the window high above fell across her father's face, making it difficult to fully make out his expression. It was easier to trace the frayed edges of his shirt collar with her eyes while he spoke.

"The provincial authorities only care about money. With enough of it, we could pay the right people to look the other way, lose paperwork, shorten a prison sentence."

Ling Fan thought of how seven oranges had smoothed the way to seeing him today. She could easily imagine that American gold would be enough to bribe officials to free Baba.

"But now Jing is gone," Aunt Fei said bitterly. "That dream of earning a fortune on the railroad has turned to smoke."

Baba flinched but otherwise ignored his sister. He put his

hands gently on Ling Fan's shoulders. "There is more than one way to turn the contract into money. It's our best chance—our only chance. Otherwise, I have no doubt I will never leave this prison. Not while I'm living."

Ling Fan had known in a corner of her mind how serious her father's situation was, but for the past few weeks she'd gotten through each day by telling herself that his arrest was just temporary, that everything would be straightened out in time. Now she felt as though all the air had been sucked out of the room. Her lungs and heart seemed ready to burst. She tried to swallow, but her throat had gone bone dry. Baba was still talking, and she struggled to pay attention.

"The ancestors smiled on us the day your brother and you were born," he said softly. "Twins! Your spirits were so much alike. Jing was always on some adventure. And wherever he went, you were at his side." For the first time since he entered the room, he smiled at her. Ling Fan's eyes filled with tears. "It was like having two boys."

Somewhere in the prison, a heavy door swung on shrieking, rusty hinges and slammed shut with a clang that shook the entire building. Ling Fan heard footsteps in the corridor beyond their room. They were almost out of time.

Her father sighed. "But you're not a boy, Ling. And I was wrong to let you carry on as though you were just like Jing. It's time you did your duty as a woman. Do your duty to your family. Obey your aunt; she has your best interests at heart."

Before Ling Fan could respond, Baba turned back to Aunt Fei.

"Go to Old Man Bao. You know what to do."

Fei nodded.

"But what can Old Man Bao—" Ling Fan started to ask.

The door opened. The guard who had brought them in entered and seized Baba under the arm.

"Don't—!" Ling Fan shouted, reaching for her father, but the guard shoved her hard against the wall, knocking the breath out of her. She could only watch as her father was dragged away like a pile of gray rags.

This time the guard didn't bother to close the door behind him.

Aunt Fei sat in the chair and sobbed softly. Ling Fan stood behind her, rubbing at the pain in her side where she'd been slammed into the wall. It felt as though something had taken a bite out of her.

Eventually the guard returned. "Come on. Time for you to go."

They shuffled after him—down another corridor, up a short flight of steps, and through a doorway that opened into an overgrown garden. The prison compound had once been the sumptuous home of a wealthy prefect. Baba had once told Ling Fan that in its glory days during the Ming dynasty, the compound had held a dozen pavilions, a lake crossed by a majestic zigzag bridge, and a magnificent rockery. The prefect's family had long ago been executed, or exiled—Ling Fan couldn't remember which. All that was left was a maze of broken walkways and a weed-choked pond. Iron-studded wooden doors closed in most of the buildings, and heavy shutters covered the windows.

Once she and Aunt Fei were outside the compound, Ling Fan felt a rush of relief, mixed with anguish. Baba was still in there, relying on her to help him . . . somehow.

They had to walk back to Lo Wai. It was torture for Aunt Fei's feet, so they paused often to rest. At midday they stopped by a small stand of willow trees that grew beside the path. There they shared a cold meal of rice and yams, passing Aunt Fei's bottle of tea back and forth.

They ate in silence while Ling Fan mulled over her father's words.

All her life she had chased after her brother, going everywhere he went, doing everything he did, even sitting in on his English lessons and practicing the language with him afterward. Aunt Fei had made her disapproval clear, but Baba brushed any objections aside. Ling Fan believed he was secretly proud of how easily she kept up with her brother. But once the twins turned fourteen, Aunt Fei stepped in with new rules. "Girls don't" was something Ling Fan heard more and more. When she complained to her father, to her shock, he started to side with Aunt Fei. Now, it seemed he wanted Ling Fan to submit fully to her aunt's restrictions. But how would that help Baba?

The shadows along the path were starting to lengthen by the time they reached the lion gate. At home, the familiar scent of old incense enveloped them as they stepped over the threshold. In her room, Ling Fan saw the paper she'd left behind that morning. She poured more water onto her ink and stirred it with her pen. With quick strokes, she wrote a few words.

We'll find a way.

CHAPTER 3

Ling Fan woke to the sound of dumplings sizzling in the kitchen. Aunt Fei was up early, cooking breakfast, and the smell of green onions in the wok made Ling Fan's stomach growl. Better get up now before Jing Fan got to the table first. She was halfway out of bed when the memory of the past few weeks flooded over her again.

She buried her face in her pillow so that Aunt Fei wouldn't hear her weeping. She wasn't sure which was worse: knowing that Baba and Jing Fan were gone, or thinking for just a moment that she had her old life again only to remember the truth.

Momo, the village cat, jumped lightly onto the bed and licked Ling Fan's ear. Voices in the kitchen—Fei's and cousin Ming's—reminded her that today was the Qingming festival. The family was supposed to visit Jing Fan's grave later that morning. She needed to bathe and dress quickly. Reluctantly, she pushed aside her heavy quilt and got out of bed.

∧ ∧ ∧

The kitchen was filled with pungent cooking smoke. Ming stood at the brick stove, stirring vegetables in the great wok while she talked to her mother in hushed tones. Aunt Fei was arranging the basket of tangerines and pastries that the family would bring to the cemetery for Qingming, the annual tomb-sweeping festival. Ling Fan hugged her cousin gingerly, careful of her bulging stomach.

"Good, you're up," Aunt Fei said. "I need you and Ming to fetch some more incense from the storeroom at Ming's house." It was still strange to think of Ming as living somewhere else. Ling Fan could barely remember a time before she'd shared a home with her cousin. Ming was like a sister, growing up beside the twins in the Tam family compound after her own father died in a farm accident.

Ming led the way down the lane, though Ling Fan could've easily outpaced her. Long before they reached the house, Ming was breathing heavily and smoothing her stomach as though to comfort the baby within. Ming's wedding had only been eight months ago, and now she was five months pregnant. All the villagers had showered words of congratulations on the couple as though they had suddenly found a pile of gold in the street.

Ling Fan knew she was supposed to be glad for her cousin, but she missed the mischievous, boisterous girl she had grown up with. Before her feet were bound, Ming had been able to run faster than either of the twins. She could spit watermelon seeds farther than anyone in the village and loved to yell good-natured insults at the sailors in the boats on the river. Ming came up with the best games. "Escape the Bandits" was a favorite, one that often got them in trouble because it involved hiding on the little-used stairs and passages that connected their compound to several others. The passages were meant to be used to evade actual bandits, Aunt Fei chided, not for games. Now, Ming spent most of her time at the beck and call of her mother-in-law, doing chores around her new home. She was always tired when Ling Fan visited her, always rubbing her aching Golden Lotuses.

As they walked Ming asked, "What happened at Peng Lu?"

Ling Fan told her. She had just gotten to Baba's cryptic instructions to Aunt Fei when they reached the Fa family's compound.

Lao Fa Seem, Ming's mother-in-law, was at the kitchen doorway, tossing out a bucket of dirty water. She was a large-boned woman who was younger than Aunt Fei, but the dour lines of her face made her look a decade older. She glared at Ming as the cousins passed by on their way to the storage shed. "Back already?" she remarked coolly. Breathlessly, Ming explained their errand. "Mind you keep track of how many she uses," Lao Fa Seem warned. "I expect as many back next week."

"Of course, Mother-in-Law," Ming replied, ducking her head. She added under her breath, so that only Ling Fan would hear, "You selfish old cow." Ling Fan giggled, but in truth the tension between the two always made her uncomfortable.

Ming yanked open the door to the shed and they stepped into the dusty room. "Do you remember how we used to pretend there were demons hiding in here?" Ling Fan said.

"I remember the time my mother thought Jing had fallen into the well and drowned but he was really in here the whole day, sound asleep while everyone was out looking for him," Ming said. "He came out covered in dust and cobwebs and Popo thought he was a real-life gui! I never thought a little old lady like Popo could scream that loudly." They laughed until Ling Fan felt tears rolling down her cheeks. She brushed them aside impatiently.

Ming pretended not to notice and changed the subject. "Are you sure your father told Mama to talk to Old Man Bao?"

When Ling Fan nodded, Ming said, "The Bao clan might not be as wealthy as they once were, but they still have some political connections. Maybe they think Old Man Bao can influence the provincial authorities to release your father."

Ling Fan felt a flicker of hope that instantly sputtered out. After the events of the last few weeks, optimism felt foolish, childish.

"Even if Old Man Bao could help us, why would he? He and Baba haven't been on good terms for years." And, Ling Fan thought bitterly, Old Man Bao certainly hadn't protested when her father was arrested.

"He would only do it if he or his family could somehow benefit from it," Ming agreed. "Look how they've shut themselves into their compound while the rest of the village sickened around them."

"Cowards!" Furiously, Ling Fan kicked at a sack of rice in the corner. Then she imagined Widow Chang's face on the side of the sack of rice and kicked again.

Ming continued to search for the incense they'd been sent to find. At last she reached into a dust-caked jar and pulled out three packages wrapped in paper. "Here it is. Come on, we'd better hurry. Mama will want to leave for the cemetery soon."

Ling followed her cousin back home, her mind turning over the events of the past few weeks. No matter how she looked at it, everything seemed hopeless.

In the courtyard, they saw two servants stationed by a sedan chair. The chair was elegant but worn; the elaborate lacquer design was chipped in several places. As the cousins stared at the unusual sight, Aunt Fei emerged from the kitchen with a tall, silver-haired man. He bowed to Aunt Fei and climbed into the sedan chair, which the servants carried off.

"What was Lao Hong doing here?" Ming wondered aloud. "I haven't seen him since he helped arrange my marriage."

The village matchmaker.

Ling Fan's stomach plunged. There could only be one reason he'd come here.

But she had no time to absorb the thought, because Aunt Fei was calling to them to help her finish packing for their visit to the cemetery.

∧ ∧ ∧

The cold little breeze that had followed them home from Peng Lu Prison the day before chased them up the winding road that led to the village graveyard. It swirled around them when they came to Jing Fan's grave marker and kept nipping out Aunt Fei's taper flame as she tried to light the incense. The incense finally caught, and Aunt Fei arranged the offerings as tenderly as if she were laying out a feast for an emperor.

Ling Fan busied herself with clearing away the winter debris from the base of another grave marker. Weather and time had worn this one down, but the calligraphy carved on the stone was still clear. Ling Fan ran her finger lightly over the characters that formed her mother's name before she pressed the incense sticks into the frozen ground. Every year for the past ten years, she and Baba and Jing Fan had come here during Qingming to clean Mama's gravestone and pay their respects. She never dreamed that one day she would be doing the same for her brother.

Ling Fan surveyed the delicacies that were spread on the ground in honor of the dead: dumplings, fruit, sliced roast pork, and an entire chicken. Sweet white incense smoke poured upward, symbolically carrying the food to Jing Fan and Mama in heaven. After she and Aunt Fei and Ming had rearranged the food several times, dashed wine from the tiny ceremonial cups onto the ground, lit all the joss paper offerings, and bowed low three times to each dead family member, they settled onto the grass a short distance away with plates of food. Her brother would eat the dumplings first, Ling Fan mused, taking one herself.

While they ate, Ling Fan found herself watching Aunt Fei and Ming, as she so often did when she was thinking of her mother. Her memories of Mama were vague and shadowy. If Mama were still alive, would she fuss and scold her as Aunt Fei did with Ming? Would she have brushed her hair and taught her how to twist it into a knot at her neck? Would she have approved of Ling Fan studying side by side with her brother? Or would she have insisted Ling Fan follow the traditional feminine path that her cousin had?

Ming sat absently rubbing the sides of her feet. Ling Fan knew that the trip to the cemetery had been brutal for both women. She insisted that they rest while she packed the remains of the food back into the bamboo carrier. They left the incense sticks burning by the markers and began the descent back to the village.

At a bend in the path, Ling Fan looked back once more. A cloud of white smoke hovered above the grave markers like a forlorn spirit that had been abandoned in the middle of a game. Ling Fan wanted to run sobbing back to her mother and brother. She would curl up between the two graves and stay there until her father came to get her.

"Ling!" Aunt Fei called from farther down the path. Ling Fan took a deep breath and hurried to catch up with them, the bamboo basket bouncing against her back.

She fell into step beside her aunt, rehearsing different versions of the question that finally burst out of her mouth. "Why was Lao Hong at the house earlier today?"

Aunt Fei sighed. "I invited him, at your father's request. We want him to speak to the Bao clan about uniting our families in a marriage between you and Young Bao."

Ling Fan shuddered. Young Bao was Old Man Bao's youngest son. Ling Fan had met him once or twice on visits to the Bao compound—a skinny, petulant boy. Once, when her family stayed for dinner, Young Bao had thrown a fit because Ling Fan and Jing Fan had been served crab legs that were bigger than those on his own plate.

"Lao Hong assured me that your birthdays are auspicious matches," Aunt Fei continued. "And he had some suggestions about good dates for the wedding."

Ling Fan closed her eyes and shook her head, wishing she could shake this moment away like a dog shaking off water.

"I'm not ready. I only just had my fifteenth birthday," she stammered.

Aunt Fei sighed again. "We've talked about this, Ling," she said gently. "Even before your father—" She looked away.

It was true. Talk about a suitable husband for her had started a year ago, even though she still hadn't gotten her first bleeding cycle. Marriage was an important part of becoming a woman, of doing one's duty to one's family.

"When we take care of our families, we benefit too," Ming reminded her, rubbing her own burgeoning stomach. "If we're lucky, we give our husbands strong sons. In turn, our husbands and sons treat us well and give us good homes."

"But what do I know about cooking a husband his meals every day, washing his clothes, cleaning his house, entertaining his friends . . ." Ling Fan trailed off. She avoided glancing at Ming's belly.

"You've been cooking and cleaning your whole life," Aunt Fei reminded her. "Everything else will come in time. All you have to do is obey your husband and be good to your mother-in-law. The Bao clan is powerful. If you make them happy, they'll find ways to reward you."

"But—!"

"And it's what your father wants."

So this was what her father and aunt had been talking about at Peng Lu Prison.

"At least with the Bao clan you know what you're getting into," Aunt Fei added. "I never set eyes on my husband until the moment he lifted the marriage veil from my face." She giggled. "I almost fainted right there from nervousness. You can be grateful that Young Bao is a familiar face."

Ling Fan only glared at her aunt. She knew she was acting like a child, but she couldn't stop the feeling that was growing in the pit of her stomach. It was a hard, tight knot of anger, as hot as a cinder.

∧ ∧ ∧

That night, Ming invited her mother and cousin to dine at her new home with her husband and mother-in-law. Ling Fan begged off, saying she was tired. In truth, she preferred to have as little to do with Ming's new family as she could. She hated the way they treated her cousin. Ming worked hard to please her mother-in-law, but nothing she did ever seemed to be good enough for the woman.

Before Aunt Fei left with Ming, she bundled the remaining

dumplings into a neat package and sent Ling Fan to deliver them to their neighbor Lao Yi Seem. Ling Fan was glad to get out of the house, glad to be alone. She crossed the narrow lane and threaded her way through the dusty vegetable garden to the back of Lao Yi Seem's house.

The house was made of mud and straw and had only two rooms and one window. Lao Yi Seem said she only needed one window and sat at it all day long. Jing Fan used to say he could tell the time of day just by looking at what Lao Yi Seem was doing at her window. In the morning, she ate a bowl of jook for breakfast, watching the villagers pass by through the steam that rose up from the soupy rice and bean curds. At noon, she chopped vegetables for her evening meal. In the afternoon she sipped a cup of tea, sometimes in the company of Momo the cat, other times with any villager who stopped to gossip.

Today, she had a visitor. When Ling Fan caught sight of who it was, she stopped in her tracks, then ducked behind a clump of bamboo that grew by the side of the house, trying to quiet the thudding of her guilty heart. Surely Widow Chang would hear it and come charging outside in righteous fury.

Ling Fan considered leaving the package of dumplings at Lao Yi Seem's door, but that would mean crossing right in front of the window. No, she would have to wait until the widow left.

". . . imagine my surprise when my manservant told me he'd chased a thief out of my orchard!" Widow Chang was saying inside.

"Aiya!" Lao Yi Seem *tsk*ed. "Did he see who it was?"

"He thinks it was a boy from the village, but more than that he couldn't be sure." Widow Chang drained the tea from her cup. "To think how low the villagers have sunk. But why should we be surprised considering who our last magistrate was?"

Ling Fan clenched her hands into fists so tight that the scars across her knuckles split and began to bleed. How dare they talk about her father like that! She would not stand around listening a moment longer. She turned to go just as Lao Yi Seem murmured something about desperate people.

"Speaking of desperation, I've heard that the Bao clan plans to make a marriage offer for Tam Ling Fan." At the sound of her name, Ling Fan paused in spite of herself. "It's about time Young Bao got married, but I can't say I think it the best possible match, all things considered."

"Why in the world would Old Man Bao want such an unfortunate alliance?" Lao Yi Seem said. "Surely there are plenty of families who are far more suitable."

"Yes, but none of them have a guaranteed Gold Mountain job," Widow Chang said knowingly. "The old magistrate went to some length to get the railroad contract for his son, you recall. You heard the stories—when so many families go into debt just to pay the fare to get to America, how did the magistrate procure such a sweet deal? But now that the boy is dead, there's no one in the family who can take his place. If Young Bao marries the girl, he gets the contract too!"

Ling Fan sucked in air between clenched teeth. They were talking about her brother's railroad contract as though it was nothing but a moneymaking opportunity. But for Jing Fan, it had been so much more. It had been the dream of a lifetime. He'd talked about the sojourn to America night and day. He'd practiced his English with Ling Fan so much that certain phrases became almost second nature to her.

"I simply cannot see Young Bao working on the Gold Mountain," Lao Yi Seem remarked. "He's only interested in gambling and drinking! Lao Fa Seem tells me he has a lot of gambling debts. Not even Old Man Bao's influence can keep his son out of trouble."

"Exactly," said Widow Chang. "The Bao clan has lost much of its fortune. They no longer hold as much sway as they once did. But there are many who would pay a handsome price for that contract to work on the railroad. If Young Bao were to sell it, he'd have enough money to pay off his debts and still have plenty left to gamble away!" She started to chortle but broke off abruptly. "What's that noise?"

Momo the cat had smelled the dumplings that Ling Fan had brought and was now circling her legs, meowing pitifully. Ling Fan tried to shoo away the hungry cat, but Momo was persistent and loud. Finally, Ling Fan dropped the dumplings on the ground and fled to the back of the house just as the door creaked open.

"It's just the cat," Lao Yi Seem said as Ling Fan scurried back through the vegetable garden toward home.

The only light in her house came from the tips of the incense sticks set before Jing Fan's altar. Ling Fan found a covered bowl of cold rice and vegetables waiting for her in the kitchen. She lit a lantern and carried it and the food back to her room. After setting everything down, she sat for a moment before she dipped her pen into freshly mixed ink and wrote, **I will never marry that snake. And I swear he'll never lay hands on our contract.**

CHAPTER
4

At noon the first day of August, the *Cormorant* rounded the eastern bend of the Pearl River. It wasn't a particularly large ship, but its deck was crowded with at least twenty men leaning over the railings. It cut through the ribbon of water easily on its way to the wooden docks at the southern edge of the village.

"It's here! Ling, look!" Ming rushed to the narrow kitchen window.

Ling Fan was already staring out the window. This was the ship that would've taken Jing Fan to the busy seaport of Guangzhou, where he would've boarded a much bigger ship bound for America—for the Gold Mountain where he would've made his fortune.

But she couldn't think about that now. Tonight Young Bao and his mother were coming to dinner, and before they arrived, Ling Fan had to speak to Aunt Fei.

Ling Fan's hand holding the kitchen knife trembled as she continued to slice white icicle radishes into long, thin strips. She tried to calm her breathing and her racing heart as she rehearsed her speech in her mind. She had brooded over it every night for weeks, trying to imagine what Fei would say and thinking of convincing replies.

"I can't see any bak gui," Ming said, leaning out the window to get a better look. "I suppose they're all in Shanghai. My sister-in-law says they have hair all over their faces like dogs. And she says when they talk, they sound like barking dogs, and they smell funny. But what does she know? She's never seen one either!"

Bak gui were the Europeans and Americans. According to the aged aunties in the village, when these foreigners first started arriving on China's shores, many people had likened them to gui—ghouls—because of their unearthly pale skin and their strange language and mannerisms. Before long, they were commonly referred to as *bak gui*, or white ghouls.

"Anyway, a ship is exciting enough even without any bak gui on it," Ming added. "I wonder if we can get a closer look before it leaves for Guangzhou tomorrow morning." Ming glanced back at Ling Fan, her smile disappearing when she saw her cousin's face.

"Jing would've been the first one on the dock," Ling Fan said, tossing the radishes into the wok. She was grateful for the hiss of oil that muffled her voice and the rising cloud of steam that hid her expression. "He would've been there at sunrise."

"With half his chores left undone and the other half done poorly," added Aunt Fei at the back door. Ling Fan flinched; she hadn't heard Aunt Fei come in from the garden. Aunt Fei put a basin of greens on the table and turned to inspect the radishes in the wok. "Remember to clean the chicken well. We need to show Young Bao that you're a good cook," she reminded Ling Fan over her shoulder as she headed back out to the garden.

Ling Fan damped down the fire in the stove and covered the simmering vegetables with the wok lid. She took a long calming breath before she told Ming, "I'll be back in a minute."

Outside, the humid air was almost as oppressive as the heat of the kitchen. Her aunt was at the far end of the garden, searching through the squash. "Bring that bucket over," Aunt Fei called as she slashed a long green squash off its stem and held it out to Ling Fan. Ling Fan took it and added it to the others in the bucket. Sweat trickled down her back as she stood by awkwardly, watching her aunt work. All the words she'd so carefully planned were clogged in her throat. Her tongue felt thick.

Finally, Aunt Fei stood up and stretched, grimacing. "Lao Bao Seem says the only soup her son will eat is winter melon. Aiya! Who has ripe winter melon now? We'll have to boil these twice as long and add extra ginger and shrimp." She snorted. "Who would ever allow their child to become that picky?" This was the first time Ling Fan had heard her aunt speak critically of Young Bao. That gave her courage.

"He's always been fussy and particular," Ling Fan ventured. "His moods change like the weather."

Aunt Fei tossed another semi-ripe winter melon into the bucket. "It's good that you're noticing these things," she said approvingly. "A wife should understand her husband's ways."

"But that's exactly the problem! His moods are unreliable. His behavior is erratic. He can't be trusted."

"A wise wife can guide her husband down the correct road."

Ling Fan swallowed her rising frustration. She and her aunt seemed to be having two different conversations. She had to make her aunt understand what a terrible mistake it would be to marry her off to Young Bao.

"I don't want to guide him. I don't want to be his wife. I don't want anything to do with him!" Panic made her voice sharper than she intended.

Aunt Fei sat down on the low stone garden wall with a sigh. "I tried to tell your father it would be like this. You were always headstrong. It comes from letting you do everything your brother did. Letting you act like a boy. But now you need to listen, and listen well." Her voice became low, as it only did when she was angry. "It's time to grow up, Tam Ling Fan. You are a woman, and you will behave like a woman. You will obey the wishes of your family. This marriage with the Bao clan is your father's only hope of getting a reprieve from his prison sentence."

"No, it's not," Ling Fan said desperately. "There are other ways! We can find someone else to take Jing's railroad contract, someone who will split the profits with us. We don't need to hand it over to the Bao clan. We just have to find someone who will make the sojourn to America, to the railroad. A sojourner would make enough gold to build a palace! Enough gold to secure Baba's release."

Aunt Fei shook her head. "There's nobody in this family to make the sojourn now. The only good that piece of paper can do us is ally an influential family to ours, and that's what we're trying to do with Young Bao."

"But he's not going to use it to get to America. He's just going to sell it to the highest bidder! How can we throw away Jing's dream like that?"

"What does it matter? We get what we need: help for your father."

"It would matter to Jing! It's what he's wanted ever since he heard of the Gold Mountain!"

"Jing is dead," Aunt Fei said flatly. She snatched up the bucket, tossing the hand trowel into it. She pushed past Ling Fan as she headed back to the kitchen.

Ming had finished slicing mushrooms, onions, and eggplant and had piled them all into the sizzling wok. Orange flames leapt high, smoke roiled, and the silver spatula flashed as Ming stirred rigorously, her face shiny with sweat. "They're here." She nodded over her shoulder. "They're in the courtyard."

Aunt Fei smoothed her tunic and tucked a wisp of hair behind her ear. "Come along," she said to Ling Fan. "It's time to greet your future husband."

∧ ∧ ∧

Young Bao and his mother sat by the edge of the small koi pond in the courtyard. Young Bao's loose, fleshy face, with its sagging cheeks and double chin, made him look older than his sixteen years. He held a bunch of crimson peonies in one hand; he thrust them toward Ling Fan as if he were passing her a poisonous snake. Ling Fan took them, trying to keep a gracious demeanor.

Lao Bao Seem, Young Bao's mother, was a tiny, birdlike woman with bright eyes. She took Ling Fan's aunt by the arm with a conspiratorial air. "I hear your cherry trees are beautiful. You must tell me how you've done it. My own trees are as bare as an old crone's head." She led the way toward the back of the compound, leaving Young Bao and Ling Fan by the koi pond.

When they were alone, Young Bao sank down on a nearby bench as though all the air had gone out of him.

"So." He licked his lips. "Mother says we should proceed with this marriage arrangement. She thinks it would be best for both families."

"Best for your family, you mean," Ling Fan said. She began to pull the petals off a flower and dropped them one by one into the tiny koi pond. "You'll reap the benefits of selling my brother's contract to the highest bidder, but what will we get?"

Young Bao sat up straighter. "You'll have the protection of the Bao clan. My father has some influence with the provincial authorities."

Ling Fan tore the bare flower head off its stem and threw it into the water after the petals. The scars on her knuckles ached. "After everything my father's done for this village, getting him out of prison is the least your family can do. Don't pretend that it's such a great act of generosity."

Young Bao's face flushed. "We're taking a big risk entering into this association with you. Plenty of people resent how your father did things around here. We could lose standing, miss out on business opportunities . . . not to mention *other* consequences of your father's poor judgment that I'll have to endure." He looked pointedly at her unbound feet.

Ling Fan threw the flower stems to the ground. She could hardly breathe. "How dare you? My father was a good magistrate. He always did his best to serve the people of this village well. People loved my father."

"If he's so good, then why is he in prison? If he's so beloved, why aren't people rising up to protest his arrest? You'll be lucky if my father can talk the authorities into lessening his sentence."

"What do you mean, *if*?" Ling Fan demanded.

Young Bao looked away. "My father," he said bitterly, "was always a big talker. The bigger he talked, the more people would listen. But that's all it's ever been. If his talk amounted to anything, do you think I would still be in so much trouble with my debts?"

Ling Fan felt as though she were a character in an opera—the one who has just been stabbed and is left onstage staring in disbelief at the hilt protruding from her heart.

"My father will *try* to sway the prefect. I just don't know what good will come of it. Treason against the emperor is a terrible crime."

Shaking with fury, Ling Fan seized Young Bao by the arm. "How dare you slander my father! He's not a traitor! He's a good man. A good man!" She must have started to shout because footsteps were suddenly hurrying back down the garden path toward them.

"Ling, what's wrong?" Aunt Fei hurried to Ling Fan's side.

"What are you doing?" Lao Bao Seem shrieked. "Let go of my son!"

Ling Fan was crying now, loud angry sobs that shook her entire body. As the women fluttered around her, Young Bao brushed at his sleeve as though there was dirt on it.

"We should come back another day," Young Bao said to his mother, "when my fiancée is not so distraught with grief over all her losses."

"Please stay," Aunt Fei urged. "You mustn't leave on an empty stomach!"

"You have such a good heart, but it's clear that Ling Fan is exhausted," said Lao Bao Seem. "We'll come back at a better time."

When they were gone, Ling Fan ran back to her room and threw herself onto her bed. She wished she could tear Young Bao to shreds just as she had shredded the flowers he'd given her. She heard Aunt Fei's footsteps stop by her doorway, but she closed her eyes and pretended to be asleep. After a moment, to her relief, her aunt returned to the kitchen.

She must have really fallen asleep, because when she opened her eyes again, it was dark. The house was quiet. Moonlight flooded her room. Instinctively she tossed aside her quilt and padded across the hall before the memory caught up with her: Jing Fan was no longer in his room.

She entered anyway, perching on his empty bed the way she used to when she'd had a nightmare. Her eyes were dry now, but she felt as though her body was a deep well of sorrow. No matter how many tears she shed, she would never run out of grief.

The moon had followed her across the hall, and in its pearly blue light she could make out the familiar outlines of her brother's room. Aunt Fei had kept everything as it had been. Ling knelt on the floor and tugged on a loose board beneath the bed. Jing Fan used to keep his prized possessions beneath it. Ling Fan groped around until her hand touched the folded piece of paper she had hidden there the night Baba was arrested.

The railroad contract.

Slowly, Ling Fan rose and unfolded the paper, her eyes flicking over the words like a moth around a flame. *Li Hing Gold Mountain agrees to pay passage to America aboard the SS California of the Pacific Mail Steamship Company . . . Li Hing Gold Mountain is honored to present the bearer of this note for employment to the Central Pacific Railroad Company . . .*

The bearer of this note . . .

The words ran together in a blur. The paper began to shake, as if a ghost wind blew against it. But the windows in Jing Fan's room were closed. Ling Fan shivered. She could imagine the cold little breeze wandering around the room, circling the furniture until it came to her, standing there with the contract in her hand. It twined around her legs, slithered up her back, and perched on her shoulder.

She looked up and found herself staring into her brother's face in the mirror.

She had been shorter than her brother but—as Aunt Fei always said—sturdy-framed and shaped like a boy. She had the same square face, strong jawline, and thick eyebrows as Jing Fan.

The room seemed to tilt under her. She felt hot and cold at the same time as the start of a wild idea seeped into her mind.

She started to pace, feeling like a caged animal. Again and again, she stopped in front of the mirror, staring at her face. At her brother's face. She knew what she had to do.

Her heart pounding, she slipped the contract into her sleeve. Moving swiftly so that she wouldn't have time to second-guess herself, she rummaged around in the wooden press at the foot of Jing Fan's bed and pulled out two pairs of cotton trousers, a couple of tunics, a jacket, and a broad-brimmed straw hat.

Back in her room, she used her brother's shaving knife to shear the hair off the front half of her head, then pulled the rest back severely into the long tight queue that was required of all men and boys in China. She found a wide strip of stiff linen that she wound tightly around her chest and secured with pins. Not, she thought wryly, that there was much to hide, but better to have the extra layer of disguise. She slipped her brother's loose-fitting tunic over her shoulders, tied the trousers, then sat down at her desk and quickly scratched out a note on a scrap of paper. When she rolled it up and tucked it into the brazier, the paper darkened and coiled like a living thing. Flames swallowed the words one by one: **I'll go to America. I'll go for you. I lost you. I'm not going to lose Baba too.**

Next, she wrote a note to her aunt and her cousin Ming.

Ming would understand. Ming would be here to take care of Aunt Fei.

She stowed her pen and ink set in a large cloth bag, along with the shaving equipment and the other clothes she'd taken from Jing Fan's room. She dropped a few coins into a small red silk pouch that she tied around her neck and tucked beneath her tunic. Its weight felt reassuring around her neck.

As she looked around the room she'd lived in for the past ten years, she felt a rush of tears that threatened to drown her nerve. Taking a deep breath to steady herself, she blew out the light and closed her door the way she did every night when she went to bed. The *Cormorant* was departing early the next morning for the daylong trip to Guangzhou. She would leave the house right before dawn, while Aunt Fei was still asleep. She sat on her bed in the darkness, listening to the night sounds of the house and turning her plan over and over in her mind.

After what seemed like an eon, the darkness beyond her lattice window turned lighter. Choosing each step carefully, she slipped down the hall and left the note on the floor outside Fei's bedroom. She walked down the set of stairs to the passage that connected their compound to the one next door. It was a simple matter to keep out of sight until she reached the last house connected to the others and exited through a side door.

The briny scent of water and fish filled her nostrils as she followed the twisting streets that led down toward the dock. Ahead of her, she could see the tops of the *Cormorant*'s masts. Holding her breath, she scanned the small group of men and boys waiting to board the ship. If anybody recognized her, her plan would be in ruins before it could begin to unfold.

After a few heartbeats she let out a long, slow breath; only strangers, probably from other villages and outlying farms. Filled with relief, Ling Fan suddenly felt light enough to be blown away by the wind that snatched at the ship's flags. Her heartbeat was still ragged, but in her mind, she could hear Jing Fan laughing with delight as she stepped forward.

CHAPTER 5

The water of the Pearl River looked dark and oily in the early morning light. It tugged at the ship, bumping it gently against the wooden pier. Ling Fan stood with a handful of men and boys at the foot of the wooden plank that led to the ship's deck. She pulled her brother's hat low and tried to stand apart from the group without losing her place in line. She had never felt so much energy surging through her body. She felt as though she could leap into the river and swim all the way to Guangzhou, where the big steamships waited to bring sojourners to America.

Ahead of her, a gnarled old man finally finished counting out coins into the captain's hand and stepped onto the gangplank. Ling Fan was next. She felt eyes on her as she fumbled with the pouch at her neck and handed over her fare. Wondering if somebody had already seen through her disguise, she resisted the urge to adjust the linen band around her chest. She pushed forward onto the gangplank, but apparently not fast enough. Someone bumped into her from behind and made her stumble. She steadied herself and shot a glare over her shoulder.

"Careful!" laughed the person who'd knocked her off-balance—a tall, skinny boy who looked to be no more than two or three years older than she was. His face might have been elegant, if it weren't so thin. He wore the same rough cotton clothes as the other men and boys, but his bony wrists dangled from the ends of his sleeves like a stick doll's.

"I *was* being careful," said Ling Fan. "You're the one who should watch your step."

He smiled broadly. "Fair point," he said, then went on as though they had been in the midst of a conversation. "I've been in a rush all morning. I took the wrong fork on the road from San Hoi Bein, my home village. Have you heard of it?"

"No." Ling Fan walked a little faster. She was sure he had been staring at her silk pouch.

"It's ten miles south of here. Good thing I left before sunrise!"

They reached the top of the gangplank.

"Wong Wei."

"What?" She whipped around again, startled. That boy still. He seemed stuck to her side like goat turd on the wheel of a cart.

"My name. I'm Wong Wei." He cocked his head expectantly.

"Tam L—" She stammered, catching herself just in time. "Jing Fan. I'm Tam Jing Fan." It felt awkward on her tongue, like putting the wrong shoe on her foot. But she'd never known a boy named Ling. Her brother's name seemed safer.

Wong Wei gave her an odd look. Was there something wrong with her disguise? The way she sounded? Perhaps she should've tried to deepen her voice . . . A knot of doubt and panic began to grow in her stomach. What was she thinking? This was a terrible idea! If she headed home now, she could be in her own room in ten minutes with no one the wiser. She started to turn back, but the crush of more passengers pushed her farther onto the deck.

Wong Wei was still talking. "I'm going to the Gold Mountain to make my fortune. Then I'll come home and build a palace with a hundred rooms. I'll have ten sons and twenty concubines!"

Anything she might have said would've been drowned out by the racket of the gangplank being pulled up by two of the *Cormorant*'s crew. Another crewman untied a rope from the pier, and the ship pulled away. A minute later, it caught the current of the river and picked up speed. A sharp blast of the ship's horn signaled that they were off. Ling Fan pushed her way through the crowd that was standing at the railing facing her receding village.

Lo Wai already looked tiny. Brown and gray houses were spread out against the low hills. Ling Fan fixed her gaze on the spot where her own house was. Then the river curved around a bend and she lost sight of the village. She had to bite down hard on her lip to keep from crying. She had never been more than a few miles from Lo Wai. Until the horror of the last few months, she had been happy in her home and with her family. The enormity of what she was doing felt like a typhoon that threatened to flatten her and drag her out to sea.

Squinting against the wind that was now blowing hard off the water, Ling Fan managed to make out the gray stones of Peng Lu Prison. From this distance, the estate's tumbled pagodas and overgrown walkways looked like a scab.

At the sight of the prison, all feelings of doubt and regret disappeared, replaced by her memory of Baba being dragged off by the guard. The wind took her breath away, and even though spray from the river threatened to drench her, she stayed at the railing staring out at the passing shore.

"So here you are!" The boy who had introduced himself as Wong Wei came up beside her. He leaned over the railing and held his hand out to the spray, grinning, then pointed toward a spot along the shoreline. "My village is ten miles just over that rise." He folded his arms on the railing and rested his chin on them. "My bride-to-be says she won't wait long, so I'd better make my fortune quick!"

"Are you going to work the railroad, or in the mines?"

"I'll do whatever gets me the most money the fastest," he said easily. "Even if that means hauling bak gui night soil with my bare hands! Who knows, there's so much gold in America, there might be some in there too!"

Ling Fan blanched and couldn't quite keep her face from showing her disapproval.

"Aiya, you're like my old popo!" Wong Wei slapped her back companionably. Too late, Ling Fan realized that she'd reacted to Wong Wei's coarse language exactly the way Aunt Fei would've. Dressing herself like a boy was not enough. She had to remember to act like a boy too.

From the corner of her eye she studied Wong Wei's loose-limbed stance and tried to copy it without being obvious. But when he scratched himself and smelled his fingers, she shuddered inwardly. Would she have to learn to belch, spit, and fart loudly too? Sweat trickled between her breasts beneath the cloth wrapped around her chest. It was starting to chafe. She forced herself not to pluck at it.

"What about you?" Wong Wei asked. "What will you do when you reach the Gold Mountain?"

Ling Fan hesitated. If she mentioned the railroad contract, he'd know she was from a family of means, and that might drive him to ask more questions. The less people knew about her—and the less reason they had to wonder about her—the safer she'd be.

"Same as you," she said. "Hoping to make my fortune any way I can."

"We sound like a couple of characters out of a fairy tale," Wong Wei said, pulling such a wry face that Ling Fan had to laugh despite herself.

Wong Wei was far leaner than Jing Fan, but he was the same height and carried himself the same way: a kind of self-conscious slouch that came out of a sudden growth spurt that he hadn't had the chance to get used to. Aunt Fei constantly berated Jing Fan for his posture, comparing him to a lumpy sack of potatoes.

As the morning wore on, most passengers sat in clumps near the bow or stern, smoking, gambling, and drinking. Wong Wei watched the dice games with the concentration of a hawk tracking a mouse. Ling Fan decided to scout out a secluded spot to relieve herself when the time came. She certainly couldn't do what she saw so many of the other passengers freely doing.

She followed a narrow set of steps that led down to the hold. It was filled with the stench of rotting fish, mildewed vegetables, and worse. She gagged at the odor but knew it would have to suffice. If she wanted to preserve her disguise, she would have to endure some inconveniences.

At sunset, she squatted around a cauldron with the other passengers while a crewman scooped out cold rice mixed with dried fish and pickled yams. They ate with their fingers and shared a jug of tea. Ling Fan found herself sticking close to Wong Wei. Twice, she caught herself about to call him Jing. Darkness fell while they ate. The night sky was like a swath of black silk cloth studded with pearls. The only light on the ship came from an oil lamp in the captain's cabin and the ends of cigarettes scattered here and there. Eventually, even those began to wink out one by one.

Ling Fan found a patch of deck between two coils of rope and settled down for the night, using her bag for a pillow. The day had been long and fraught. The creaking of the wooden vessel soon lulled her into a deep, dark sleep. In her dream, somebody kept calling for Jing Fan. "He's dead," she kept trying to explain. "It's just me." Then a hand like iron grabbed her ankle.

She woke with a yelp, gripping her bag tightly and kicking out as hard as she could. She'd heard tales of thieves robbing unsuspecting travelers of everything, including their lives. She wished she'd thought to bring a knife or some other weapon with her. She kicked again, and this time her foot made satisfying contact with something solid.

"Aiya! Ow! Tam Jing Fan, it's me, Wong Wei!"

Dizzy with sleep, Ling Fan sat up, but kept her bag between herself and the coil of rope. In the starlight, she could just make out Wong Wei. He was doubled over, clutching his nose, but laughing softly. A stink of cigarette smoke, dried sweat, and whiskey clung to him like a shroud.

"Aiya, Tam Jing Fan, you sleep like an old sow! I've been calling you for five minutes! Move over."

Wong Wei plopped down beside her on the warped wooden deck. He reached under his shirt and pulled out a coin. A piece of braided silk string ran through the square hole in the coin's center and looped around his neck.

"A good day's haul," he murmured to it. Then he pressed it to his lips and slipped it back under his shirt. He had the same self-satisfied smile Aunt Fei had after a good night playing mah-jongg with some of the village women. A minute later, he began to snore.

All drowsiness melted out of Ling Fan, replaced by the knot of panic and doubt growing once again in her stomach. She sat up and hugged her knees to her chest, shivering. She could still feel the sudden grip around her ankle. She was mostly shaken by how deeply asleep and vulnerable she had been. She was lucky that Wong Wei seemed friendly, but she couldn't count on anybody else she met to be trustworthy. She shivered again, thinking of stories Aunt Fei used to tell of what happened to women and girls who were caught by mountain bandits. If anybody ever discovered her secret, simply sending her home would be the kindest thing they could do.

∧ ∧ ∧

Sometime in the middle of the night, the ship entered the Pearl River Delta. With luck, the captain said, they would dock at noon. Dozens of vessels sailed by: junks with their elegant fan-like sails, Western schooners with white sails like the wings of magnificent albatrosses, large and small fishing boats, and a fair share of houseboats. Far in the distance was docked the biggest ship Ling Fan had ever seen.

It was easily the size of several houses and had a large round column rising up between two stout masts. English lettering adorned its side, and Ling Fan, with a racing heart, could just make out the name: SS *California*. This, according to her railroad contract, was the steamship to America.

As they drew closer to the port, Ling Fan strained to catch her first glimpse of American bak gui. She had never in her life seen one. Baba had gotten the railroad contract through Chinese intermediaries in Guangzhou. Jing Fan's English tutor had been a scholar from Shanghai. She wondered if the bak gui were indeed covered in hair like dogs, as Ming's sister-in-law had insisted.

She didn't see any especially hairy people on the bustling quays, but she did see a number of people dressed in Western-style clothing. Many of them had beards or mustaches, but from this distance she couldn't see much more than that. Nervously, she ran through some of the English phrases she had practiced with her brother: *Good morning, How are you, I am well, I am sick, I am hungry.*

After a breakfast of watery jook, Wong Wei turned eagerly back to the dice games. He tried to persuade Ling Fan to team up with him. "Twice as much money in the pot means six times the winnings," he insisted. "Last night I put in ten wen and won fifty! It's easy money!"

Ling Fan considered it. Why wait for the Gold Mountain? More money now meant more money for Baba in the long run and quite possibly a shorter stay in America. She followed Wong Wei to three men squatting by the stern. They recognized Wong Wei and made room for him, waving Ling Fan in as well.

Coins were fished out of pockets and pouches and tossed into a chipped bowl. But when it came time for her to ante in, Ling Fan backed away, unable to part with one precious wen. Wong Wei threw her a look of utter contempt but seemed to forget about her once the game began. He did well in the first few rounds. Each time he won, he pulled the coin that hung around his neck out from under his tunic and kissed it.

After the fourth round, he looked up at Ling Fan. "If you want, I'll lend you the ten wen, and you can pay me back from your winnings later. You'll see. It'll be fun!" She was tempted— not by the pile of coins at his side, but by the sly, cocky grin he cast up at her. Jing Fan used to have the same smile whenever he tried to lure her into an adventure. She'd come to learn that his assurance—*You'll see, it'll be fun!*—almost always meant they would end up in trouble. That never kept her from following him, because despite the consequences, it *was* fun.

But this boy wasn't Jing Fan. That became clear as Ling Fan studied his expression. His thin face looked as sharp as a bird of prey's. Her hand went to the little pouch around her neck as she shook her head. Wong Wei shrugged and tossed the dice with a snap of his wrist.

The dice rolled to a stop. Shouts and groans rippled through the crowd that had gathered around the players. Wong Wei's grin flickered like a candle in a breeze, but it flared up again when the dice came back to his hand. He continued to smile even as the pile of money by his side melted away.

When he had no coins left, Wong Wei got to his feet and bowed to the other players. He joined Ling Fan by the rail, where she'd been dividing her attention between the dice game and the growing panorama of the Port of Guangzhou. The *Cormorant* was angling toward an empty berth beside the SS *California*. The crew hustled with final preparations before landfall.

Wong Wei leaned against the railing and stared at the bustling port. His hand clutched at the coin beneath his shirt, but he didn't pull it out. His face was chalky in the noon sun.

"Hard luck now," Ling Fan said gently. "But things will be better once we get to America."

Wong Wei balled his hands into fists. "Maybe for you. I won't be going to America."

"What do you mean?" Ling Fan stared at him.

Wong Wei turned his back to the railing and slumped to the wooden deck. His hands dangled over his skinny knees.

He mumbled through clenched teeth, "To get to America, you have to pay for passage, and to pay, you need money."

"Do you mean you lost *all* your money? What—?" Ling Fan bit back the rest: *What were you thinking? How could you be so foolish?* None of that would help him now. Instead she squatted down beside him and asked, "What are you going to do?"

A muscle in Wong Wei's clenched jaw worked. "I know I can win my money back. I know my luck will turn. I just need a little help." His eyes drifted to the sack of coins she wore around her neck.

"No," she said, jerking away as though a snake had suddenly uncoiled at her feet.

"Please, Tam Jing Fan. I'll pay you back the instant I win."

She wavered, struck again by how much Wong Wei reminded her of her brother when he begged for favors.

"I only need ten wen," he said.

She wanted to help her new friend, but not if it meant jeopardizing her chances to help Baba. Besides, after what she'd seen of the game, she had little faith in Wong Wei's luck.

"No," she said. "Ten wen is what got you into this mess to begin with."

Wong Wei's face turned red. "You not joining with me in the game is what got me in the mess! If you'd been playing and we'd split our winnings, my odds would've been that much better."

A blast from the ship's horn interrupted them. The *Cormorant* had pulled up to the pier. Once the gangplank was secured, passengers disembarked and set out in a dozen different directions. Some men went straight over to the SS *California*, docked at the pier to the right. From her vantage point on the deck, Ling Fan had a clear view of the activity surrounding both ships.

At the stern, crewmen streamed back and forth like a line of giant ants, loading cargo into the SS *California*'s hold. Closer to the bow, there were two gangplanks for passengers instead of one. At the foot of the farther one, passengers wearing Western-style suits and narrow-brimmed hats stood near boxes with handles and ornate crates. They didn't look like laborers at all, but rather like the merchants who'd sometimes visited Ling Fan's father. Many of them were giving orders to workers who scurried about, carrying boxes and parcels onto the ship.

One man, with hair the astonishing color of new copper, seemed especially irate. He was surrounded by half a dozen large crates stuffed with straw. Several Chinese workers were busy prying open these crates and rearranging their contents. The man's attention was divided between his possessions and the crewman he was haranguing. As she watched the drama unfold, an idea as wild as disguising herself as a boy grew in Ling Fan's mind.

"Would you do anything to get to America?" she asked Wong Wei.

"Of course, but—?"

"Then do everything I tell you."

∧ ∧ ∧

Ling Fan descended the gangplank and joined the crowds on the dock. She pushed her way toward the SS *California*, toward the redheaded merchant she had seen from the deck of the *Cormorant*. Workers were sifting through the man's crates, removing and repacking vases, lacquered cabinets, and statuettes. Some of the crates were almost empty, except for the straw.

"I didn't pay a hundred extra dollars to have these crates go into your godforsaken hold!" the redheaded merchant raged at the SS *California* crewman. "These items are going into the cabin next to mine. Now!" He turned to survey his crates. "You'd damn well better make sure those things are packed correctly this time! If anything's broken, I'll break your heads!"

Ling Fan edged closer to one of the crates and, with a quick movement, tipped it over. Straw and vases tumbled out onto the dock. "Aiya! How clumsy of me! Let me help you!" She proceeded to kick and toss straw and vases into further chaos, very nearly tipping over a second crate. The merchant and the workers frantically tried to contain the mess and check for damages, while behind their backs, a skinny figure climbed into one of the emptier crates. Ling Fan heaved a huge handful of straw into it and slid the lid into place.

"Come here, you damned river rat!" By now the merchant's face was as red as his hair. He reached for Ling Fan's arm. "I'll have the port authorities throw you in the brig!"

Ling Fan danced out of reach and plunged into the mass of people. She ran past carts, rickshaws, and quayside food vendors. She dodged around cages of livestock and stacked barrels. When she was sure no one was still pursuing her, she doubled back and hid behind a pallet of dry goods, where she had a decent view of the merchant's crates. One by one, each crate's lid was tied shut with rope and lifted onto the SS *California*. Triumph glowed like a sun in her chest. Her plan had worked! Wong Wei was on board. Once the ship was underway, he would escape the crate he'd hidden in and join the other Chinese travelers.

Satisfied, Ling Fan made her way over to the second gangplank, where two SS *California* crewmen were inspecting the papers of Chinese passengers waiting to board. All the Chinese passengers were men or older boys, dressed in loose tunics and cotton pants of the same style that she wore. Still, Ling Fan nervously pulled her hat low over her eyes.

Finally it was her turn. Without looking up, she held out the contract to the inspector, glad that at least her hand wasn't shaking. The inspector unfolded the paper and read it silently, frowning slightly. Ling Fan shifted from foot to foot, waiting. Was there something wrong with it? He folded it back along its creases and tapped it against his front teeth. "Where are you going, boy?" he asked in English.

Surprised, Ling Fan looked up into the man's tanned face. Was this a test? Was there some kind of secret answer she was supposed to supply? But the inspector had mild blue eyes that seemed genuinely curious. For a second she wanted with all her heart to say, "I'm going to the Gold Mountain to save my father." She licked her lips, thinking through which words to use in English. This was the first time she had ever spoken to a bak gui.

Aloud, she said, "To America, sir. To work on the railroad there."

The inspector nodded, stamping her contract with a black stamp before handing it back to her, and waved her aboard the SS *California*.

CHAPTER
6

Two *Cormorant*s, with room for a house or two from Lo
Wai, could have easily fit inside the SS *California*. Ling Fan
would have liked to explore the top deck, but a crewman at the
top of the gangplank waved her and the other Chinese passengers toward the stern. She glimpsed a row of cabins on a deck
above their heads as they filed by. The bak gui who looked like
merchants were settling themselves and their luggage into the
tiny rooms. Ling Fan caught sight of a familiar pile of flimsy
crates and the red-haired merchant beside them.

In single file, the Chinese passengers climbed down a set
of rickety wooden steps that led into the hold. Her eyes slowly
adjusted to the darkness, but her nose did not. The SS *California*'s hold didn't reek as much as the *Cormorant*'s, but even so,
she couldn't help gagging as she descended.

The man in front of her looked back at her wearily and without sympathy. "Welcome to the bak gui's bounty," he said. He
was a large, doughy man with sleepy eyes nearly covered by a
dusty brown hat. "The best thing about this passage is that if this
clunker springs a leak, we get to be the first to drown!" He guffawed at his own joke before disappearing into the murky room.

The hold stretched across the breadth of the ship. Kerosene lamps hung on timber posts scattered here and there.

Light peered through two portholes set high on the starboard wall like distant candle flames. There were no berths or bunks as far as Ling Fan could tell. Around her, passengers settled themselves on patches of floor that were out of the way of passing feet and not too wet.

Remembering how Wong Wei had grabbed her the previous night while she slept, Ling Fan pushed deeper into the hold until she reached the wall farthest from the entrance. There, she found a space between a coil of tar-covered rope and a pile of dirty rags. She kicked at the rags, trying to make more room.

"Aiya!" the pile of rags howled. A man sat up, pulling his hat off his face, and glared at her. It was the sleepy-eyed man who'd joked about drowning. He grabbed her arm. "Watch where you're stepping if you don't want to have your skinny legs broken!"

Ling Fan tried to break free, but the man had a fist of granite. "Let me go," she cried, kicking out as hard as she could. "Let me go!"

One of her kicks landed on his stomach, and he dropped her arm with a curse. Ling Fan scrambled backward, out of reach. They glared at each other—he bent double and wheezing, she panting. Then, inexplicably, the man burst out laughing, a deep belly laugh that made his shoulders heave.

"Aiya, you look like a wet rabbit," the man declared, slapping his thigh. "And you fight like one too!"

"Better to fight like a wet rabbit than a clumsy old water buffalo!" She closed her mouth with a snap, shocked at herself. Aunt Fei's voice hissed in her mind: *A proper woman does not speak like that!* She expected the man's rock-crushing grip to descend on her again, but he burst into another roar of laughter.

"The name's Tan Din. And you'd better sit down."

Above their heads, feet hammered across the wooden deck. The SS *California* seemed to shudder. The room began to bob. Ling Fan felt as though a giant hand had suddenly pressed down on her brain and given it a spin. She closed her eyes, waiting for the dizziness to pass, but it didn't.

"Sit down," the man said again, "before you fall on top of me." The room tilted hard to port. Ling Fan sat.

A horn sounded three times, long and low. They were off.

∧ ∧ ∧

Ling Fan longed to watch the southern coast of China recede into the distance, but when she climbed the steps to the main deck, a crewman sent her back down to the hold with a curse. She was sure fresh air would cure her dizziness, but the Chinese passengers were not allowed to wander around the ship as they'd done on the *Cormorant*. Water and food were brought to them in the hold twice a day.

"They treat us more like livestock than passengers," Ling Fan grumbled to Tan Din.

"Don't fool yourself," Tan Din said around a mouthful of rice. "The livestock get better food than we do!"

This was Tan Din's second sojourn to America. He had worked in a mine for a year. Nobody was more shocked than he to discover he had returned to China with a sack of worthless fool's gold. This time, he declared, he would be no one's fool and would make his fortune working on the railroad.

"That's my plan too," Ling Fan said, though she stopped short of mentioning the contract. If the other passengers knew about it, they might try to steal it.

"The bak gui are fixing to run that railroad of theirs

through the mountains, you know," Tan Din said. He drew a quick map on the dirt-covered floor with his knife. "From what I heard, the Central Pacific Railroad Company started their railroad here, in a place called Sacramento. They're trying to build it to a place called Utah over here, where it'll meet up with the tracks laid by another railroad company. In between there's a mountain range. Four hundred miles long and forty to eighty miles wide. The Sierra Nevada."

"They must think we're mountain goats, to build railroad tracks over a mountain," she said.

"I didn't say *over* the mountains, boy, I said *through* the mountains. The bak gui want to dig tunnels."

Aghast, Lin Fan asked, "How are they going to get through all that rock?"

Tan Din barked his cavernous laugh. "They'll do it with us!"

"My cousin says they use gunpowder," chimed in a big-bellied man named Gwon Ho. "They use it to blast huge chunks out of the mountain. My cousin says they need to dig ten or more tunnels across the mountains before they finally get through."

"Gunpowder," Tan Din echoed. "Dangerous stuff, that. I've seen plenty of miners using it wrong, and *BOOM!* There went an arm. Or a leg. Or worse."

"Gunpowder's bad, but my cousin says the bak gui just created something even more powerful," Gwon Ho said. "Even the bak gui are afraid of it."

"You're telling big tales! What's more powerful than gunpowder?"

"My cousin says it's some kind of yellow liquid that's five times stronger and ten times more dangerous. The bak gui call it *nitroglycerin*." His mouth and tongue stretched awkwardly around the word.

Tan Din shook his head. "Going back home to China, I met so many people who worked on the railroad. A lot of them had injuries: missing fingers, broken bones, crushed limbs. The stories they told of fallen comrades! You'd think they were soldiers in a war! Railroad work is already dangerous. Trust the bak gui to make it even worse."

Ling Fan suppressed a shudder. What was she getting herself into?

∧ ∧ ∧

On their second day at sea, a commotion above them was followed by a body tumbling down into the hold. A crewman shouted down in English: "Next time we find one of you coolies where you don't belong, we'll toss 'im over the side of the ship. Captain's orders!"

Ling Fan pushed through the crowd to get to the body that lay limp and unmoving. "Wong Wei!" She turned him over. His face was gray. Instantly she was transported back to the moment when she realized her brother lay dead in his bed. Terrified, she shook Wong Wei as hard as she could.

He groaned and sat up, bruised but otherwise uninjured. Ling slowly let out the breath she'd been holding. She stumbled to the water barrel and stood over it for an eternity, willing her hands to stop shaking.

By the time she returned with a tin cup full of water, Wong Wei sat propped against a wooden support column sucking on a piece of dried fish Tan Din had handed him. "Well, I managed to break out of the crate and sneak out of that bak gui's cabin," he told her. "But right away a crewman caught me wandering the decks looking for the other sojourners." He licked his fingers clean, then took the cup from her and gulped down the water. "The bak gui passengers eat with the captain. I saw them sitting there eating meat and fresh vegetables. That's what I'm going to do when we get to America, eat roast pork and fresh vegetables every day."

Tan Din scoffed. "You're lucky enough you're sitting here eating the same slop as us instead of sitting at the bottom of the ocean eating with the fish. If the crew had realized you were a stowaway, that would've been your fate."

Ling Fan gnawed on her bottom lip, feeling guilty that she hadn't considered the danger Wong Wei would've been in if her plan had gone wrong.

She looked around at the other passengers. Surely everybody in the hold knew Wong Wei had stowed away. "Don't worry," said Tan Din. "Nobody's going to turn him in to the bak gui."

He was right. There seemed to be a kind of unspoken brotherhood among the Chinese passengers. It made Ling Fan half-ashamed of keeping her railroad contract a secret. But most of the other sojourners were traveling with relatives or friends. She was alone among strangers, and she couldn't be certain that jealousy and self-interest wouldn't win out over fellow feeling.

Five days into their journey, a squall hit, tossing the SS *California* around like a child's toy boat. As the ship pitched and heaved, Ling Fan's stomach did the same. It was impossible to keep down the overly salted rice and fish until Tan Din managed to turn it into a kind of porridge that he spooned into her mouth himself. Even so, she was so weak that she couldn't stop shivering. Wong Wei borrowed a blanket for her from another passenger. It was scratchy and smelled of wet hens, but Ling Fan was in no position to complain. Tan Din and Wong Wei rarely left her side. Their attention reminded her of the last nightmarish days when she and Aunt Fei watched over Jing Fan.

She was able to keep her senses enough to insist on using the latrine corner on her own. Despite the close quarters of the hold, the stench and accumulated filth in that dark corner was so unbearable that nobody ever lingered nearby long enough to notice her crouching beneath her blanket to relieve herself.

One evening, as Ling Fan lay curled up near Tan Din, she noticed he was whittling a figure out of a piece of wood.

"What are you making?" she croaked. Anything to distract her from her own wretchedness.

"Something for my daughter. She's four. She doesn't understand yet why I had to leave her behind."

A lump rose in Ling Fan's throat. She forced herself to ignore it. "I'm sure she'll understand as she gets older. Her mother can explain to her—"

"Her mother died last month," Tan Din said flatly.

"Oh. I'm sorry." It was on the tip of her tongue to say her brother had died recently as well.

He paused in his whittling, though he kept staring at the block of wood. "My wife was always the first to help any ailing neighbor. When the coughing sickness came to our village, she nursed others until she came down with it."

Tan Din told her how, after his wife's death, he'd bundled the family's possessions into a single pack that he slung across his shoulders, settled his daughter on top, and followed the road to Guangzhou. He couldn't bring his daughter with him to America, so like so many other sojourners before him, he'd left her at an orphanage in Guangzhou.

"You'll be back for her soon," Ling Fan said.

"In two or three years, if I'm lucky. I'm aiming to make twenty thousand wen, a few hundred American dollars, and that'll take time."

Two or three years? Ling Fan's throat closed. She herself needed at least twenty thousand wen to secure Baba's release. She knew she could earn it faster on the Gold Mountain than anywhere else. But up to now she hadn't thought much about just how long it might be before she would see her home again. Would Baba even survive that long in prison? What if he died there—from poor treatment, from despair—before she even got back? She gritted her teeth. *Two years,* she vowed. *Three years at the most.*

Slowly, unbelievably, she began to feel a little stronger and hold down more food. One day she discovered she could sit up without feeling as though everything was spinning around her.

"About time, boy," Tan Din chortled when she told him. "We're going to make landfall in America within the week. You don't want the first thing you do on the Gold Mountain to be tossing up last night's half-eaten dinner. That just doesn't seem the auspicious thing to do in the new country."

CHAPTER
7

Perhaps the imminent landfall made the bak gui sailors more lenient, or perhaps there was something soothing in the late-summer fog that filled the air in the mornings, but the Chinese passengers were allowed to make longer forays out onto the deck as the SS *California* sailed closer to America. Ling Fan took full advantage of this every day. The fresh sea air cleared the last dregs of dizziness out of her head and stomach, and she spent as long as she could staring into the distance.

Ling Fan knew perfectly well that America was not literally a mountain made of gold, but even so, she expected to see a grand sight rising out of the ocean. What she saw was a smudge on the horizon that grew thicker day by day until it resolved itself into masses of green and brown hills.

The knot in her stomach grew larger, and she wasn't sure whether to call it excitement or fear. What now? She knew she would have to report to the offices of the Central Pacific Railroad Company once the ship docked in San Francisco, but aside from that she had no idea what to expect.

One day, when Tan Din was standing with her by the railing at the stern of the ship, she said, "You've been to America before. What's it like?"

Tan Din didn't answer right away. He looked into the

distance as though he were searching through his memories, or perhaps searching for the right words to explain them. "It was different from anything I ever lived through before," he finally said. "Wonderful, but terrible too. The first time I came, I wasn't much older than you. My old ba told me to just hurry on over to the Gold Mountain, fill my hat with as much gold as I could, and get back home. I really thought that was all I had to do!" He spat into the water. "Well, it turns out I was in too much of a rush. Or maybe I was too eager to chase after easy money . . ."

"Or maybe you just didn't get in with the right people," said Wong Wei. Ling Fan hadn't heard him approach. Lately, he'd taken to appearing suddenly at her elbow, like a gui. It made her jumpy. She couldn't help worrying that he'd startle her into doing something that would reveal her secret.

"Who's to say which people are the right people?" Tan Din shrugged.

"Oh, you get a feel for it after a while," Wong Wei said, fingering the coin around his neck. He had been in high spirits for the past week, ever since one of the passengers recognized him from the *Cormorant* and let him into a game on credit. He'd won back almost double the money he'd lost. "Then again, some people never do learn. They're the ones who get played for fools time and again." He smirked.

"Are you calling me a fool, boy?" Tan Din drew himself up to his full height, head and shoulders above the younger man. Wong Wei shrugged, feigning indifference, but his body was taut as a bowstring. Ling Fan tried to distract them both by pointing out something on the horizon. Shortly after that, Wong Wei left them, muttering about a game, to Ling Fan's relief. Her two friends seemed to have nothing in common except a willingness to bicker.

Back in the hold, when a crewman brought down their dinner of dried fish, Ling Fan ventured to ask him how long it would be before landfall. His reply—"Three days"—filled her with joy.

"What were you talking about with that bak gui?" Wong Wei asked. His narrow face was half in shadows, his expression unreadable.

"I asked him how many days left on the ship," Ling Fan said lightly.

"I didn't know you could speak American English."

"A few others here can speak it too," Ling Fan said, shrugging.

"They know some words," Wong Wei said, "but you sound like you know a lot."

The familiar knot of cold dread twisted in her stomach. The days she had spent huddled in a corner with seasickness had been a blessing in disguise, allowing her to keep mostly to herself. So far she'd managed to stay unnoticed, in the shadows. Now, as Wong Wei pressed her, she felt herself in a precarious spot. Too much explaining would open her up to more scrutiny, and that could make her vulnerable to discovery.

"My father was a merchant who had to deal with bak gui," she told him, thinking fast. "I learned it from him." That sounded reasonable.

"Ha! I knew it!" he crowed. "Your hands give you away. It's always the hands."

She resisted the urge to hide her hands behind her back, realizing just in time how girlish that gesture would appear. She tried to remember how her brother had acted when he was in trouble.

"What about my hands?" she asked coldly, crossing her arms.

"Anybody can see you never worked a day in your life. Merchants' hands are as soft as a woman's." Wong Wei spread out his own fingers. His hands were gnarled and thick, the skin pitted and scored, stained with scars. They looked strong enough to crush a skull.

He pointed to a thick scar that crossed his left palm. "I got that when I was nine. Sliced it almost down to the bone while gutting fish for baba. My family's hauled nets and worked the fishing boats for generations. No fancy merchants in my family. Railroad work will be ten times harder, I hear. Are you sure you're up for it? Maybe you should look for other work."

The knot in Ling Fan's stomach doubled in size. He was looking at her so knowingly—so coldly. Her mind raced. Was this it? Was she discovered? Should she try to run up the steps and jump overboard? Throw herself at the mercy of the captain?

No, she told herself firmly. Wong Wei hadn't guessed anything. All she needed to do was keep calm.

"Don't worry about me," she snapped.

His words gnawed at her, though. She was not a dainty girl. Aunt Fei had always bemoaned this even while Ling Fan herself relished being able to wrestle her brother to the ground or outrun him in a race or reach the top of the tallest guava tree. She had always stood side by side with Jing Fan in play and work. But it was true that as they grew older, he outmatched her in feats of brute strength, lifting two sacks of rice to her one or yoking a neighbor's water buffalo in a matter of minutes while she struggled to even lift the wooden harness.

Until now, the reality of facing hard manual labor hadn't sunk in. All her energy had been focused on leaving home and maintaining her disguise. Now, as she surveyed the passengers in the hold, she saw that most of the men looked to be in their prime and fit as mules. Aside from herself and Wong Wei, there were two or three other boys, but they too had the burnt-log look of lifelong laborers.

Doubt, like a great python, settled across her shoulders and started to whisper in her ear. She wasn't afraid of hard work, but she couldn't help wondering if she would be able to keep up with the other workers. What good would the precious contract be if the railroad bosses decided she was unfit for the job? What good would she be to Baba?

Between the pitching ship and her own roiling stomach, Ling Fan found it impossible to get any sleep. Finally, after what felt like an eternity, she gave up and stepped over snoring bodies to reach the steps that led onto the deck. The rain had passed, leaving behind a fierce wind that ripped at her hair and clothing. The water was choppy, but the fresh cold air cleaned all ill feeling out of her. She stood at the railing, watching the clouds stream past the moon like tattered rags.

A hand fell on her shoulder. It was Wong Wei. He had a flask in one hand and smelled as though somebody had thoroughly doused him with the contents of another.

"Tam Jing Fan! I've been calling your name from halfway across the ship!"

Inwardly she flinched. She still wasn't used to answering to her brother's name. She had to work on that. As always when she felt exposed, she scrambled to deflect attention from herself. Fortunately, that was never difficult with Wong Wei.

"A good haul tonight?" she asked, pointing her chin at the flask in his hand.

"The best!" Wong Wei saluted her with the flask. "Come, I never thanked you for helping me get onto the ship."

He handed her the flask. It would be unmanly to refuse, so Ling Fan tipped it back and gulped twice.

"See? What did I say? The best!" Wong Wei smacked her cheerfully on the back as she coughed. She was amazed that fire didn't spew out of her mouth; there was certainly enough blazing down her throat! After a third swallow, the fire faded into a fluid warmth that rooted in her stomach and spread outward to her limbs. She sat down, leaned her head against the bulwark, and watched the stars appear between the shreds of clouds.

"At least the stars are the same," she remarked, the weight of homesickness in her voice. She expected Wong Wei to jump on her with a sarcastic retort, but he didn't.

"On my last night at home, I was invited to my intended bride's house for dinner." Wong Wei's voice was soft in the darkness. "I thought her father had accepted our intentions at last, but I was wrong. At the dinner table was Fee Gou, the son of the fishmonger. Mei's father said . . ." He paused to take a long pull on his flask. "He said I had three years to prove myself."

"Prove yourself?"

"Fee Gou's father owns three fishing boats, you see, and they're the wealthiest family in the village. Mei's father doesn't think I'm worthy of her hand. He thinks I'm too poor. But Mei's a stubborn girl. She told him she wants to marry for love." Ling Fan heard the smile in his voice.

"Her father gave me three years to make a fortune worthy of Mei." He pulled the coin on its string out from under his shirt. It glinted dully against the dark sky. "That night, Mei and I went up in the hills behind our village. The stars were above our heads just like now. She said she knew we were destined to be together. She said she believed in me." His voice thickened.

"Nobody ever told me that before. Then she gave me this and told me that so long as I have this coin, I will never run out of luck while I'm in America."

Ling Fan thought of the note she'd left for Aunt Fei and Ming. She wished she could know for sure that they would understand her reasons for leaving—that they believed in her the way Wong Wei's sweetheart believed in him.

"I can't waste a minute," Wong Wei went on. "I'm here to make my fortune, but every day more Chinese arrive on the Gold Mountain with the same thought in mind, just with a different story. I have to stay ahead of the crowd. I won't let Mei down." He pressed the coin to his lips before slipping it back under his shirt. "But enough about my sad story. What about you? Why are you here on this ship? What's your story?"

"My brother was supposed to make this sojourn instead of me, but he died from the influenza that's killed so many. My father—" She shut her mouth with a snap, shocked at her loose tongue. She had been about to tell Wong Wei everything. What was wrong with her? Her brain felt sluggish, but words spilled out so easily. Only a slight change in Wong Wei's face had stopped her. Perhaps it was just the shifting of shadows, but he had taken on the hunting hawk expression again.

Ling Fan continued, carefully measuring the words before letting them out. Everything she said was true, but ripped apart and stitched back together to make a new tapestry of truth.

"My father has fallen on hard times. He's been wronged." Yes, she could say that much. The times being what they were, so many could say as much. "The money from America will help him. He doesn't deserve what's happened to him. He's always followed his conscience, even if it means making enemies. Once, there was a boy who kept stealing eggs from the villagers' hens.

When he was caught, the village demanded that m—that the village magistrate give him a public whipping. That's the law, of course, but my father insisted on talking to the boy first. He found out that the boy lived with his grandmother and two little sisters in a mud hut that the boy had made. My father paid for all the stolen eggs himself, then asked a friend to take the boy on as a helper on a farm."

She remembered how angry the villagers had been that her father had cheated them out of a public spectacle. Yet he had been adamant. He'd told Ling Fan, "People who do desperate things do so because they have no better option, not because they're wicked."

"Your father sounds like an honorable man," Wong Wei said. "He's fortunate to have a son like you. That reminds me." Wong Wei pulled something out of an inner pocket. Ling Fan recognized his money pouch. He fumbled with the elaborate knot. "Here."

Ling Fan stared at the coin he held out to her. "What's that for?"

"My luck turned the day I met you. I wouldn't be here if it hadn't been for you."

"But you need it."

"Thanks to you, I'm on my way to a mountain of it." Wong Wei took her hand and closed her fingers around the coin. "Think of it as my fare. Or as a token of what's to come in America."

The moon was now a hazy pearl glowing just above the horizon. Its light lay reflected across the water like a finger pointing after their ship. Wong Wei raised his flask to the sky. "Here's to our sojourn on the Gold Mountain! May we find the fortune we deserve!"

CHAPTER
8

If the Port of Guangzhou had been overwhelming, San Francisco Bay was a hundred times worse. Massive ships edged their way to the docks, some with the help of smaller boats. Horns blared incessantly, and collisions seemed constantly imminent.

The SS *California* docked in the late afternoon. Ling Fan wished she could watch the final approach to the mainland from the deck as she had on the *Cormorant*, but the Chinese passengers were ordered to remain in the hold. Feet hammered across the deck above their heads amidst the crewmen's shouts, curses, whistles, and occasional mysterious thuds. The ship groaned as it bumped lightly against the pilings of the dock. In the twilight of the darkened hold, passengers bundled up their possessions.

"Where will you go?" Ling Fan asked Tan Din. She felt as though she was losing a dear friend, even though she'd only known the man for three weeks.

"Du Pon Gai," Tan Din said. "There are a few streets in San Francisco that have a lot of Chinese businesses. Du Pon Gai is the oldest. It's the best place to go to get a bead on work. That's where I went last time. Come with me. There'll be plenty of jobs suitable for a wet rabbit like you!"

Heat crept up the back of her neck. She had kept the railroad contract hidden throughout the voyage. Now she felt awkward about revealing it to Tan Din. He might resent her for having an unfair advantage in their mutual quest for fortune. On the other hand, it felt wrong to keep him in the dark, especially after all he'd done for her.

"Well, actually . . ." Ling Fan chewed her lip. "I already have this." She reached deep into her bag and pulled out the railroad contract. Tan Din looked at it blankly. Wong Wei, who had been repacking his own sack nearby, was suddenly by her side. He snatched it from her hand.

"Is this—?"

"It's mine!" Ling Fan cried, lunging at him. Wong Wei was taller by half a head, and he easily held it out of her reach. There was a nightmarish familiarity about this: Jing Fan used to play to his extra height too, holding things above her head and laughing as she jumped helplessly around him. But this boy wasn't Jing Fan, and the paper he held aloft wasn't a toy. It was Baba's life. Shaking with fury and panic, Ling Fan curled her hand into a fist.

"Nah, nah, nah." Tan Din stepped between them like a long-suffering parent and deftly retrieved the letter. "What is this?"

Still glowering at Wong Wei, Ling Fan explained.

Tan Din let out a roar of laughter and nearly flattened her with his congratulatory back slap. "Well done, boy!"

"Yes, what good fortune, Tam Jing Fan," Wong Wei chimed in. "I suppose your merchant father got it for you?" His voice was light, almost teasing, but Ling Fan shuddered at his expression. She had seen tension in his thin face before, but this time, she saw something else. Something hungry.

"Yes, he did," she said. She felt his eyes on her as she pushed the contract deep inside her bag and knotted it shut.

The doors to the hold were flung open. A young man with

straw-colored hair and gold-rimmed glasses descended the steps, followed by another man wearing a little round pearl-colored hat. He had a fleshy, florid face that was almost completely covered by a rich layer of brown hair. A fine blue suit stretched across his round stomach. The hold quickly filled with smoke from the cigar clamped in his mouth.

The younger man spoke in rudimentary Cantonese, then repeated himself in two other dialects. "Those of you with papers from Li Hing Gold Mountain will be working with their American business partner, Mr. Cornelius Koopmanschap. Stand to the side over there. We'll escort you to the railroad as soon as we've sorted out your papers and you've cleared the customs inspection. The rest of you will now disembark."

About a dozen passengers approached him and presented papers like Ling Fan's. While he spoke to each of them and wrote notes in a small book, the other passengers climbed up the steps and disappeared into the sunshine.

Tan Din and Wong Wei were among the last to go. Wong Wei didn't even glance in her direction. Tan Din grasped her shoulder as he passed. "Good luck to you, boy." He clapped his dusty brown hat on his head and followed Wong Wei toward the steps.

A wave of misery rose up in Ling Fan. Those two were the only familiar faces in this foreign land.

"Wait! Tan Din, Wong Wei, wait!" They paused, confused, as Ling Fan ran over to the young bak gui. "Excuse me, sir, but there's been a mistake. My cousins"—she pointed at Wong Wei and Tan Din—"were promised railroad jobs too, but the person who told us this only gave us one paper." She pulled her contract out of her bag and held it out to him, relieved that her hand didn't shake.

"Don't try to play your coolie tricks on me," he said coldly in English, then added in Cantonese, "It's one contract per person. Nobody would've promised otherwise."

By now Tan Din and Wong Wei were by Ling Fan's side, listening to the exchange.

"My uncle paid three times the price and was promised that the three of us would have railroad jobs when we arrived," Wong Wei said, catching on. "He worried you bak gui would go back on your word, and now we know who's been tricked."

"And I'm saying that's impossible," the man retorted. "Keep it up and I'll rip this contract up entirely. Then you can all go find a job in the mines together!"

The words were like a dagger of ice in Ling Fan's chest.

"No need to do that," Tan Din said sharply. "There's your contract. One per person, you say. Here's the person." He gave Ling Fan a little push forward. Ling Fan hardly heard him. Aunt Fei's voice hissed in her mind: *Only a girl would've made such a risky gamble. Only a girl would've lost a golden opportunity the moment she set foot on the Gold Mountain. This is what happens when girls try to act like men!*

"Is there a problem, Mr. Thayer?" The man with the cigar strode over.

"These coolies are trying to pull a fast one, Mr. Koopmanschap." The young man explained the situation in English.

Koopmanschap listened, rolling his cigar from one corner of his mouth to the other, looking the three of them up and down as though they were mules at the market. "I tell you what, Thayer," he said, "I've been in this business for years now, importing all manner of things: flour, provisions, and now coolies! You know what I've learned?"

Thayer shook his head.

"There's a whole damn country full of coolies who'll do just about anything to get a job here in America. There are thousands who'll be happy to sign away two years, five years, even eight years of their heathen lives just for a monthly wage of fifteen or twenty American dollars. Ha! Add these two to the list, it makes no difference to me. Crocker and Strobridge'll pay me a hundred dollars a head just the same." The round little man put his cigar back in his mouth and strolled away, humming.

"Yes, sir." Thayer did not look happy, but he did as he was told. "Your names?"

Next he asked for their home villages and their ages, which he scribbled down in his notebook. Then he ushered the whole group of contract bearers off the ship and into the bright San Francisco sunshine.

Descending the gangplank to the dock, Ling Fan felt as though she were walking into the maw of a giant creature made of a million writhing parts. She had never seen so many bak gui in one place: crewmen, dockworkers, merchants, officials, all intent on accomplishing their tasks in a hurry. Her eyes were drawn to the bak gui women with their boldly colored dresses and their long, easy strides—so different from the mincing walks of women Ling Fan knew back home. As she paused at the foot of the gangplank, gaping at the activity around her, a dockworker buried beneath a load of wooden boards brushed past her.

"Out of the way, y'damn coolie!"

She jumped to the side only to come face-to-face with another worker carrying a trunk on his back. "Move!"

Hundreds of sojourners crowded together on the wharf, waiting. Craning her neck, Ling Fan spotted bak gui men in blue uniforms, holding wooden batons at the ready. "What's going on?" she whispered to Tan Din.

"They search everyone for contraband," Tan Din said, using the American word. "They say we try to sneak in opium or other illegal things, but"—he pointed with his chin—"who knows what they decide is illegal?" Ling Fan followed his gaze and watched one bak gui run his hands along a sojourner's arms and legs, while another dumped the sojourner's sack of possessions on the ground and kicked through it with his feet. He scooped something from the pile and shook it at the sojourner. She couldn't hear what was said, but the sojourner was led away, protesting loudly.

Ling Fan's throat closed. She hadn't expected this! The band of cotton cloth wrapped around her chest suddenly felt ridiculously flimsy—it would never withstand the groping of those bak gui hands.

While she was frantically trying to think of what to do, Thayer pushed his way to one of the bak gui conducting searches and murmured in his ear. An envelope passed between them. The bak gui nodded and Thayer waved for their group to follow him past the searchers and off the wharf. Ling Fan's breath left her in a rush of relief.

As Thayer led the sojourners through the dusty streets, she felt people watching their progress. Many looked up with as much open curiosity as she herself felt, while others tried to seem indifferent. More than once somebody spat tobacco juice at her feet. Again and again, she heard the word *coolie*.

"It's the bak gui's term for laborers like us," Tan Din said when she asked. "They say we're out to steal their jobs, when the truth is their own bosses hire us because they can pay us half as much for the same work."

"Why? If it's the same work, it should be the same pay!"

Tan Din pushed his hat to the back of his head and scrubbed his face like a bear scratching an itch. "That's the way it is. And even so, it's more than we would dream of making back home. Welcome to the Gold Mountain."

They arrived at a wooden building with a painted sign over the door that read KOOPMANSCHAP IMPORTS. Three wagons stood waiting, each hitched to a team of mismatched horses. A short, thickset Chinese man waited in the doorway. He was dressed in a long blue tunic and loose gray pants, and his hair was tied back in a long, tight queue. When he took the notebook from Thayer, Ling Fan tried not to stare. Two of his middle fingers were gone, and the remaining fingers were swollen like sausages.

"Chin Lin Sou is the Chinese foreman you'll be reporting to," he told them. "I'm Ah Sook, one of his assistants, and you'll be getting your job assignments from me when we get to base camp. For now, climb aboard a wagon. We're headed to Sacramento first. From there we'll ride the train to the End o' Line in the mountains."

As the wagons rolled onto the main thoroughfare, Ling Fan glimpsed tall, dark ship masts clustered together in San Francisco Bay like a forest of leafless trees. Beyond the open mouth of the bay was the Pacific Ocean, and beyond that was home.

She bit down hard on her lip to keep the tears from flowing.

When the bay was finally out of sight, she took a shuddering breath and let it out slowly as she turned to face the men in her wagon.

Tan Din, with his hat pulled over his face, had settled into a spot in the corner. He sighed too, then let out a long, tuneful fart.

∧ ∧ ∧

They arrived at the Central Pacific Railroad's base camp in the Sierra Nevada mountains at the tail end of a drenching rainstorm. Ling Fan's ears still rang from the wild clatter of iron wheels against the rails. Riding the train had been like being inside an untamed metal animal that bellowed and hissed as it flashed across the countryside, faster than she'd ever moved in her life. Her spirit soared at the thought that soon she would have a hand in carving out a path for it! The wooden wagons they'd boarded for the final leg of the journey seemed dull and tedious in comparison.

It was close to sunset when they stopped in front of an expanse of sopping gray tents that spread outward like an untidy, unplanned village. The tents were thrown up every which way, with no apparent order or plan. In some places there were straight rows, while in others the tents were all in a huddle. Dirt paths, turned to ankle-deep mud by the rain, wound around them like the threads of a spider's web.

The sojourners climbed out of the carts. Ah Sook began pulling down rolls of tent cloth and tossing them at the newcomers. "Pitch your tents, then report to the cooking area for your dinner."

Ling Fan took a roll for herself. "Everybody shares," Ah Sook barked at her. "We're not running an inn with private rooms. Two or three to a tent."

Ling Fan stared in dismay at the boys and men around her. Two or three to a tent would leave them practically cheek by jowl. How would she keep her secret in such close quarters?

Tan Din seized the tent out of her hands. "You're with me, boy," he told her. "Can't think anybody else would put up with what I had to when we were on the ship." He hoisted the rolled tent and his bag over his shoulder and strode off. Ling Fan followed, relieved to be sharing a tent with someone she could trust, someone who would give her space.

Wong Wei pushed farther into the encampment with two other men, talking about an upcoming round of games, while Tan Din found a spot beside a windblown sapling and began to set up. Around them, more men trickled into the camp, workers finished with their shifts. These men spent a few minutes at their tents, then gravitated toward a bowl-shaped clearing dotted with fire pits and trestle tables. Ling Fan, Tan Din, and the other new arrivals followed them.

At the farthest edge of the clearing was a long, open-sided tent where a large table stood laden with covered cauldrons. The unmistakable scent of food made Ling Fan's stomach give a tiny mewl of anticipation. An old man in a filthy apron, standing near a stack of bowls at one end of the table, gestured for the workers to serve themselves.

Ling Fan took a bowl and a thick-handled soup spoon. Her exhaustion fell away as she peered into each pot. Rice! Bok choy! Chicken, stir-fried and mixed with slices of bamboo and scallions! Tiny pieces of home drifted up to her on the wisps of fragrance. She had to bite down hard on her lip to keep tears from dropping into her bowl.

"Ingredients from San Francisco are shipped up here by railway," one of the more seasoned workers explained. "Our cooking staff gets to prepare everything the way we want it."

Ling Fan nodded at him, then looked away. He seemed friendly, but it would be wisest to keep to herself. The fewer people she got to know here, the better her chances of keeping her secret. She'd already befriended Tan Din and Wong Wei. They would have to be enough.

Most of the men didn't even bother to sit before shoveling food from their bowls into their mouths as fast as they could. Ling Fan followed suit, then filled her bowl with a generous helping of soup. But Tan Din stood aloof, peering into each pot with an expression of disdain. "Burnt ginger. Meat the size of fists—no wonder it's half raw."

"Aiya! This isn't a noodle shop." The aproned man glared at Tan Din. "I'd like to see you do better!"

"Of course I can. I've worked plenty of years in restaurants from Guangzhou to San Francisco." Tan Din glared back, arms crossed.

"Well then, go right ahead." The old man took off his apron and tossed it at Tan Din. "The men will be expecting breakfast at five o'clock." He stomped out of the clearing and vanished into the tent village.

Ah Sook raised an eyebrow. "Looks like I won't need to figure out which job to give you!"

Tan Din pushed back his hat, scrubbing at his broad red face. He thrust his chin at the cooking crew milling around behind the serving table. "Do they listen?" he demanded.

"They're all good men."

"Then breakfast will be ready at four."

Ling Fan thumped Tan Din on the back, happy that her friend had found a job that suited him. As she looked out across the work camp, she wondered if she would be as lucky.

∧ ∧ ∧

Ling Fan stood with Wong Wei and a half dozen others in front of the entrance to a railroad tunnel. It looked like a ragged mouth punched out of a rocky giant's head. Ling Fan knew that several hundred yards away, out of sight beyond the rising ground, another work crew was excavating the facing that would be the tunnel's exit point. Eventually, the two winding ends would meet in the middle, uniting to form a continuous tunnel. She'd been astounded to learn that this was only one of a total of fifteen tunnels that would eventually cross the crooked back of the Sierra Nevada. Several were in various stages of excavation now.

Other work crews were busy clearing the roadbed for the train tracks that would connect them to the rest of the Central Pacific Railroad, back at the End o' Line. Ling Fan imagined a great iron serpent making its sinuous way through the wooded foothills, hugging the mountainside as it swept along sharp bends and disappearing into the dark cavernous tunnels that led it to Utah.

Excitement coursed through her veins, making her shift from foot to foot.

"The blasters have done their part," Ah Sook told them. "Now you'll join the crews hauling the granite rubble out." He handed each worker a long-handled shovel and then a wooden yoke with two iron buckets suspended on each end.

Ling Fan settled her yoke across her shoulders and followed the others in her group as, one by one, they were swallowed by the gaping black hole of the tunnel. The air was thicker inside. Her eyes gradually adjusted to the darkness. Every few yards, great wooden beams braced the tunnel walls and ceiling. Shadows cast by lanterns licked at Ling Fan's feet. Voices echoed up out of the darkness ahead along with the hiss and scrape of metal on stone.

At last they arrived at a point where the tunnel seemed to pinch shut. Broken rock lay strewn about in shoulder-high piles. Ling Fan's crew joined the men who were already shoveling the rubble into buckets and hoisting laden yokes across their shoulders, then staggering back the way they had come.

Ling Fan set her buckets down beside a pile and thrust her shovel beneath the rocks. She tried to lift, but the shovel didn't budge. She heaved. The shovel twisted in her grasp. Perhaps the rubble wasn't loosened enough. She tugged the shovel out and tried again, this time thrusting harder. Again, she heaved. Nothing.

Sweat slid down the side of her face. All around, men from her group were topping off their buckets and heading back to the tunnel entrance. Panic seized her. What would happen if she fell behind? Would she be exposed for the impostor she was? Would she be replaced? No! She'd come this far. She couldn't fail now!

Ling Fan took a deep calming breath and studied the rubble around her. The stones were incredibly heavy, she realized, hefting one in her hand. *Granite*, Ah Sook called it. Ling Fan scanned the ground until she found a pile of smaller chunks to slide her shovel beneath. With a grunt, her heart hammering in her chest, she lifted the pile and poured it into her bucket. She scooped up another small load, and then another.

By the time her buckets were finally filled, sweat was pouring down her back, and the muscles of her shoulders and arms burned, but she felt a sense of triumph.

Ling Fan leaned her shovel against the wall of the tunnel, arranged the yoke over her shoulders, and stood up. Or tried to stand up. It felt as though she'd lifted the entire mountain on her shoulders. She took a step. The buckets dragged across the dirt floor. Another step. She stopped, gasping. Her face burning with shame, she tipped each bucket to let some of the stones fall back to the ground. Only then was she able to join the line of men heading to the tunnel entrance. As she emptied her buckets outside, she braced herself for comments from the others, but none came. She turned and trudged back into the tunnel.

At noon, a donkey cart loaded with food arrived. Most of the workers ate where they were, shoveling the food into their mouths with their fingers. Ling Fan worried that if she sat down, she would never be able to stand up again. Besides, she had to relieve herself. Her nose quickly showed her the area being used as a latrine, but she circled farther out, trying to look unobtrusive as she searched for a secluded clump of bushes or rocks. She was glad her bleeding cycles had still not started—something Aunt Fei used to fret over, now one less thing to worry about.

After her shift, Ling Fan crawled into the tent she shared with Tan Din, arms and legs trembling. It had been a grueling ten hours. She threw herself onto her bedroll, meaning to close her eyes for a few minutes before dinner.

The next thing she knew, early morning light was streaming through a crack in the tent and Ah Sook was once again calling out workers. Every muscle in her body screamed in protest as she sat up. Tan Din had already left hours earlier to start the cook fires. Her fingers trembled as she tightened the knots around her linen chest wrap, smoothed her tunic, and stood up to begin another day.

CHAPTER
9

Payday was the last Sunday of the month. Ling Fan had been on the Gold Mountain less than a week, but she was just as excited as the workers expecting a full month's wages.

Men rose early to line up before a trestle of squared-off logs set up for the paymaster. He arrived around noon, wrapped in a great fur cloak and flanked by two rough-looking men dressed in buffalo skins. Ling Fan heard a sojourner saying they'd come from Illinoistown, the place where Central Pacific's fully functional tracks came to a temporary end.

The paymaster uncinched two bulging saddlebags from his horse and brought them over to the trestle table. He laid open a large leather-bound book on the table and settled down next to Chin Lin Sou, the foreman of the sojourner work crews, who had already taken a seat.

One by one the workers approached the table. Chin Lin Sou quietly affirmed the name of each worker while the paymaster made a note in his book, then formed a stack of coins on the table for the worker to scoop up. The worker bobbed a hasty thank-you, stuffed the coins into his pocket, and walked away. It wasn't long before men squatted in groups, laughing, smoking, and gambling anew.

Until arriving on the Gold Mountain, Ling Fan had never

heard of a day of the week reserved for rest. No work on the railroad was permitted. Most of the sojourners treated the day like a festival day, hunched around dice or card games, staggering down the dirt lanes between the tents clutching bottles of spirits, or visiting the tents that seemed to overflow with thick clouds of sickly-sweet opium smoke.

Some used the time more productively, mending and washing their clothing. Ling Fan crouched over wet stones in the nearest shallow streambed to scrub the tunic and trousers she'd worn all week. Others followed the same stream with fishing poles over their shoulders and returned with strings of wriggling trout. Occasionally, gunshots rang out from the nearby trees and Ling Fan wondered if a lucky sojourner had bagged a rabbit or squirrel for supper. That evening, Ling Fan's mouth watered from the scent of smoked fish and game filling the air. As campfires sprang up in the dusk, the sojourners who had trekked out to Illinoistown for the afternoon staggered back in twos or threes, singing bawdy songs and reeking of liquor.

When the last glow of light was wavering over the jagged teeth of the mountains, men sat around fires, smoking or crouched over dice games. A few sat on empty crates beside the open flaps of tents. It was a cool fall night, and the tiny, smoky fires provided more light than warmth. Heavy plumes of smoke floated upward and hung like a dark cloud against the even darker bulk of the mountains.

The stink of whiskey and stale tobacco hung in the air, along with other odors brought out by the close crowding of tired men. Every so often a roar of hoots or groans rang out: a dice game was starting to pick up. Ling Fan stood at the edge of the group of men watching two players. No surprise that one of them was Wong Wei. He waved her over to join him, but she shook her head and turned to thread her way along the paths through the ragged tent village.

Clothing scrubbed clean earlier that day was still draped everywhere to dry: on the tops of tents, on ropes knotted between poles, even on the scraggly bushes that grew near the base of the rocky mountain wall. Laughter, shouts, bits of raucous song, and curses drifted out from some of the tents. Others were as dark and silent as dungeons. Once in a while, Ling Fan caught the scent of opium pipes.

The tent Ling Fan shared with Tan Din was empty. She crawled in and collapsed on her bedroll with a sigh. Her body felt as though she had been working for a year. In the dim light, she sat up and gently worked her gloves off. They were Tan Din's gloves, huge leather mitts that fit over the strips of linen wrapped around her hands.

She unwrapped the cloth, hissing as it caught on the half-healed blisters that covered her palms. Each night, Tan Din helped her change the bandages, but they were often so encrusted with mud, sweat, and blood that she had to soak them in warm water for half an hour before they could be removed.

The first night they did this, she had clamped her teeth closed to keep from screaming, focusing on the image of her father being dragged off to his cell. Tonight, her hands felt stiff, but they were no longer a mass of agony. She slathered on the pungent ointment that Tan Din had mixed for her and wrapped each hand in fresh bandages.

Fumbling a little with her bound-up hands, she lit a candle and took out her ink set. **Jing: I don't know what's worse, waking up to Tan Din's snores or waking up to his farts. But I'm getting so much stronger. I feel like I could lift an ox!**

Most days she was too tired to write, or her hands hurt too

much. But when she did manage it, she felt lighter, as though an invisible harness had lifted from her shoulders.

She burned her note in the flame of her candle, letting her doubts and fears float skyward with the ashes. **We're like ants digging at the feet of sleeping rock giants. What if the mountains woke up and decided to crush us?**

For what must have been the hundredth time, she pulled the silk bag from beneath her tunic and shook out the coins the paymaster had given her just that morning. The gold felt comfortably heavy in her hand.

Tomorrow, she would give most of these wages to the Chinese Benevolent Society money man for safekeeping. He would keep track of her earnings until she was ready to make arrangements with Li Hing Gold Mountain to transfer the money to China. But for now, Ling Fan counted each coin as she slipped it back into the bag. Tomorrow was Monday, and she had another long exhausting week in the tunnels ahead of her. She fell asleep with the bag in her fist.

∧ ∧ ∧

Ling Fan stood in the center of Tunnel Two, bowed down by the load of rubble slung across her shoulders. In the distance, the beat of the picks and hammers as they chewed their way through the mountain echoed faintly against the rocky walls. The tunnel entrance was only twenty feet away, but it might as well be twenty miles. The wooden yoke dug into her shoulders as she forced herself to take step after step. She kept her eyes on the entrance—a bright, ragged hole that slowly grew larger. At last she burst through. The sun blazed blindingly as she staggered to the dumping area.

She paused for a moment after unloading her latest batch of rubble and wiped her face with a rag. Sweat ran down her aching back. The stiff wind blowing down from the Sierra Nevada peaks felt as good as a long drink of cold water. Behind her, workers from her crew emerged from the tunnel like a line of giant ants. Each face was coated in a layer of dust, each back bent with a load of rubble. Some had tied rags over their noses and mouths to keep from breathing in the fine granite dust that infused the tunnel air. Without breaking stride, they dumped their loads and turned back to the tunnel, empty buckets swinging. Ling Fan hurried after them.

She passed Wong Wei on his way out with a load. Their eyes met briefly, but neither wasted energy or time with talk. She arrived at the pile of loose rubble and began shoveling granite into her buckets. She'd been at this particular assignment for two weeks now, and she was pleased that while she was still exhausted at the end of the day, her stamina and strength had grown. At least she was keeping up with the other workers.

Every part of the job had become routine: shovel, carry, dump, return, shovel, carry, dump, return. Today felt different, though. Something felt off. She noticed it on her third trip back into the mountain. Dust and grit were trickling down the walls and sprinkling from the ceiling of the tunnel. This happened from time to time—a patch here, a patch there. But now it was happening all along great stretches of the tunnel. Sand and dirt began to accumulate in tiny drifts along both sides.

On her fifth trip, Ling Fan heard a tremendous crack followed by a thunderous boom. Suddenly, men with black-smudged faces were running past her, shouting, "The tunnel is collapsing! Get out! Drop your buckets! Run!"

Somebody stumbled into her, knocking her hard against

the craggy tunnel wall. She fell to the floor with her yoke and buckets on top of her. In the darkness, several feet stampeded over her legs and outstretched arms.

Then Ling Fan felt the cold stone vibrate beneath her hands. Everything began to shake. Dust and small rocks rained down from the ceiling with a hissing roar. She could only see a few inches in front of her face. It became almost impossible to take a breath. Ling Fan clawed at the harness that pinned her to the ground until she was able to squirm free.

She burst out of the tunnel entrance, into the harsh sunlight, gasping for air. Behind her, other members of her work crew dashed out, threw themselves down on the ground, thanked their ancestors that they had made it out alive.

"Make way! Move!" somebody cried. Ling Fan turned to see two men dragging a third away from the tunnel. His legs were bloody and twisted. She saw a tall, thin boy stagger toward her, one scarecrow arm dangling uselessly while he screamed in agony. For one icy heartbeat she thought it was Wong Wei, but it wasn't. Wong Wei was nowhere to be seen.

"Where is Wong Wei? Have you seen Wong Wei?" she kept asking as she rushed from group to group. Blank stares, shakes of heads. The trickle of men coming out of the tunnel slowed, then stopped. The last ones to emerge was a man staggering under the weight of a worker he'd slung over his shoulders. Ling Fan ran to them as the rescuer carefully laid down his gasping burden. She gagged and almost fainted at the sight. The person she stared down at was hard to recognize because his head had been crushed like an egg, but she could tell from his build that it wasn't Wong Wei.

Two men on horses thundered up the path from the base camp. One was Ah Sook, looking like a sack of yams hunched over his saddle. The other was Chin Lin Sou. Ling Fan had never spoken with him but had often seen him giving orders to the hundreds of Chinese workers in the camp. He was tall—taller than most of the workers—and he spoke American English better than any sojourner she'd ever heard. He was dressed like the bak gui bosses, in a heavy button-down shirt and vest, with trousers tucked into black boots. A crease appeared on his high forehead as he surveyed the injured crew.

"What happened?" Chin Lin Sou demanded, swinging down from his saddle.

"Tunnel collapse," a worker gasped.

"What? Impossible!" Ah Sook growled. "Those tunnels are reinforced every step of the way."

"Is everyone out?" Chin Lin Sou asked grimly.

The worker who'd spoken up said, "There may still be people trapped or buried."

Which meant that if Wong Wei wasn't out here, he must still be under the mountain.

Ling Fan's legs began moving before the thought was complete. They propelled her past injured and uninjured workers, back to the tunnel. She thought she heard somebody shouting at her, but she didn't stop.

There was almost no light inside. Most of the kerosene lamps lay extinguished on the ground, but Ling Fan found one that was still lit and carried it with her as she went deeper into the mountain.

"Wong Wei?" she called. The tunnel was strewn with rubble, but she was able to pick her way through. Sand and small rocks were still falling from the ceiling, still sliding down the walls. Every so often larger clumps of stone came down, setting off little avalanches of movement around her. Farther in, she encountered larger mounds of rock that she had to crawl over on her hands and knees. At the base of one large pile was an unmoving foot. Ling Fan gasped, then called again. From faraway came a sigh, like wind whistling through a crack. Was that a voice? "Wong Wei?"

"Here! I'm here!" a voice called back from the darkness. Ling Fan came to a pile of rock that blocked the tunnel from wall to wall and from floor to ceiling. "Tam Jing Fan, is that you? I'm here!" Wong Wei's voice sounded as though he was right behind the newly fallen stones.

Relief surged through Ling Fan like a wave. He was alive! "Are you hurt?"

"I don't think so, but my leg is caught under something. One of the wooden beams, I think." Ling Fan climbed up the pile of rocks that blocked her way, trying to find a gap wide enough to crawl through. A chunk of granite under her right foot dislodged as she put her weight on it, and she slid back down to the ground. Rocks, gravel, and sand skittered down the mound around her. The air was filled with dust. She raised the lantern high, trying to scan the top of the blockage. Close to the right side of the tunnel wall was a large black space that looked like a gap. She set the lantern on the floor and started to climb toward it.

She slipped twice but managed to keep herself from sliding more than a foot each time. Finally, she reached the gap. It was just wide enough for her head and shoulders to fit through. The tunnel was pitch-black on the other side of the blockage.

"Wong Wei?"

"Here!"

He sounded close. Ling Fan wriggled hard and managed to pull the rest of her body through the gap. It was like crawling into a deep empty well on a moonless night. For a dizzying second Ling Fan lost complete track of up and down. She clawed frantically at the rock as her feet slipped. She half slid, half tumbled down the slope and landed on something soft. She groped blindly at it. A leg. A leg that didn't move.

"Where are you?" she shrieked in panic.

"I'm right here!" his voice replied a few feet from where she'd landed. A little light from her kerosene lamp filtered down through the gap. Her eyes adjusted to the darkness enough for her to make out the jagged remains of one of the wooden braces. Beyond it was another mass of fallen rock. She crawled forward until her hand bumped against something wrapped in fabric. To her relief, it gave a little jerk.

"My leg is caught," said Wong Wei. "I can't get free."

Ling Fan probed with her hands, finding the rocks and wood that had pinned his leg. She pushed and pulled with all her strength, but it was no use. "I can't move it by myself. I'll go get help—"

"No!" Wong Wei grabbed her tunic. "Don't leave me here!" Sand and rocks continued to roll down the sides of the tunnel. The air was thickening, filling with fine dust that set them both coughing and gasping. Far in the distance they heard a muffled boom as part of the ceiling deeper in the tunnel collapsed.

"The others will come quicker if they know exactly where you are and that you're still alive," she tried to reassure him.

"What if the rest of the tunnel collapses after you leave?" Wong Wei's voice was high.

"It won't," she said, making herself believe it as she said it. "But I have to go now." There was no time to lose. The rain of sand and rocks was intensifying.

A soft sound drifted out of the darkness. It could've been

a sob or a sigh. "You're right. But can you do something for me first?"

"Of course."

Ling Fan could just make out the Wong Wei's darker shape sitting up and fumbling at his neck. "Take this with you."

"Your coin? Why?"

"Take it for luck. And"—Wong Wei swallowed—"if you happen to pass by my village, San Hoi Bein, when you're back in China, perhaps you could give it back to Mei and tell her I tried." There was sadness in his voice but no fear.

Ling Fan felt her throat close. It was the sort of thing her brother would've said. Tears rolled down her cheeks, mixing with the grit and sweat that caked her face. The air seemed to grow heavier in her lungs. She forced it in and out through clenched teeth as though she were breathing for both of them. She was not going to let Wong Wei give up.

"You'll tell her yourself, after we get out of here."

"Yes, of course," Wong Wei said softly. "But for now, I just want you to have it—for luck. Please."

Ling Fan reached toward him. Her hand fumbled through the rubble, colliding with a piece of splintered wood. It was long and heavy. A memory tickled the back of her mind. With the right lever, you can move the world, Baba used to say. She tested the wood in her hand. Yes, it might work!

"What are you doing?" Wong Wei coughed.

"Trying something." Ling Fan picked up the wood, wedged one end beneath one of the granite chunks that pinned Wong Wei, and threw her weight on the other end. Slowly, the chunk shifted to one side. She yanked the wood free and this time wedged it in more carefully. The granite chunk shivered and rolled off the pile.

"It's working!" Wong Wei cried. A piece of granite the size of a wagon wheel crashed down from the ceiling. "Hurry!"

Swiftly, she felt around. Two more rocks and the wooden beam still pinned Wong Wei's leg. She angled her lever and wedged it between the two rocks. Once again, she threw her weight on the lever and one of the rocks rolled aside.

"I think I can move the beam a little now," Ling Fan panted. "But you'll have to pull your leg out when I lift it." She wedged the lever and heaved. Wong Wei scuttled back just as the lever snapped in Ling Fan's hand. The timber beam crashed down again. One end raked against the wall as it fell, bringing a huge chunk of stone down with it.

"Come on! Climb!" Ling Fan shouted, yanking at Wong Wei. They scrambled up the mound of rubble toward the gap Ling Fan had used earlier. Wong Wei wriggled through and rolled down the other side, with Ling Fan right behind him. Rocks and sand sloughed down the mound with them. Something slammed into Ling Fan's right arm as she reached the bottom. The pain was so sharp it made her head swim. She could barely move.

Wong Wei looked back over his shoulder and screamed, "Run!" He limped out of sight ahead of her.

Ling Fan could barely pick herself up off the ground, let alone make her legs move. Behind her, rocks were cascading down the rubble heap like a tidal wave. Chunks of ceiling showered down around her. She tried to crawl forward but her lungs were burning with every breath. It felt as though the mountain itself was reaching out rocky tentacles to keep her from escaping.

Dizziness and pain forced her to stop. She put her head down and closed her eyes, waiting for the tunnel to collapse on top of her. "I'm sorry, Baba," she whispered. She wondered what she would say to her brother when she saw him again.

Then suddenly there were lights and voices. She felt hands drag her across the rocky floor, until she felt deliciously cool air against her face.

She was outside, staring up into a night sky filled with thousands of stars. Somebody put a canteen to her lips and she drank deeply. The familiar taste of tea soothed her despite its bitterness. She tried to lift her hand to take the canteen, but the pain almost made her scream. Her arm hung like a swollen sausage. Wong Wei crouched in front of her, saying something, but she couldn't make sense of any of it.

Time blurred. Wong Wei was helping her to her feet, then she was being lifted into a wagon, then she was in a large tent.

At least a dozen men were sitting or lying on the ground around her. A constant buzz of groans filled the air, punctuated by sharp cries of pain. She glanced over at the person beside her, then wished she hadn't. She rolled over and threw up.

"Easy now. Let's have a look at you." A man knelt beside her. Streaks of white hair twined through his long queue. He briskly ordered an assistant to mop up the mess she'd made while he rolled up her tunic sleeve and examined her right arm. He probed gently, but she gasped with the effort to keep from screaming. "Your arm isn't broken, just badly sprained at the elbow." He slathered it with a poultice of medicinal herbs and wrapped it in rags. The sweet, pungent aroma unexpectedly brought tears to her eyes; Aunt Fei's home remedies had smelled much the same.

"You're lucky your friend saved your life," the healer added, leaning back on his heels. "He came running out of Tunnel Two screaming that you were still in there, and wouldn't stop until they pulled you out."

Ling Fan's relief that they'd both gotten out of the tunnel in one piece was cut short when the man continued. "Central Pacific will provide transportation back to San Francisco free of charge—no deduction from your pay."

"Why would I want to go back to San Francisco?" she asked blankly.

"Your injury will take several weeks to heal, boy. You won't be able to work at full capacity, and the bosses can't afford to have people just sitting around."

"But I want to work! Isn't there anything I can do here?" She twisted around as though she could conjure a job if she looked hard enough.

He shook his head.

"But I have to make money!" The dread that spread through her like frost left her feeling far worse than the pain in her arm. Two weeks' wages would not be enough to help Baba!

"That isn't the railroad's problem," the healer said, not without sympathy. "Look, you can reapply for a spot back here once you've healed properly."

He helped her to her feet, led her out of the medical tent, and gestured to a wagon that held several wounded workers. "It's going back to San Francisco in the morning. Safe travels."

Ling Fan shuffled toward the wagon, but once the healer had turned away, she headed back to the tent she shared with Tan Din.

She was shaking by the time she arrived. Her arm blazed with pain, as if a thousand knives were digging into it. She crawled through the flap and wrapped herself in her blanket, biting down hard on a corner to keep from crying out.

The pain was nothing compared to the waves of anxiety that poured over her. She could barely move her arm; using it to work was out of the question. But any time when she wasn't earning American dollars was more time Baba had to spend in Peng Lu. The distant incessant sound of men hammering against iron spikes and railroad ties reminded her of the sound of prison doors slamming closed.

The tent flap was wrenched aside. "Jing Fan!" Tan Din's bellow filled the tiny space. He pushed a lantern ahead of him as he crawled inside.

She scrubbed her eyes with the back of her hand before sitting up. "I'm here."

The lantern light threw strange shadows across Tan Din's face, but there was no mistaking the look of relief that swept across it. He sat back on his heels. "I heard there was a tunnel collapse. I saw the bodies go by in carts. I thought you—" His raspy voice broke and then turned into a growl. "Damn these bak gui and their flimsy tunnels! How many more of us have to be crushed like insects before this railroad is done?"

"I'm fine."

He eyed her cloth-swathed arm. "Is it broken?"

"No, but it might as well be. You need two good arms to work on the railroad. What am I going to do now? I need this job!"

"There are other jobs that pay good money and won't be nearly as dangerous."

"The railroad pays the most!"

"You won't get paid anything if you're dead. Even I had no idea how dangerous it is here. This is no place for a—"

"I'm not dead, and I can take care of myself!"

Tan Din took his hat off and scrubbed at his face, muttering something under his breath. It sounded suspiciously like *stubborn donkey*. "There are safer, easier jobs in San Francisco.

Jobs more suited for a—a—young person like you. Especially an injured young person." He scowled at the crumpled hat in his hands, his stubbly jaw working as though he were chewing through a few more choice words.

Ling Fan drew a shaky breath and held it; her heart hammered against her ribs like a caged, angry bird. Her voice remained steady. "Tan Din, my father's life depends on the money I make here on the Gold Mountain. I'm never going to turn my back on a chance to get it for him, no matter what it takes." She locked eyes with him until Tan Din looked away.

But to her surprise, when he crushed the hat back on top of his head, a smile was slowly spreading across his sunburned face. "Aiya, of course! Why didn't I think of this in the first place?"

"What?"

"Do you know anything about cooking?"

"A little," Ling Fan replied truthfully, thinking of the family meals she'd helped with back home.

"Good. Then you'll start in the morning. Meet me at the cook fires before the sun rises." Tan Din rolled himself up in his own bedroll. "And don't be late. I can't stand a lazy cook."

CHAPTER 10

Ling Fan woke just as the sky took on the lighter shade of blue black that comes right before dawn begins its glow. Tan Din had already left the tent by the time she crawled out. Heavy snores and grunts filled the air like a chorus of bullfrogs as she threaded her way through the camp, down the faint path that led past the latrine to the enormous oak whiskey casks that the workers used for bathing.

Once a week, late at night or early in the morning, she took her turn. This meant that the water was always tepid and soiled from those who'd used it before her. She tried not to think about it and bathed as quickly as possible, careful of her injured arm.

Afterward, in the shadow of a tall spur of rock, she shook out the long band of cotton and wound it tightly around her chest again, pulled on the stiff undershirt that she tucked into the waistband of her loose-legged pants, and buttoned up her tunic. With only one fully usable hand, all this took longer than she would've liked.

The first faint, peachy glow outlined the dark craggy mass of mountains to the east. As she walked toward the cooking area, Ling Fan dragged her fingers through her wet hair, pulling it back into a queue. Two crows took to the air, their harsh scolds echoing off the cliff walls around them. She watched the dark shapes dart and swoop wildly through the sky, reminding her of the days not so long ago when she and her brother raced around the family compound. As she idly traced the birds' path across the horizon, a flash of light caught her eye. It was some distance away, near the western edge of the campsite where the supply wagons stood. Ling Fan could just make out a figure moving around one of the covered wagons.

The person wore a long blue-gray coat and a brown hat pulled low so that it was impossible to make out his face. He could've simply been another early riser, but Ling Fan noticed something odd about the way he moved. Every few steps, he stopped to look around. He circled the wagon twice before he climbed up and disappeared under the canvas.

Curious, Ling Fan crept closer. She crouched behind some barrels about fifty yards away from the wagon, waiting for the figure to emerge.

A pair of booted feet dropped back down onto the ground. In a moment he'd turn and she'd see who it was.

"Tam Jing Fan!" The shout was like the crack of a whip. Ling Fan looked around, feeling as though she'd been caught sneaking an extra treat from the kitchen.

"There you are!" Tan Din bellowed from beside a cook fire. "I told you not to be late!"

Ling Fan waved hastily at Tan Din to signal she'd heard. When she looked back at the wagon, there was no sign of the person in the long coat.

Ling Fan spent the rest of the morning being chased around the cooking area by a never-ending stream of Tan Din's orders. He peppered his commands with commentary about the quality of ingredients, the weather, the laziness of his cooking staff, and the workers' appetites. "They're bottomless wells," Tan Din complained, pouring a bag of black-eyed peas into the soup that bubbled over one fire. He stirred vegetables in the broad, open wok beside it and stooped to add some more twigs to the flames. "Start another pot of tea after you finish chopping those scallions, then bring this pot out."

Through the steam rising from the pots around her, she could see sojourners crawling out of their tents, stretching and scratching at themselves and starting to amble toward the cooking area. A line had begun to form even before Ling Fan finished setting out the first batch of food. The men ate quickly, barely pausing long enough to chew and swallow. Within half an hour, most of them were headed up the narrow footpath to the tunnels. A handful of latecomers trickled over and wolfed down the last of the food.

Tan Din set her to scrubbing bowls in a tin tub big enough to bathe in. She worked mostly with her left arm to spare her injured elbow. It still ached, but she was grateful not to be following her old work team back into the tunnels to haul granite. Even more grateful that she was still here on the railroad at all.

A shadow fell across the tub's soapy water. "You! Boy! What is this slop?"

Ling Fan squinted up from under her hat at two workers, barely men themselves. One was holding a bowl half filled with rice and vegetables at arm's length as though he had a skunk by its tail. The other stood languidly by, a smile playing across his face as though he was watching a scene from an opera unfold.

"Don't eat it if you don't like it," she said with a shrug and turned back to her scrubbing.

"Good money is taken out of our pay for every meal we eat here," the worker said. "I expect better. Pigs eat better than this." He turned his bowl over and the food fell into the tub with a splash. Water sprayed upward, drenching Ling Fan. "Make me something better."

Furious, Ling Fan wiped her face with the back of her hand, then groped through the greasy water for something, anything that might help her. Her fingers closed on a long, thin handle that ended in a heavy wedge of flat metal. She pulled it out and swung it back. "Make it yourself," she growled.

The two workers stared in shock, then burst into laughter just as Ling Fan realized the object she was brandishing in her hand like a cudgel was an oversized spatula.

A third figure stepped through the thick smoke that hovered over the cooking area like banks of low-hanging storm clouds. Ling Fan's heart lifted when she recognized Wong Wei, dressed in a long blue coat like the ones many of the bak gui wore. A brown hat with a floppy broad brim hung on a cord around his neck. Ling Fan thought the outfit looked familiar, but she didn't have a chance to dwell on it.

"Aiya! What's going on?" said Wong Wei to the other two workers. "I sent you to get better food, not stand around giggling like a couple of girls!"

The first worker was clutching his sides while his friend wiped tears from his eyes and pointed at Ling Fan. "We were trying to get something better, but the cooks are nothing more than jesters. No wonder the food tastes like dung!"

Only then did Wong Wei seem to realize who was standing by the washtub. "Tam Jing Fan!" he cried, bouncing up on his toes. "What are you doing here? I thought you were sent back to San Francisco!"

"I'm working with Tan Din. He—"

"Doesn't know a pig's tail from its ass," one of the workers said.

Ling Fan's cheeks flamed and she raced around the tub, spatula raised high.

"Nah, nah, nah," Wong Wei cried, stepping between them. Turning to the worker, he added, "Don't talk about my friends like that."

The man's eyes widened. "But you said—"

"Never mind. If you don't like it, you can go hungry. Just get out of here. Go on."

The two workers stood dumbfounded, then exchanged dark looks and turned away.

"Don't expect any more favors, Wong Wei," one of them called back. Wong Wei watched them go, a frown creasing his brow.

"What was that about?" Ling Fan said.

Wong Wei shook his head and clapped his hands together. "Forget them. Now for breakfast! What's on for today?"

Ling Fan stared. "Didn't you already eat breakfast?"

He pulled a wry face. "I got here so late, nothing was left but a few burned noodles and some vegetable stems. Isn't there anything else?" He looked pointedly over her shoulder at the table Tan Din had set aside for the cooking staff. The scent of fresh jook wafted over with the steam. He reminded her so much of her brother wheedling extra helpings out of Aunt Fei that Ling Fan had to laugh. She scooped out a brimming bowl for Wong Wei and one for herself.

The jook was made of thick broth full of chunks of chicken and black-eyed peas, mixed with long ribbons of wrinkled bean curd and poured over boiled puffed rice. Just breathing in the woody aroma of cilantro, green onions, and nuts was like taking a trip back home to the family kitchen.

Wong Wei finished his portion with a sigh and a belch. "The

best thing about Tan Din's jook is that you get to taste it twice."

Ling Fan prickled in disgust. "Fine thing to say about an extra meal."

"Aiya, you're talking like my popo again," Wong Wei retorted.

Another slip. What would her brother say? She knew what he would've said in front of the family. But was that what he would've said among his male friends? There was so much more to acting like a boy than she had ever realized. She resorted to what Jing Fan always did when he was cornered. She shrugged, digging back into her own bowl in silence.

A few yards away, two bak gui bosses rode by on mules. "Tunnel Three coming along well," one said. "I heard Tunnel Two had a cave-in yesterday, but we'll be starting on Tunnel Four before week's end." Ling Fan translated the comment for Wong Wei.

Wong Wei looked at her appreciatively. "You must know more American English than anyone who works at this site, except Chin Lin Sou. We always have to go to him if we want anything from the bak gui, and he always tells us what Strobridge and the other bak gui bosses want us to do." For a second, the muscles in Wong Wei's thin face tightened, reminding Ling Fan once again of a bird of prey.

"Does he seem unfair to you?" asked Ling Fan.

It was Wong Wei's turn to shrug. "I wouldn't say unfair. But he thinks he can run the camp his way, and that's not how everyone wants it." He set his bowl on the ground and shouldered a canvas sack that clanked dully. "There's a game outside Li Bo's tent tonight. See you there?" Without waiting for a response, Wong Wei turned up the path that led toward the tunnels, whistling.

Ling Fan picked up Wong Wei's empty bowl and stacked it with her own. As she walked to the tub of brown dishwater, Tan Din emerged from behind a mound of hundred-pound rice sacks. He circled the food supplies stored in boxes, barrels, and crates, pausing every so often to make some marks on a piece of paper. Acutely aware of his scrutiny, Ling Fan picked up the long-handled brush beside the tub and began to scrub the bowls.

Tan Din came up behind her and banked the cook fires. The red tongues of flame shrank back into bright fissures that snaked through the nests of blackened logs.

"It's none of my business, boy," Tan Din said after a moment. "I've known plenty of men like your friend Wong Wei. He's a great joker and a better talker . . . but get on the wrong side of him, watch out! He's as slippery as an eel."

Ling Fan didn't look up but fished out a bowl from the murky water, swirling the little brush around the inside once, twice, then around the outside, once, twice. "He saved my life. I wouldn't have gotten out of the tunnel yesterday if not for him."

"Seems to me you wouldn't have needed saving if you hadn't gone back in to find him."

Ling Fan frowned down at the water. It became murkier the more she stirred it.

"He's my friend. Friends look out for friends." That's what Baba had always told her. *Wong Wei is a troublemaker, but he's also a piece of home.* She fished out another bowl and set it to the side, facedown, to dry.

Tan Din sighed. "Yes, but all I'm saying is, be careful."

CHAPTER 11

For the next few hours, Ling Fan helped prepare lunch. Rather than have the workers waste valuable daylight walking back from the tunnels to the cooking area, Tan Din rigged together a train of several donkey carts by lashing the halter rope of each donkey to the cart in front of it. He and Ling Fan packed each cart with bamboo baskets full of rice, vegetables, boiled chicken, and a cauldron of fresh tea, and brought lunch to the work site. The men ate standing up, leaning against the rough walls of the tunnel that was slowly chewing its way through the mountain.

"Boy! Hurry up with that tea!"

Ling Fan quickly filled two wooden buckets with tea from the cauldron. She hooked the handles of the buckets to the ends of a long pole, balanced it across her shoulders, and went from crew to crew with the tea. The noon sun beat down, heating the air. Sweat streamed down the faces of the workers, turning black as it mixed with dirt and gunpowder ash. Ling Fan was grateful for the shade of her broad-brimmed straw hat.

When the work crew was done eating, she helped Tan Din turn the empty carts around, and they headed back down toward the camp. They didn't stop at the cooking area as Ling Fan expected but instead continued along the path, past the tents and around the shoulder of the mountain to the south. There, the path broadened and joined the cleared roadbed that work crews had formed for the oncoming train tracks. On either side of the wide dirt road, enormous oak and redwood trees towered over their heads, soaring a hundred feet straight into the air. The road wound down steep inclines and past sudden drops filled with the tips of fir trees.

"Where are we going?" Ling Fan asked. She sat beside Tan Din on the first donkey cart.

"Illinoistown. There'll be a food shipment there for us from San Francisco," Tan Din replied.

Illinoistown! That was where the End o' Line was. It was also the temporary headquarters for the bak gui bosses, like James Strobridge, the construction supervisor whom Chin Lin Sou reported to. Each day trains made the fifty-mile trip from Sacramento carrying supplies and workers fresh off the boats from China. Ling Fan vaguely remembered passing through the town on the way from Sacramento to the base camp, but the caravan had moved so quickly that she'd gotten only a vague impression of dusty streets and raw wooden buildings.

The early afternoon sun slanted through the leaves and branches of the trees overhead, forming a dappled path for them to follow. Invisible insects trilled from the brush at the edge of the road. The dull thump of donkey hooves mingled with the rattle of the little cart as they swayed and bumped along the uneven dirt road. The stink of hot donkey sweat hung over them like a cloud. Ling Fan's eyelids grew heavy.

After a while, a sound like water thundering down a waterfall began to filter through her hazy dream. Strange—she didn't remember there being a waterfall near Illinoistown.

"We're here."

Ling Fan jerked awake and realized the source of the noise she'd been hearing in her sleep.

Illinoistown was a sprawl of timbered buildings that smelled of tar and fresh-cut lumber, surrounded by swarms of people. Skeleton frames of more structures stretched farther than she could see.

The sudden bustle made the donkeys skittish and sullen. Tan Din had to get down from the cart and pull on the lead donkey's halter until it finally shuffled forward. They passed a building twenty feet high and twice as long. A board on the front read ILLINOISTOWN GRANARY DEPOT. Next to it was a building with a wide covered porch lined with barrels of tools, nails, and seed. Farther on was a smithy with three fire pits. The sound of hammer against metal rang through the air.

Tan Din pulled the donkey cart up to a length of log that had been hammered into the dirt road. He looped the reins loosely around it and with a quick "Stay here," he disappeared into the stream of people moving up and down the road.

Ling Fan clambered off the wagon and looked around. Most of the people were clearly laborers, judging by the amount of dust and dirt that covered their clothes, boots, and hands. Most were bak gui; some were her countrymen. Once or twice, her eye caught the bright flash of a woman's long skirts.

Back home, Ling Fan had always disliked wearing gowns and finery for special occasions. The stiff embroidered material felt like a prison, hampering her every move. The bak gui dresses were fuller but heavier. She wondered what it would feel like to have to wear one. She imagined a wide skirt weighing her down, pinning her to the earth, and a rigid bonnet blocking her view like the blinders on a horse. Dusty as they were, she loved the loose, blocky tunic and soft trousers she had on now. She had never felt so free.

She heard a nearby giggle and turned around just in time to see her hat whisked off the wagon seat where she had left it. It was firmly clapped onto a small head of tangled curls, bobbing up and down as it dodged around a sea of legs and turned the corner of the nearest building.

"Aiya!" Ling Fan shouted and took off after it. The tiny thief didn't look back but slipped through the crowd like a shadow. Ling Fan, on the other hand, felt as though she was running through a wall of living molasses. Bak gui suddenly seemed to spill out of every doorway and alleyway between buildings just in time to block her path. She almost lost sight of the culprit as she dodged around a farmer and his overburdened mule, but caught a glimpse of her hat again as it ducked beneath a wagon and headed straight toward the End o' Line.

The End o' Line really was the very end of Central Pacific's rails. Every day, more track was added, and every day, the massive steam engine, the Pioneer, rolled eastward a few more yards. A gravel-filled roadbed had been laid ahead of it, and on either side, the raw material for train tracks was piled high: stacks of lumber waiting to be cut into ties, mountains of twenty-foot-long iron rails, and hundreds of crates and barrels filled with spikes, nuts, bolts, and nails. Bak gui and Chinese workers flowed around and along it like waves of ants, hauling rocks and gravel for the roadbed, tamping down the loose dirt, driving iron spikes through the wooden ties with every swing of their twenty-pound sledgehammers. Ling Fan almost lost track of the thief in the sea of workers.

They sped past the Pioneer and dodged behind the dozen boxcars that served as living quarters for many of the bak gui work crew. Ling Fan raced alongside the track, following the pair of feet that pelted across the gravel on the opposite side. She still didn't have a good view of the thief, but she was determined to get her hat back.

At the end of the chain of boxcars, Ling Fan skidded to a halt, struck by the sight of the caboose. The car was painted sky blue, and red gingham curtains hung in every window. A set of wooden stairs led up to the entrance at the back, and a canvas awning stretched over the threshold, creating a shady porch. A bright yellow canary sat in a little bamboo cage that hung next to the door.

Ling Fan couldn't take her eyes off the little house on wheels. As she stared, half a dozen children of all sizes burst out the door, shrieking with laughter. They were followed by a tall, yellow-haired woman in a simple blue dress. She was laughing too, just as the thief ran full into her.

"Clara Strobridge, what in the world are you doing?" she demanded, hands on hips.

"Look, Mama, I found a Chinaman hat," the tiny thief declared, tilting it upward to reveal a smudged, pointed face framed by blond curls.

"Hmmm," the woman said and shot a sharp glance at Ling Fan. "Mr. Chinaman, do you know anything about this hat?"

"It's my hat, madam," Ling Fan said in her best English.

Clara's face crumpled. "I found it," she insisted, stamping her foot. Wordlessly, her mother held out a hand. Clara threw the hat to the ground, raced up the steps of the pretty little caboose, and slammed the door behind her.

The woman sighed and picked up the hat. She brushed the dust off before handing it to Ling Fan. "Please excuse my daughter, Mr. Chinaman. She's not a bad girl, just one who runs a little wild. It comes from being out here for so long." She gestured ruefully around them. "It serves me right for following my husband into the wilderness."

"No harm done, madam." Ling Fan bowed low in gratitude.

The other children were in the midst of a chasing game. Ling Fan counted five altogether. She wanted to ask about their ages, who was oldest or youngest, the sort of details she once would've discussed with any auntie in her village, but she contented herself with bowing again and went to find Tan Din.

He had moved the team of donkeys a few streets over to a supply depot built of logs and rough boards. "Where were you?" he growled. "You're here to work, not take in the sights."

Ling Fan described what had happened while she helped him load up the carts with barrels of dried goods, crates of live chickens nestled in rank-smelling hay, and hundred-pound sacks of rice. "I didn't know the bak gui brought their families to the railroad," she finished.

"Only if you're Strobridge," Tan Din said. "He reports directly to the Big Four—Crocker and that lot. From what I hear the foremen saying over their meals, he pretty much gets what he wants."

While Tan Din filled out papers and checked off the inventory, Ling Fan stowed bins of tea leaves, boxes of dried cuttlefish, and sacks of mushrooms, abalone, and seaweed. As she worked, she tried to ignore the curious looks from people around her. There were far fewer sojourners in Illinoistown than were up in the work camps near the tunnels. From time to time, some of the bak gui even stopped in their tracks to stare at her openly. She was tired of being looked at. From the moment she stepped off the ship in San Francisco, every bak gui who'd crossed her path had regarded her as though she were an exotic oddity.

Today, though, Ling Fan felt that the looks were different. The skin on the back of her neck prickled as though she were being watched by a tiger. It took all her willpower to continue filling the carts and not look back over her shoulder.

Finally, Tan Din had finished his paperwork and she had packed the last of the supplies. They clambered back up onto the first cart and were just about to pull away from the depot when Ling Fan noticed the commotion at the far end of the wooden loading platform.

"Tan Din, wait. Something's happening."

Workers were gathering around something on the ground, and more were coming from every direction. Voices were muffled by the mass of gathered bodies, but Ling Fan heard an edge to the words that made her nervous.

She slid out of her seat. "I want to see what's going on."

"It's bak gui business, not ours," said Tan Din. "We have to get back to camp."

"I'll be right back. This could be important."

Tan Din sucked on his teeth irritably but stopped protesting.

Ling Fan slipped through the growing crowd. Once again, she felt eyes turned on her, and she heard someone mutter "Damn coolie." Just as she started to think that Tan Din was right and she should turn back, the crowd thinned in front of her.

A fresh hole had been dug next to one of the logs that supported a corner of the loading platform. Beside it, on the ground, was a small wooden barrel still covered in bits of mud. Both ends of the barrel were sealed shut, but a long strand of thin rope ran out of it through a tiny opening and was wrapped several times around the base of the support log. Ling Fan recognized this as the kind of keg that held the gunpowder used to blow up tree stumps and blast tunnels in the mountainside.

What was it doing here, like this?

Two workers with shovels stood over the hole. They looked angry, as did most of the onlookers. Someone called, "Here comes Stro. He'll get to the bottom of this."

The crowd parted for a bearded man with a chiseled, stern face made sterner by the black patch he wore over his left eye. He carried himself with the assurance of a man accustomed to getting his way. This must be James Strobridge, the main bak gui foreman of the entire Central Pacific Railroad. He knelt down by the gunpowder keg and ran a finger along the fuse. He was silent for a long time, and when he finally looked up, his scowl was enough to make some of the men take a step back.

"Are there any others?" he asked.

"Naw, sir," one of the men holding a shovel said. "This here's the only one we seen. Lucky for us Luke here's got such good eyes. He only saw a little bit of the fuse wrapped around the leg over there. Thought it was mighty strange so we started digging and—"

Strobridge cut him off with a wave of his hand. He seemed to make up his mind about something as he stood up and faced the crowd.

"No point in pretending we aren't all thinking the same thing," he began. "There's been too many accidents these past few months. Broken tools, collapsed tunnels, now this."

The crowd's muttering sounded like the distant roll of stampeding oxen.

"Starting today, I will personally hand over five dollars to any Central Pacific worker who can give me information about any damage done to the railroad, or anyone planning or carrying out such damage. Ten pieces if you catch the rogue red-handed!" The crowd shouted its approval. Ling Fan slipped back to the donkey cart, feeling the back of her neck prickle.

"This is not good," Tan Din said when Ling Fan reported what she'd heard. "We should've gone back when I said so." He urged the lead donkey forward with a sharp lash of the reins across its rump. Ling Fan had to grab for a handhold on the lurching cart.

"What's—?" she started to say, but then caught sight of three workers striding toward them.

"The way I sees it, gotta be the work of them Chinamen. They'll do anything for a little money," said one of the workers, a red-faced, sandy-haired man. He spoke to his companions, but his eyes flicked over Ling Fan, Tan Din, and their donkey carts.

Tan Din started to steer past them. A worker grabbed the lead donkey by its halter.

Tan Din said in clumsy English, "We're no trouble."

The sandy-haired man came around to Tan Din's side. "Weee no t'lubble, weee no t'lubble," he brayed while his companions laughed. "Guess what? Weee no care, coolie." He reached up and swatted Tan Din's hat off. Tan Din sat still as a statue, his knuckles white as he gripped the reins.

"Stop it!" Ling Fan shouted. "Leave us alone! We haven't done anything!" She leapt out of the cart.

"Ooh, lookee here! A coolie who talks proper American!" the sandy-haired man crowed. The other two edged closer, grinning. Ling Fan felt a stab of panic.

A tall man with a long tangle of brown hair stepped forward. His face was slashed by a long, jagged scar that stretched from his left ear to the side of his mouth. He walked with a slight limp that looked more like a swagger.

"What's going on now?" he said. Beside him was a boy with red hair who looked about the same age as Ling Fan. He had a round, open face covered with reddish spots. Unlike his companion, he looked nervous.

"We found us a couple of them troublemakers," the sandy-haired man said. "We was just about to bring 'em over to Stro."

"We didn't do anything!" Ling Fan burst out.

"Aww, who can trust them coolies?" the sandy-haired man said dismissively. "They come over here stealing our gold back in '49, and now they want to steal our railway jobs. They'll do any fool thing for a bit of money—any manner of mischief. You know how they are."

"How's that then, friend? Did you see them do the thing?" the newcomer asked, sounding mildly curious.

"Well, no, but Harry here saw both of 'em on the loading platform being sneaky. Tell 'em, Harry." The sandy-haired man pushed one of his companions forward. Harry looked startled to find himself suddenly the center of attention.

"Do tell us, Harry," said the tall stranger. "Exactly how were they being sneaky? I'm only asking because Strobridge will want details, of course."

"They seemed in an awful hurry," Harry mumbled. "And they were talking funny."

"Ah. Sounded a bit like a whole other language, did it?"

Harry looked confused.

The sandy-haired man broke in. "What difference does it make? We never saw any of this mischief until Crocker started bringing his pet coolies over. I still say a coolie done the mischief. Coolies got their hands on that gunpowder all the time, and a coolie is what I'll bring him."

"Are you sure Strobridge will see it that way?" The redheaded boy spoke up for the first time. The tips of his ears turned red. "Me and Uncle Jonathan use that gunpowder on the tree stumps blocking up the roadbed."

Harry glared at him. "I don't see as it's any business of yours." The boy ducked his head, and the crimson that began at his ears slowly spread across his cheeks.

"He's right, Thomas," the tall stranger said abruptly, turning toward his companion. "It's none of our concern if he has to deal with Stro's temper once Stro realizes he's wasted time on the wrong person."

Harry and the third bak gui muttered uncomfortably and started to back away.

The sandy-haired man jabbed a thick finger at Tan Din. "This ain't over." He whipped around and scuttled after his deserting friends.

The redheaded boy let out a slow breath as he took a square of cloth out of his pocket and mopped his face with it. "All's well that ends well, right, Uncle Jon?" He looked up at the older man.

"Fellows like that will still be trouble," said the stranger. "Best watch your back, friends."

Tan Din studied the other man's scarred face, then nodded. He said in slow, deliberate English, "Thank you, friend," and held out a hand, American style. The stranger grasped it firmly.

"Our pleasure. We're all just guests on this land, even the men who think they own it. Any time you could use some help from a fellow guest, just let out a holler. The name's Jonathan O'Brien, and this here's my nephew Thomas O'Brien." Thomas nodded at them before he and his uncle walked away. Jonathan O'Brien's long shadow stretched before him, jerking awkwardly as he limped back toward the glinting bulk of the Pioneer.

Ling Fan and Tan Din turned the donkeys and started the trek to the mountain work camps.

CHAPTER 12

"**S**torm's coming," Tan Din said, more to himself than Ling Fan as their cart trundled up the mountain path. The warm, still air had been replaced by a cold wind blowing down from Donner Pass. It whipped the tree branches overhead, making the leaves thrash wildly as though waving the supply caravan onward.

Ling Fan was still trying to sort through the day's events. They kept tossing through her mind like the windblown leaves that swirled around the donkeys' hooves.

"Tan Din, why would anyone want to cause problems for the railroad?"

Tan Din sucked on his teeth. "It's the way these American bak gui like to do things. Everyone's out to get what's best for themselves. Even if that means clawing over everyone else to get it. Building this railroad is like running a race. One racer, the Central Pacific Railroad Company, started out of Sacramento. The other, the Union Pacific Railroad Company, is coming in from the East. Whichever one gets to a certain spot in Utah first gains enormous prestige."

Ling Fan couldn't help snorting. Two groups of men racing to a finish line. It sounded so childish.

"Scoff all you like," Tan Din growled. "Prestige brings

money. Mountains of it! And that's on top of all the land they'll get control of wherever tracks have been laid. A lot of American bak gui dollars have been put into this project, but that's nothing to the money they'll get out of it when it's finally finished."

In her mind's eye, Ling Fan saw the two railroads flowing across prairie and hills like two ravenous snakes. Everywhere they passed, wagon trails, buildings, houses, and stores sprang up and spread deep into the countryside for miles around. So much wild, jagged land flattened to make room for the people to come.

Something Jonathan O'Brien had said nibbled at the edge of her mind. "Tan Din, whose land is it?"

"What do you mean?"

"That bak gui in Illinoistown said even the men who think they own this land are guests. So whose land is it really?"

"I suppose he's thinking of the Indians." Tan Din shrugged. "I don't know much about them—just that they lived on some of this land before the bak gui came. But when the bak gui in charge of the railroads finish their work, the land will be theirs."

Something about Tan Din's explanation didn't feel right, but Ling Fan decided to drop the subject. The day had been fraught with too many emotions and new ideas. None of this made sense to her, but she was too tired to wrestle with it.

That night, she wrote to her brother: **I don't know why most of the American bak gui seem to hate us sojourners so much. But you'd like the O'Briens and Mrs. Strobridge. I think Baba would too.**

∧ ∧ ∧

Day by day, summer turned to fall, and Ling Fan's arm grew strong again. Tan Din gave her more responsibilities, including hauling water from the nearby stream. From there, she had a clear view of the camp's north edge, where extra supplies and tools were kept. One day when she arrived as usual to fill the water buckets, Ling Fan saw three new wagons covered by burlap tarps. At this distance, she could just make out bundles of what looked like narrow wooden rods poking out from the covering. Four men ducked in and out from beneath the tarps, carrying tools. They seemed to be building something. Ling Fan thought it strange that they were working under the canvas covering instead of out in the open. Stranger yet, the men seemed to be keeping others away from the wagons, waving off anyone who strayed too close.

"Tan Din, have you seen those wagons?" she asked when she returned to the cooking area. Tan Din shrugged from beneath half a side of salted pork. His breath blew out in white clouds as he dropped the meat onto a table and began slicing it into huge cubes for soup. Ling Fan squinted against the afternoon sun. "They look like they're full of reeds. Why would anybody need reeds up here?"

Tan Din pushed his hat back and scratched at his head. "You ask a lot of questions, boy. If you worked as much as you ask questions, we'd be done in half the time."

"Don't you think it's strange?" Back in China, people sometimes used reeds to make bedding. For a moment, Ling Fan had an image of men sleeping in the tunnels on reed mats at the end of a shift, not bothering to waste time walking back to their tents. "Aren't you curious?"

"We're not paid to be curious. We're paid to work. Didn't you learn your lesson back in Illinoistown? Curiosity will get you killed here."

Illinoistown had never left her mind. It was like a lump of hot coal lodged in her memory. She had known that the work here in America would be hard, but she'd never thought there would be so much hate in the hearts of the Americans.

"Hurry up with that water, then come help me get started with dinner."

Ling Fan hustled through the work, but she couldn't stop thinking about those men working so secretively near the wagons. What if it had something to do with the "accidents" that kept happening? Strobridge had offered a reward for any information about people damaging the railroad. Ling Fan was disappointed by Tan Din's lack of interest, but she could think of at least one person who would want that reward money. Wong Wei would help her get to the bottom of whatever was going on.

The trouble was she'd barely talked to Wong Wei since the cave-in more than a month ago. Tan Din kept her hopping during mealtimes so that she barely had a moment to spare. And Wong Wei had fallen in with a rough crowd that stank of whiskey and more. Around his new friends, he was ebullient and rude, boasting of his latest gambling wins, quick to lash out at anyone and everyone.

Ling Fan had learned to keep away from him when he was like that. But just when she decided that Tan Din was right about his true nature, Wong Wei would show up alone, subdued, but attentive and pleasant to her. It was as though there were two Wong Weis. She wondered which one she would find tonight.

Men covered in dirt and dust from the tunnels began to arrive for dinner. They heaped their bowls with rice and topped it with bok choy, bean curd, and chicken. The little clearing rang with laughter and voices telling "big tales" from China, or even bigger tales of work in the tunnels. Ling Fan hustled to refill kettles and stir pots until finally Tan Din began to damp down the fires for the night. Tiny spots of light flared up in the darkness as men sat back and lit pipes and cigarettes.

Slowly, in twos and threes, men trickled off to their tents, but Wong Wei was still nowhere to be seen. Ling Fan brought the last stack of dirty bowls to the washtub and began to scrub, trying not to worry. If there had been any major accidents or injuries in the tunnels, she would've overheard the diners gossiping about it.

By the time Ling Fan had tossed out the dirty dishwater and helped bank the last of the fires, there was still no sign of Wong Wei. Ling Fan bade Tan Din good night, picked up a small tin pail and canteen she'd set aside earlier, and headed out to find Wong Wei's tent.

After a couple of wrong turns and an inquiry or two, Ling Fan arrived at a patched tent. The flap was down but not tied shut.

She knelt and called softly through the flap, "Wong Wei, are you in there? It's Tam Jing Fan." The smell of old whiskey mixed with an older, sweeter smoke drifted out of the dark tent and made her gag.

"What do you want?" a voice said thickly.

"Come out here, I want to talk to you." Ling Fan waited, shivering in the cold mountain air. The tents surrounding Wong Wei's were just as dark as his, and just as silent.

After what seemed like an eternity, Wong Wei emerged, blinking, a blanket clutched around his bony shoulders.

Ling Fan stifled a gasp as she took in the thin, stinking scarecrow standing before her. "Are you all right?"

"I'm fine." Wong Wei pulled his blanket closer. "I've been ill, but I'm fine now."

"I'm sorry," Ling Fan said softly.

"Why are you sorry?" Wong Wei asked. He sounded annoyed.

"I didn't know. I would've come sooner." She stared down at the pail in her hand. "I didn't see you at dinner tonight. I thought you might be hungry."

Wong Wei snatched the pail. He ate like a starving animal, scooping the food out with his hand, not even bothering with the soup spoon or chopsticks Ling Fan had also brought until he came to the last morsels at the bottom of the pail. When he was done, he wiped his mouth with the edge of the blanket.

Ling Fan pretended not to notice any of this while she busied herself with building up a little fire over the ashes in front of his tent. She dragged a log over and perched on it to tend the growing flames. Wong Wei sat down beside her, still wrapped in his blanket. Silently, she handed him the canteen of cold tea. He finished it in three swallows.

"Where's your coat, Wong Wei? It's freezing tonight." She tried to keep her tone even and matter-of-fact, the way Baba used to whenever he spoke to a sullen villager who'd fallen on hard times.

Wong Wei shrugged and mumbled something about losing it in a game. Ling Fan stared into the growing flames, deciding not to press further. Wong Wei was in more than just a bad mood. As magistrate, her father used to come across problems like this, but never in her life did Ling Fan imagine she would see it herself. "It's the opium," she'd heard Baba remark once. "It's like an invisible leash that drags a person into actions he'd never dream of doing and robs him of his best intentions."

"*Feh*," Aunt Fei had spat. "Anyone foolish enough to eat opium gets what he deserves. And anyone with any sense would keep out of his way." Back in China, living in her own comfortable family compound, Ling Fan had privately agreed. Here on the Gold Mountain, sitting at the feet of an ancient granite dragon the sojourners were supposed to conquer, she wasn't so sure.

"At least you still have that." She nodded at the coin on the silk string around Wong Wei's neck.

Wong Wei lifted the coin and studied it in the firelight. The corners of his mouth twitched. "This, I'll always have."

"And it can remind you of what you'll have when you go back home," Ling Fan said. "Not everyone is fortunate enough to have their future so assured." She was thinking only of her own family's uncertain prospects, so she wasn't ready for Wong Wei's scowl.

"Nothing is sure until the day I return to my village with enough gold to satisfy Mei's father."

"You'll do it," Ling Fan said stoutly. But Wong Wei shook his head, hands hanging over his knees like a scarecrow's. Ling Fan remembered another day when he'd sat as dejected as this. *Not again . . .*

"How much did you lose?"

Wong Wei didn't look up as he slid his coin back and forth on its string.

"How could you be so foolish?" she exploded.

Wong Wei's head snapped up. His jaw clenched. "I'll win it back. Twice as much. I've done it before!"

"You can't keep doing this—"

"I said I'll get my money back. My luck will change." The firelight made the hollows in his face even darker. He tugged at the coin on its silk thread. "Besides, I already have a plan. There's always extra money to get around here if you know how to play things right." He flicked his hand as though he were tossing invisible dice. Ling Fan glanced doubtfully at the dirty blanket wrapped around his shoulders but decided not to push. She gathered the dinner dishes and stood to go.

Food, tea, or the prospect of future winnings seemed to have brought back Wong Wei's old spirit. He scrambled after her. "If you want, I can get you in a game too. We could be a team. We could double our money. What do you say?"

Wong Wei's spurt of enthusiasm made Ling Fan's mind race. Double the money meant less time in America, and less time Baba would have to spend in prison. As she weighed her options, she caught a whiff of stale smoke mixed with whiskey, vomit, and opium. The smell, coming from Wong Wei's tent, was so strong that she almost retched.

It was enough to clear her mind. What was she thinking? She was desperate for fast money, but not that desperate! She shook her head.

"You don't trust me," Wong Wei said, pulling the blanket tighter around his shoulders and drawing himself to his full height. "After everything we've been through, you don't believe in me."

"What? I never said that." Keeping up with Wong Wei's shifting moods was exhausting. She cast around for a safer topic. "Of course I believe in you, and I trust you. That's why I came looking for you." Quickly she described the tarp-covered wagons and the reeds—and the reward money for useful information. Wong Wei listened, sliding the coin back and forth on its cord.

When she was done, he said, "If you saw gunpowder sitting

around unattended, that'd be worth reporting. But what harm can reeds do to the railroad?" He turned back to his tent with a shrug that felt like a slap.

"Don't you want to know what they're for, though?" she called after him. She knew she sounded like a small child tugging at the sleeve of an elder, but she had to try.

Wong Wei didn't look back over his shoulder. "I don't know about you, but I'm here to make as much money as I can, not waste time chasing after profitless mysteries."

Jing, she wrote that night, **each day Wong Wei becomes less the boy I met on the *Cormorant*. It's as though the Gold Mountain has eaten his dreams and left behind a money-obsessed gui.**

∧ ∧ ∧

After that, Ling Fan avoided Wong Wei. It was easy enough to do when hundreds of hungry men came crowding in for a meal. And it seemed that he no longer wanted anything to do with her either. On the rare occasions when they crossed paths, he looked through her as though she was a ghost.

One night, when the cook fires were banked and glowing dully, and Ling Fan was hunting for empty bowls and cups left by careless workers, Chin Lin Sou and Ah Sook came for their dinner. Ling Fan was surprised to see them so late in the evening. Most of the men had already finished eating and gone back to their tents, or to the nightly games. A handful lingered in the clearing, smoking over their cups of tea. Chin Lin Sou stopped to have a few words with each before settling down to his own meal with Ah Sook.

"The last two wagons arrived this afternoon," Ling Fan

heard Ah Sook say. "Pu Tong thinks they have enough reeds to finish." Chin Lin Sou nodded in satisfaction.

Reeds! They were talking about the covered wagons! So perhaps whatever was going on wasn't meant to damage the railroad. But then why the secrecy? She continued collecting discarded bowls from the surrounding tables, careful not to seem interested in the quiet conversation.

Ah Sook tipped the last drop of pale liquid from a metal flask into his tea. "So you think this idea of yours is going to work?"

Chin Lin Sou shrugged. "It'd better. I told Crocker and Strobridge that we could drill and blast twice as fast as the Irish bak gui if we did it our way."

Ah Sook snorted. "Those Irish bak gui are pretty fast just using ropes and harnesses. Can you really say our way will be any better?"

Chin Lin Sou gulped down a mouthful of rice before he answered. "What would you do? The bosses are happy to dangle men on the end of a rope like buzzard bait. They don't care who ends up at the bottom of Cape Horn so long as there's someone else to take his place the next time they need more gunpowder set. My idea will at least give the driller more support, and he can work faster."

"But it'll be a lot more weight to pull up, and the driller will be sitting like an emperor instead of scrambling back up the line."

"It's worth a try. Pu Tong and Fong He are already weaving the reeds. In the meantime, keep an eye out for good candidates. We only need three. Remember, we're looking for light but fast."

Ah Sook shook his head. "Only a fool with a death wish would take on that job."

"Tell them about the bonus," Chin Lin Sou said. He wiped his mouth on his sleeve and headed back toward the tents.

Ling Fan's heart was beating in her throat the same way it had the day she stepped aboard the ship for America. She'd heard that bonus pay for dangerous jobs could be as much as an extra dollar a month. Whatever Chin Lin Sou had in mind, she was going to be a part of it. Every extra cent she earned meant less time her father had to suffer.

That night, she wrote to her brother, **I will do whatever it takes to get that bonus money!**

CHAPTER 13

Now more than ever, Ling Fan wished she could talk to Wong Wei. He'd be able to figure out a way to get in on Chin Lin Sou's project. But she hadn't seen Wong Wei for several weeks. She wondered if she should seek him out again at his tent, but the memory of her last visit filled her with dread. No, she would have to find a way by herself.

Just before dinner the next evening, she loaded up a flat wooden board with several heaping bowls of food and a pot of steaming tea. Then, as workers converged on the cooking area, she watched for Ah Sook. As soon as she spied him walking toward the serving table, she hefted the board onto her shoulder and pushed her way through the crowd to meet him.

"Ah Sook!" she called, trying her best to imitate Tan Din's gruff friendliness, which went over so well with everyone. "No need to wait for your meal. I have it ready for you right here!" A large worker suddenly blundered into her, almost knocking the makeshift tray out of her hand. Ling Fan managed to steady the bowls on the board, and she held the food out to Ah Sook as if nothing was amiss.

"Huh. You're fast," he muttered as he accepted her offering. He narrowed his eyes as he scrutinized her from head to toe. "You look familiar."

She fought to keep her expression neutral even as she ran a nervous mental hand over herself, praying her disguise could withstand his attention. "I joined Tan Din's crew after I injured my arm in the tunnel collapse a couple of months ago," Ling Fan said, then snapped her mouth shut, dismayed. She didn't want him to think she was weak!

But Ah Sook was nodding in approval. He sat down at the nearest table with his board of food in front of him. "Yes, you helped rescue that trapped worker. That took fast thinking and nerve. And you've worked hard even with your injury. We like that around here."

"Yes, sir. I mean thank you, sir," she stammered.

Ah Sook took a bite of rice and asked around his mouthful of broken teeth, "How much do you weigh, boy? Hundred ten, hundred fifteen pounds?"

"That sounds about right. Why?" She knew why. *We're looking for light but fast.* She held her breath.

"We're down a man or two at one of our other work sites. You'd be right for the job. There's bonus money if you prove to be good at it."

This was it! The chance she'd been hoping for. Wong Wei would've said it was about time her fortunes changed. In her place, he would've grabbed at the opportunity, shouting, "When do I start?"

But thinking about Wong Wei's impulsiveness made her hesitate. There was something strange about how Ah Sook sat there, not quite looking at her. A fragment of the overhead conversation sifted through her mind: *They don't care who ends up at the bottom of Cape Horn.*

Ling Fan licked her lips. "What's the job?"

"We need to run railroad track around the side of the

mountain at Cape Horn. To do that, we have to cut a lip out of the mountain wide enough for the track to go on. It's a difficult area to get to. We've had workers going at it from the top on special harnesses. They drill as much as they can, set the powder to do the rest, and then get pulled clear of the explosion." *On the end of a rope like buzzard bait.* "It'll be dangerous, but that's why we're offering the bonus money."

"Working on the railroad is already dangerous," Ling Fan said. She couldn't help glancing at Ah Sook's clawlike hand. "How much more dangerous is this job?"

Ah Sook scowled. "We've lost a dozen men in the past week." Ling Fan wasn't sure whether he was upset over the loss of good workers or just annoyed that she'd pressed him to reveal specific information. "Some were caught in the blast before we could pull them up high enough. Some . . . there was trouble with the harness and they fell." He added defiantly, "But now we've worked out a new method. It'll be more secure."

Ling Fan swallowed. She'd never worked with gunpowder before, but she'd overheard plenty of talk from sojourners who'd had to use it. Nothing about this situation sounded secure. "How much?"

Ah Sook glanced around again. Although nobody was in sight, his gravelly voice dropped to almost a whisper. "You're getting twenty-four dollars a month now. Chin Lin Sou says he can give anybody who works on this project an extra two dollars a day on top of that. Most likely it'll take a month. Maybe two."

Ling Fan gaped. For the railroad to offer such a fortune meant this particular job was incredibly deadly. Sweat trickled down the back of her neck. "Can I think about it and tell you in a day or two?"

"Chin Lin Sou needs to know by tonight how many men are willing to do this. It's now or never."

Ling Fan rubbed her damp palms against the rough cloth of her trousers. Forty extra dollars, maybe as much as eighty. To be back home that much earlier! To see Baba again! To know he was safe! To be with Ming again and meet Ming's baby. Her heart ached.

She took a deep steadying breath. She would not end up at the bottom of Cape Horn.

"Tell Chin Lin Sou I'm in."

Ah Sook nodded. "Hao! As it turns out there are a few candidates. We only need three. Chin Lin Sou wants to send only the very best, so we'll be holding a trial of skill tonight."

Ling Fan felt her heart plummet to her feet. How could she win in a competition against other workers? She could barely keep up in ordinary jobs! She felt a twinge of pain in her right arm.

"Come to Chin Lin Sou's tent at nightfall. If you're one of the lucky ones, you'll be heading out to Cape Horn in the morning."

"I'll be there," she promised, sounding more confident than she felt.

∧ ∧ ∧

Chin Lin Sou's tent was pitched at the edge of the camp, next to a rock wall. There was plenty of space around it, unlike the ordinary workers' tents. By the time Ling Fan approached it in the deepening dusk, eight other sojourners were already clustered in the little clearing. She was surprised to see Wong Wei among them.

They locked eyes, but then Wong Wei looked away, as though he didn't know her. Ling Fan bit her lip but knew better than to try to talk to him. Instead she surveyed the others. Most were boys who looked close to her age. A few were clearly older, but all had the same thin, wiry build. Tension was in the air, but not hostility. They eyed each other silently, warily, as they waited.

Dismay tugged at Ling Fan. All these candidates looked strong and capable. How would she ever stand a chance against them?

Chin Lin Sou emerged from his tent, followed by Ah Sook. Everyone's attention turned toward them.

"Thank you all for coming tonight," Chin Lin Sou began. "You've heard the deal: three men needed for drill and blasting work at Cape Horn. I won't lie to you. We've lost a lot of men there already. There's no shame if you decide it isn't worth the risk. But I will say that this time we're trying a new approach that may make the work easier, and we're willing to give extra money to anyone who tries it."

It struck Ling Fan that her father would've liked Chin Lin Sou. The foreman looked each worker in the face, speaking the truth frankly. He clearly regretted the loss of his men but just as clearly had faith in this new method, whatever it was. He was, her father would've said, an honorable man. If Chin Lin Sou believed his plan could work, then Ling Fan did too.

Looking around at the men, who hadn't budged, Chin Lin Sou nodded, a faint smile twitching the corner of his mouth. "Well then, we'll have to narrow you down to the quickest and toughest." He turned and pointed at the craggy wall of rock behind him. Ah Sook hung a lantern on a nearby pole to provide more light. The rock wall stretched about forty feet high.

The lamplight illuminated three ropes dangling from the top. "We will time each of you as you climb to the top of this rock face and back. Take one of the red cloths up there to prove you made it all the way. The three fastest climbers will go to Cape Horn in the morning. Good luck."

Alarmed, Ling Fan stared up. Around her, the others laughed nervously. Some rolled their shoulders or swung their arms in circles, stretching and warming their muscles.

"Make three lines," Ah Sook ordered. He held a pencil and a scrap of paper at the ready, while Chin Lin Sou took out a pocket watch.

Ling Fan moved to queue up. Wong Wei pushed past her, almost knocking her down. She ended up as the third and final person in the left-most line. Wong Wei was in the middle line, behind two other men. Their turns would come at the same time, in the final round of this strange race.

At the front, three men stood tense, waiting for Ah Sook to give the signal. One man, the tallest in the group, took off his tunic and tied it around his waist. His muscles rippled across his back and shoulders. Ling Fan rubbed her arm, clenching and unclenching her right fist. Her arm felt as good as new after two months of healing, but she hadn't tried lifting anything heavier than a pot of dirty dishwater or an armful of logs for the cook fires. She swung her arm in circles: forward, then backward. Was that a twinge she felt in her elbow?

Chin Lin Sou raised an arm above his head and counted down from five. When he dropped his arm, the first three men ran forward, grabbed their ropes and began to climb. At first, they were even, shimmying up the ropes like a trio of acrobats. Gradually, though, one of the climbers pulled ahead. He reached the top of the cliff, yanked off one of several cloths attached to the top of his rope, and slid back down. His feet touched the ground just as the second climber grabbed his cloth.

Ah Sook, peering over Chin Lin Sou's shoulder at the pocket watch the foreman held, wrote down the times of all three men. The next set of climbers stepped up.

Ling Fan watched these men closely as they climbed. Two relied on their arms to pull them up the ropes, muscles bulging with effort, but the third used both feet and arms. That climber seemed able to move with less effort. She studied his feet, fascinated by the way he almost seemed to walk up the rope.

Now it was her turn. She stepped up, trying to shake the tension out of her arms and legs. Beside her, she was aware of Wong Wei spitting into his hands and rubbing them together. She could feel the energy crackling off his body. Next to him she felt as sluggish as a turtle. She knew without looking that he was flashing that hawklike grin he always wore when he was deep in a game.

Ling Fan took a long breath and fixed her mind on her father's face. She thought of his gentle eyes and easy smile. She took another breath and pictured her brother, face alight at the prospect of traveling to America.

Chin Lin Sou's arm dropped, and they surged forward. Ling Fan leapt as high as she could and grabbed her rope, her hands and arms pulling upward. Her feet clamped together, bending the rope as she had seen the others do so she wouldn't slip as she pulled upward again and again. Out of the corner of her eye, she saw Wong Wei beside her, slowly pulling ahead. The muscles in her arm began to burn, and her elbow felt as though an iron skewer had been shoved in it. She kept her eyes trained on the red cloth loosely tied to the top of her rope.

A chant started in her head that matched the rhythm of her arms and feet. Pull with her arms: *for Ba*. Push with her feet: *for Jing*. Pull: *for Ba*. Push: *for Jing*. Pull: *Ba*. Push: *Jing*. *Ba*. *Jing*. *Ba*. *Jing*. *Ba JingBa JingBaJing*.

She caught up to Wong Wei.

His partially shaved head gleamed with sweat and he was breathing hard. Ling Fan's arms trembled. She hauled herself up and up and up. Wong Wei's rope writhed like an angry snake as he redoubled his efforts. He surged ahead again, his feet pressed together against the rope like a pair of tongs.

Ling Fan had barely registered his odd posture when his reaching hands suddenly slipped, and he slid down the rope two feet. Then, unbelievably, her right hand touched the soft patch of fabric at the top of her rope. She was at the top! With a gasp of relief, she grasped the cloth with one hand, loosened her grip on the rope with the other, and slid downward—past Wong Wei, past the unknown man who was still struggling near the midpoint of the third rope. When her feet finally touched the ground, she didn't dare let go of the rope. She wasn't sure her knees would keep her upright, she was shaking so hard—from exhaustion or exuberance, she wasn't sure which.

"First!" Ah Sook shouted, and wrote her time down on his paper just as Wong Wei landed beside her. Ah Sook wrote his time too, as well as the last climber's. Chin Lin Sou put away his pocket watch. He studied Ah Sook's paper for a moment before he turned to the workers.

"Bing Lai, Fei Gei, and Tam Jing Fan will be our blasters at Cape Horn," he announced.

Bing Lai and Fei Gei looked stunned, then exhilarated. Several of their competitors graciously congratulated them and thumped them on the back.

Ling Fan's legs had turned to water. She clung to the rope, not knowing whether to laugh or cry.

"The rest of you," Chin Lin Sou added, "can join the support crew for regular wages. Be at the wagons on the north side of camp at four tomorrow morning. Ah Sook will explain your assignments when you get to Cape Horn."

Chin Lin Sou disappeared back inside his tent, and the rest of the workers melted into the darkness, leaving Ling Fan by the smoldering ashes of Chin Lin Sou's fire wondering if she had dreamed the whole thing.

Finally, she let go of the rope. She threw her arms into the air and let out a whoop that rang against the rocky wall. With the bonus money from this assignment, her sojourn would be over so much sooner than she'd planned! Oh, to see Baba and Ming and Aunt Fei again! She spun around in a wild pirouette, laughing. The tales she would tell!

A tiny light hissed into life, briefly illuminating Wong Wei's sharp features as he cupped his hands around a cigar butt clenched between his teeth. "Well, somebody had a lucky day." He drew in a deep lungful of smoke and let it out slowly.

Ling Fan stopped; her arms dropped to her side as she regarded him warily. In the short time she'd known him, she had come to realize that Wong Wei's moods rose and fell like the tide. At times he was cheerful and friendly, charming and eager to please. Other times he was sullen and sarcastic, cutting down anyone with a few harsh words. Given that she had just beaten him at this competition, she decided to tread carefully.

"Your luck will turn. It always does, you say so yourself," she said, but the look on his face made the words feel hollow in her mouth. She rushed on. "The support crew is at regular wages now, but maybe that will change . . ."

"Don't worry about me, I'm not going. Something more interesting just came up. It sounds like a better bet than hanging off a cliff."

He took a deep pull from his cigar. "But seriously, I hope you keep your good luck. From what Chin Lin Sou said, being unlucky on this particular assignment is the same as being dead." He turned and sauntered off into the darkness.

∧ ∧ ∧

Back at her tent, Ling Fan told Tan Din that she would likely be away for a month or two. "I guess this means I get the tent to myself for a while," Tan Din rumbled cheerfully.

Ling Fan smiled and got out her writing set. **Jing: Wong Wei is wrong. Our luck has finally turned for the better. I know it!**

CHAPTER 14

Well before first light, Ling Fan packed her travel bag and made her way down to the circle of wagons that waited to depart for Cape Horn. Other workers must've had the same idea; Ling Fan counted no fewer than seven bodies sprawled in an untidy array of sleep. Most had pulled their wide-brimmed hats over their faces, and Ling Fan could see long, dark queues snaking out from beneath them. She clambered aboard a wagon, curled up between two heaps of coiled rope, and went to sleep.

She woke to a blur of cloud-strewn sky and endless scrub brush on either side of the trail. The steady rocking of the wagon reminded her of being aboard the SS *California*. But the shrieks of hungry seagulls and the flap of wind-filled sails was replaced by the newly familiar rattle of metal and wood as wheels rolled over uneven ground.

Ling Fan's wagon closely followed four others loaded with supplies. Behind it trailed two more carrying workers, most of them Chinese, but some bak gui too. Judging by the slant of sunlight, the wagons had been on the move for an hour or two, winding eastward and upward. The base camp and Tunnel Three were nowhere in sight.

The patches of scrubby grass that dotted the landscape gave way to barren brown earth and tumbled rock. Around noon, the wagons pulled off the trail onto a work site and everyone piled out on stiff legs.

They were on a wide, windy plateau several hundred feet higher than their main campsite. Ling Fan had never been so high. How close were they to the summit? She squinted into the wind. It was fierce, stinging her eyes and cheeks and cutting through her padded jacket.

Ah Sook seemed to be everywhere, shouting out orders or bellowing at men for being too slow, too clumsy, too careless. Canvas tents were pitched beside a spur of granite wall that curved south, and many of the bak gui were already settling into them and starting small fires. Ling Fan and the other Chinese workers joined a group of sojourners at a cluster of tents set apart from the bak gui.

From their sacks they pulled out packages of dried seaweed and cuttlefish that they softened in hot water and steamed over boiled rice. A jug of cold tea passed from hand to hand, and everyone took a swig. "This swill will have to do until more supply wagons catch up with us in a few days," Ah Sook remarked as he handed the jug to Ling Fan. "It'll be real food, none of that boiled cardboard the bak gui eat. Oysters, abalone, fresh bamboo shoots, noodles . . ." He stared morosely into his bowl.

Ling Fan glanced toward the bak gui workers. "Why don't we eat with them?"

Ah Sook shrugged. "Why would we want to? We can't even speak each other's languages."

Ling Fan was tempted to point out that she actually knew plenty of English, but she stopped herself in time. Better to drop the subject. No need to draw more attention to herself.

Ah Sook was giving her a sharp look. "Those bak gui have

their ways, we have ours. They always let us know quick enough that we're not one of them."

His tone made her prickle, but she couldn't dispute what he'd said. The bak gui kept the Chinese workers at arm's length, interacting only when absolutely necessary. And her fellow sojourners seemed fine with that arrangement.

In some ways it was a disappointment. Baba had always been intrigued by Westerners, and he had shared that interest with his children, going so far as to teach them English. And Jing Fan had absorbed all that curiosity. If they were here now, they would've been over at the other cook site, making small talk and sampling American food. But perhaps it was just as well; Ling Fan couldn't take the risk of socializing with too many people anyway.

She nodded at Ah Sook, and to her relief he turned his attention elsewhere. Ling Fan finished her meal, silent but watchful.

The wind kept snatching her breath. Clouds scudded across the sky like tattered sails. Far to the east, she glimpsed twin craggy blue shadows that rose even higher than where she now stood. Donner Pass, the high point where the railroad would finally crest the mountain range and begin its way down toward Utah.

The plateau was mostly bare soil studded here and there with patches of brown grass. Beyond the tents to the east, the ground had been churned into a dusty pit that looked like a huge open-air workshop. There, several men, mostly bak gui, were uncoiling a rope that was as thick as Ling Fan's arm. One end of the rope was knotted around an anchor buried in the ground. The other end was attached to a leather harness. As she watched, a worker strapped himself into the harness and walked twenty feet eastward to where the ground suddenly disappeared. He turned to face the other men and, by manipulating the rope, gradually lowered himself over the edge of the cliff. Mesmerized, Ling Fan watched the man slowly sink from sight.

She went to the ragged edge and looked down. Fifty feet below, a wide ledge was beginning to emerge along the side of the mountain. From this height, the swath of freshly chiseled granite was distinct from the rest of the rocky mountainside. Half a dozen workers hung in midair by their harnesses, pounding at the stone wall with drills and hammers. She gathered that once a big enough hole was made in the cliff wall, it would be filled with gunpowder and ignited. The blast would gouge out an enormous slab of cliff wall, lengthening the ledge.

Farther below, Ling Fan could make out the writhing gray ribbon of the American River. It wriggled out of sight around the base of the mountain. As she stared at the whirling water, feeling the wind rip at her hair, clothing, even her breath, it began to seem as though the ground itself was spinning beneath her feet. Ling Fan staggered backward with a gasp.

"Watch it!" Strong hands pushed her downward so that she found herself sitting on firm, flat ground, a few feet away from the edge of the cliff. She struggled to keep a wave of nausea from pulling up the lunch she'd just eaten. Blinking, she tried to focus on the pale freckled face and red hair of the bak gui peering down at her anxiously.

"You all right?" he said. The tips of his ear reddened as he spoke.

"Thomas O'Brien!" she exclaimed. The nephew of the bak gui who'd helped her and Tan Din that day in Illinoistown.

She'd never expected to see him again, least of all here at the edge of the world.

"Good memory. I don't think I caught your name."

"Tam Jing Fan." Her brother's name rolled off her tongue easily now.

Thomas handed her a canteen of water, but she pushed it away, whispering, "Tea?" Thomas waved over a Chinese worker with a bucket of cold black tea, and she gulped down a cupful. Thomas stayed beside her, his round face filled with concern.

"I don't know what was the matter with me." She hoped Ah Sook hadn't seen her reaction. She knew that at least half a dozen men would eagerly step up should Ah Sook decide she wasn't fit to do this work after all. She couldn't risk losing the bonus money.

"Uncle says it hits a lot of folks like that the first time," Thomas said, gesturing at the jagged cliff edge. He replaced the stopper in the canteen that was still in his hand. "You'll get over it quick enough."

"I didn't mean to be rude just now," Ling Fan said. The tea had stopped the spinning sensation and cleared her mind. "It's just that we feel there are . . ." She groped for the right English words. "Bad spirits in the water. The old sojourners tell us to never drink water that hasn't been boiled. They say the water makes you sick."

Thomas looked thoughtfully at the bottle in his hand. "Hmm, you Celestials may be right about that. Hold on there," he added as Ling Fan stood up shakily. "Sit a spell and get your breath back at least." He nodded toward a tarp-covered supply wagon that Ah Sook hovered around like an anxious hornet. "Are you part of the mysterious Celestial project?"

She decided "Celestial" sounded friendlier than "coolie."

"I suppose I am," she said. "But I don't know much about it yet."

"Really? Uncle Jon has been in such a sweat over it these past few weeks. He moved heaven and earth to get us jobs up here just so he could see it all himself. He says that Strobridge and your foreman—Chin Lin Sou, is it?—came up with a newfangled Celestial way of carving out Cape Horn faster than we've been able to so far. Nobody knows exactly how, but looks like we're about to find out."

Ah Sook pulled the tarp off the supply wagon. Thomas's jaw dropped. "JesusMaryandJoseph. What in heaven's name are those?"

There were three of them: tightly woven reed baskets that were three feet deep and two feet wide. Characters for luck and good fortune were written in red paint along the four sides. The top of each basket was pierced by four brass rings large enough to be bracelets for dancers at the imperial court. Workers threaded more of the thick rope Ling Fan had seen earlier through each of the rings, then twined the four strands together into a single braid to form a long tail. This was then wound around a metal spool that had a large spiked wheel attached to its side. The wheel's long-handled crank surely needed two men to operate it. The whole contraption reminded Ling Fan of the inner workings of a clock her father had once shown her. By turning the wheel, she guessed that workers would wind and unwind the rope, which in turn would lower and raise the basket as it hung over the cliff.

Thomas let out a long appreciative whistle. "By God, you Celestials are a clever bunch, aren't you?" Seeing Ling Fan's blank expression, he added, "Don't you see, this'll give a worker more stability to hammer at the rock. I'll wager you could do three times the work in one of those baskets than we could dangling in our puny harnesses. Wish I could have a go in one."

Maybe we should trade places, Ling Fan wanted to say. Now that she had a better grasp of what she was in for, she couldn't suppress a sense of dread. She couldn't imagine doing any task at this height, much less creating a controlled explosion . . .

"I'd better get back," was what she said instead, standing up and dusting herself off. Ah Sook was glaring at her.

"As well should I," Thomas agreed. "Good luck to you then, Tam Jing Fan." He headed over to the bak gui working with the harnesses. He nodded to Ah Sook as he passed, but Ah Sook didn't return the gesture.

"What were you talking about with that bak gui?" Ah Sook demanded when Ling Fan reached him.

"Nothing," Ling Fan said, surprised by Ah Sook's irritation. "He offered me some water."

"Never accept any favors from the bak gui. Never take anything that you haven't earned. They are not our friends. Now come on."

He led her over to the other basket candidates. "Fei Gei, you'll work the first basket, Bing Lai the second, and Tam Jing Fan the third." He explained what they would need to do, and the three of them helped assemble and check the materials they would use for the job. Ah Sook dismissed them in time for dinner. "We'll start at first light tomorrow."

After picking at her food, Ling Fan headed to her assigned tent. She stepped over the men already inside and wrapped herself tightly in her bedroll. She wasn't tired or hungry. Shutting her eyes only made tomorrow's imagined work all the more vivid. She sat up and pulled out her pen set. **Jing, what have I gotten myself into?** She tucked the note away to burn later and closed her eyes. Once again, she felt the ground spinning, felt as though she was falling and shouting . . .

It must have been well past midnight when she realized the sound of shouting and the smell of smoke were not coming from her nightmares, but from outside her tent.

She scrambled out of her bedroll, dimly aware of flickering orange light beyond her tent flap. People were running here and there, and she thought she heard metal clanging against rock. She pushed her way outside, where a terrible odor filled the air, making it hard to breathe. Smoke was everywhere. Her eyes began to sting. She grabbed at the nearest person as he ran past her.

"What's happening?" she cried.

"Fire! Bring anything that can hold water, hurry!" He tore away. Ling Fan grabbed the first vessel she spotted—a teapot—and ran after him.

The heat was fierce. Ahead of her, barely visible, a ragged line of men stretched from the tiny stream at the edge of their work site all the way across the plateau. They were passing pails, pots, and kettles of water along as fast as they could. At the end of the line, a tower of flame blazed into the night sky, orange and red tongues writhing hungrily through what was left of a basket at the edge of the cliff.

Ling Fan joined the line as men threw the pots of water against the flames, but it was like trying to put out a campfire by spitting on it. A new cry broke out from the workers as sparks, blown by the strong wind, landed on crates and sacks. Men abandoned the water line and ran to pull away the supplies.

By the time the last flame was put out, the baskets were nothing more than sodden black lumps. The sky began to glow orangey peach, as though the fire had forsaken the plateau and taken to wispy, feathery flight. Ling Fan sat on a rock to rest while a few of the men prodded piles of debris with sticks, checking for smoldering embers.

Ah Sook walked up to Ling Fan and perched on the rock beside her. His face was covered with soot, and his eyes were red from the smoke. "I sent a rider back to base camp with the news," he said. "Chin Lin Sou will probably come up himself." He adjusted his hat with his clawed hand, squinting at the ghostly landscape around them as though he was looking for something long lost. "Months of planning gone in just a few hours. Months." His shoulders slumped, and suddenly he looked like a tired old man. "They never tell you," he said softly, and lapsed into silence.

"They never tell you what?"

"How this place eats you." Ah Sook's voice was savage. "It eats you up and spits you out." He sighed and shook himself. "You might as well get some rest, boy. We won't have a new plan until Chin Lin Sou arrives." He bent down and picked something up from the ground. It was her teapot. She stared at it as he pressed it into her hands.

The miasma of wet, smoky bodies inside her tent made her retch. Still, she curled up alongside her tent mates, grateful for their warmth despite the odor. Her whole body suddenly felt as though it were made of rock; her mind drifted sideways in blessed relief and she slept. A moment later someone was shaking her and bawling in her ear, "Get up! Ah Sook wants you at the basket now!"

The basket? The baskets were gone. Burned. Or had she dreamed the whole thing? No, the acrid tang of smoke still hung in the air. She sat up, and every bone in her body screamed in protest. "Hurry up, Tam Jing Fan. Chin Lin Sou is waiting. Strobridge will be here soon." Strobridge here? Ling Fan crawled out of the tent and blinked against the glaring sun.

To the north, bak gui workers were moving about with their harnesses, pausing every so often to take in what was happening to the east, where the sojourners concentrated on their work. The plateau seemed crowded with twice as many men, donkeys, and horses as there had been yesterday. Most of last night's wreckage had been pushed to one side. Ling Fan caught sight of Chin Lin Sou deep in conversation with Ah Sook next to . . . a basket! Had Chin Lin Sou brought another one from the base camp?

This one seemed odd. It didn't look quite right. For starters it was much smaller than the others had been.

Ling Fan hurried to join the men. "I thought all the baskets were destroyed in the fire!"

"They were, but we were able to salvage enough of each basket to put together a new one," Chin Lin Sou said.

On closer inspection, Ling Fan could make out the places where the basket was clearly patched together; one entire side was darker than the rest, as though it had been toasted. The splendid calligraphy that had adorned the original three was now a series of random red hashes that crisscrossed the sides. They looked, Ling Fan thought with a shudder, like bloody claw marks.

The new basket looked pathetic in the harsh mountain light. It looked like the bottom would fall out should anyone be so foolish as to try to climb into it.

"Strobridge is on his way," Chin Lin Sou continued. "We have to keep this basket work going. We have to show him what we can do." He nodded at Ling Fan. "Fei Gei was badly burned last night trying to put out the fire, and Bing Lai can't fit inside this one. It'll have to be you, Tam Jing Fan."

In her mind's eye she saw the fierce winds knocking this flimsy basket into the side of the cliff. She saw herself bursting through the bottom of it, like the meaty kernel from a peanut shell, and tumbling head over heels along with the charred reeds into the raging American River.

Ling Fan tried to swallow, but her mouth was too dry. She hoped her face didn't show the panic that blew through her like the winds gusting around them. If she didn't accept this job, there went the bonus money. *Think of Baba*, she told herself. *Remember Jing.* She nodded once. "I'm ready."

CHAPTER 15

A h Sook sent her to help some of the other workers prepare the rope that would be used to lower her over the cliff. Two of them were in the midst of a heated discussion.

"I saw them with my own eyes!" said a boy with a broken nose. Ling Fan recognized him as one of the rope climbers she had beaten the other night. He looked to be about twelve years old.

"You were dreaming," an older man retorted.

"No, I wasn't. I was coming back from the latrine, and I saw them clear as day."

"Saw what?" Ling Fan asked.

"I saw who started the fire," the boy said.

Ling Fan had assumed the fire had been an accident—the unfortunate result of campfire ashes blown by the wind. Now she thought of all the *accidents* the railroad had had in just a few months. The idea that anyone would deliberately wreak havoc seemed monstrous to her. But the boy was adamant.

"Have you told Ah Sook or Chin Lin Sou?" she asked.

The boy scowled down at the rope in his hands and shook his head. "They wouldn't believe me. Nobody ever believes me. They just laugh at me."

"I won't laugh. Tell me."

The boy did not look up at her as he continued to coil the rope. "The ghosts did it," he whispered.

"The ghosts?"

When she didn't laugh, as promised, the boy let out a deep breath. "The ghosts of all the workers who've died here. The guhun yegui."

He was talking about the spirits of men who had been killed but whose bodies were never properly buried because it had been impossible to recover them. Some were trapped beneath tons of rock, some were blown up, others had fallen from the cliffs to the river below. Many sojourners believed that the spirits of such men became wild, lost ghosts, doomed to wander eternally.

"I see them," the boy whispered. "I hear them. I saw one last night before the fire started."

"What did that one look like?" Ling Fan asked.

The boy looked abashed. "It was dark and hard to see. But there was a man-shaped form that moved from shadow to shadow."

Ling Fan frowned. The boy's story reminded her of the morning she started working with Tan Din, when she'd seen the figure in the dusty blue coat moving amongst the covered wagons.

"You believe me, don't you?"

"I believe you saw something," she said.

"Tam Jing Fan, we're ready," Ah Sook shouted, waving her back to the basket. She stood up and started toward him, but the boy grabbed her hand.

"Be careful. I don't know why the ghosts are so angry, but . . ." He seemed to struggle with finding the right thing to say. "Make sure you keep an eye on the fuse."

Ling Fan nodded. She'd heard about workers who'd misjudged the amount of fuse needed to ignite the gunpowder and gotten caught in their own blast when it detonated sooner than they expected.

She ran over to the basket. It was so full of picks, drills, and hammers that she could hardly squeeze herself into it. Ah Sook shouted a command, and several other men lifted the basket and carried it to the cliff's edge. Ling Fan wrapped her fingers around the ropes that were knotted through the iron rings just as everything she saw began to tilt and swing. Her stomach felt ready to turn itself inside out. The men who'd been so close a second ago suddenly rose above her head as the basket was lowered down the mountainside.

The wind made the basket sway. Every so often, the basket bumped against the craggy face of the cliff wall and began to whirl, first one way, then another. Twice, the basket was caught up in the gnarly branches of a wind-stunted bush that had somehow taken root in the thin soil of the mountainside. Ling Fan had to hack at the leathery limbs with the ax from the pile of tools before the basket could move again. And still she went down.

The ribbon of the American River grew wider, and now she could hear its steady roar. She could barely make out the workers high above her, outlined against the deep blue sky. They looked like round beetles scurrying around the rim of a vast bowl. Just as she was wondering if she should signal them to stop the basket, it jerked to a halt. In the distance to her right, she could just make out an echo that sounded like the high-pitched twang of metal striking metal. It was the sound of the bak gui in harnesses hammering spikes into the granite wall. She'd better get started too.

Quickly, Ling Fan scanned the expanse of rock in front of her, looking for the longest, deepest crack to begin her drilling. She found one that looked promising and set to work with iron spike and hammer. After what seemed like an eternity, she stopped to take stock of her progress.

Sweat poured down her back and dripped along the side of her face. As the dust cleared, she stared in disbelief. The rock face in front of her showed numerous white marks where her pick axe had scored and pitted the surface, but despite all her hammering, she had only managed to make a dimple the size of an acorn cap in the granite wall.

The metallic sound of hammers on either side of her echoed off the mountainside and drifted by on a cold breeze. She pushed her hat back and let the blazing sun beat down on her bare head. She drank heavily from the canteen of tea she'd set in the bottom of the basket along with a packet of dried fruit and nuts. Her hands, arms, and shoulders felt as though weights had been tied to them.

Blisters had blossomed across her palms where she'd gripped the hammer. She ripped a strip of cloth off the bottom of her tunic and wound them around her hands. She didn't know how she would ever get herself to start again, but somehow, she did, forcing her right arm to bring the hammer against the pickax over and over.

Hours later, the tiny hole she'd made in the granite wall was large enough to fill with gunpowder. Her hands shook as she picked up the sack holding the powder.

It was her first time handling gunpowder. Her tongue felt like a piece of old leather as she licked her lips, running through Ah Sook's directions from yesterday. She tried not to think of the charred stumps on men who had survived blasting accidents.

The powder was in place. Leaning over the lip of her basket, she whistled to the men above and waved the red cloth that signaled she was about to light the fuse. A watcher from above whistled back and waved his red cloth.

Ling Fan cut a length of fuse the way Ah Sook had instructed her. She carefully pressed one end deep into the powder in her little hole, tamping it down tightly. She struck a flame from her tinderbox and lit the end of the fuse. It caught on the first try, and Ling Fan could feel her heart hammering as she watched the flame crawl swiftly toward the gunpowder in the stone wall.

She waved her red cloth again and waited for the basket to be lifted.

Wind whistled past her ears. It knocked the basket gently against the cliff wall. The basket twisted on its rope once. Twice. She waited.

What was the problem? She shaded her eyes, trying to see if the men above were signaling to her, but there was no one in sight. The sputtering light had traveled almost a quarter the length of the fuse.

No more time. If she didn't move now, she would be too close to the blast. Heart beating in her throat, Ling Fan gripped the rope holding the basket and started to climb as fast as she could.

Her arms felt like dead weights, but she gripped the rope with her feet and legs and somehow managed to make progress.

A fantastically loud crash filled the air around her. Rocks and dirt started to rain down the side of the mountain, hitting the rope, hitting her. She clung to the rope, head ducked. Suddenly she felt herself moving, but in the chaos, it was impossible to say in what direction. She closed her eyes, picturing herself splattered at the bottom of the cliff, where she would lie buried beneath a ton of splintered granite.

As suddenly as it started, the noise and the shower of rocks stopped. Cautiously, Ling Fan looked around. She was back at the top of the cliff, surrounded by her crew. Everyone was talking at once, grinning and pounding her on the back. Chin Lin Sou himself pried her hands loose from the rope and pressed a flask of whiskey into them. She tried to take a swig but spilled most of it.

Satisfied that she was unharmed, Chin Lin Sou joined Ah Sook and several other workers next to the iron wheel. They were taking the wheel apart piece by piece and arguing over every step. Finally, Chin Lin Sou gestured for silence. "That's enough. I don't care whose fault it is. I just want to know why that wheel jammed in the first place, and I want to know before Strobridge gets here." He marched off. He hadn't raised his voice—hadn't bellowed and cursed as Ah Sook would have—but the anger vibrating off him made the air around him crackle.

"I know why the wheel jammed," a voice by Ling Fan's elbow said softly. It was the boy she'd spoken to earlier. He was kneeling on the ground, winding the remains of the broken rope into a neat coil.

"What did you see this time?" Ling Fan said to him.

"Nothing—but this morning everything was working fine, and just now they couldn't use the wheel to pull the basket up again. So the crew started to pull the rope up by hand, but by that time you had climbed most of the way back up." He looked at her admiringly. "You sure can climb fast."

"You would too if a mountain wall was about to blow up in your face." Ling Fan got to her feet, though her legs shook under her weight. "So you think a gui jammed the wheel?"

The boy nodded. "It makes sense, doesn't it? After what I saw last night?"

Ling Fan wasn't sure what to say. The boy's comment that the gui were "man-shaped" made her suspect that the damage had more to do with ordinary people than spirits. "I'll talk to Chin Lin Sou," she said.

"He won't believe you if you tell him about the gui."

"Maybe not. But he should know there's a chance the equipment was tampered with." She set off to find the foreman's tent.

It was pitched next to Ah Sook's by the leeward wall of the plateau. As she drew closer, she saw a horse tethered just outside it and heard a deep voice rumbling within.

". . . only agreed to let you try this idea because you promised me results," the voice was saying in American English. "You told me you'd get ten times more work done in a day than the men in harnesses could do in a week."

Chin Lin Sou's higher voice said something without rancor.

"All I see here is a whole hell of a mess over in your corner of the plateau." The other man would not be soothed. "And now you want me to give you more time and money so you can make another expensive mess?"

Ling Fan heard Chin Lin Sou say something about "more baskets."

"We're already months behind schedule and thousands of dollars over our budget. The Big Four are breathing down my neck. Crocker's coming out here himself from San Francisco. I already took a big risk letting you try this coolie trick and look where it got us. I want you to clean up and get back to base camp. As far as I'm concerned there were never any baskets at Cape Horn!"

Ling Fan jumped back as the tent flap was thrown aside and Strobridge shouldered his way out. He strode past her without a glance and mounted his horse. Turning the horse slowly, he took in the sweep of the surrounding plateau. Between the eye patch and the thick beard, it was difficult to read his expression, but Ling Fan doubted it was anything good. He took one last long look before clucking to his horse and setting off for the trail that led back down the mountain.

Chin Lin Sou emerged from his tent, looking weary. "You heard Mr. Strobridge, Tam Jing Fan. Spread the word that we're to pack up and head back down in the morning."

Ling Fan wanted to tell him what the boy had told her, what she suspected. But something about his expression, implacable as the mountainside, made her stare down at the tops of her worn boots. "Yessir."

"Tell Ah Sook I want the place spotless. Not a sign that we were ever up here with our baskets."

The next day, Chin Lin Sou's tent was gone. The ground where it had stood was now churned by wagon wheels and donkey hooves. Once more, Ah Sook was rushing around, chasing barrels, boxes, and supplies back into carts and wagons. By midmorning, they were on the trail back down to the base camp.

CHAPTER 16

"**Y**ou said there would be bonus money! Two extra dollars a day for a dangerous job! Where's my money?"

Ah Sook stood in front of Chin Lin Sou's tent, arms folded across his thick chest. "We said there would be bonus money for completed work."

"I did the work. Now I want my money!"

"You got your money."

"This?" Ling Fan shook the coins in her fist. "It's a quarter what you promised!"

"You're lucky you got anything at all, since the job was canceled."

"That's not my fault! I was almost killed!"

"Boy"—Ah Sook pointed a finger in her face—"that's exactly my point!"

"I demand to see Chin Lin Sou!"

"I told you, he's not here."

"I'll wait."

"Make yourself comfortable. He won't be back until the day after tomorrow." With that, Ah Sook ambled off, leaving Ling Fan fuming.

It was Sunday, a week after she'd returned from Cape Horn. For days, she'd been filled with a fierce, wild energy. She'd returned to Tan Din's cook fires, but stories of what happened at Cape Horn had spread and it seemed like everywhere she turned, somebody was clapping her on the back or shouting her name—her brother's name. She told him, **I feel like the hero of an imperial opera! I could take on a dragon!**

Then reality set in, like a collapsing tunnel. The bonus money in her pay was only fifty cents. Staring down at the coins the paymaster handed her, she was sure there'd been a mistake. Granted, she had only worked at Cape Horn for a day instead of the month or two she'd expected, but even so, she was owed more than this!

Of course, no amount of arguing or cursing changed a thing. The bosses had made their decision. Or at least Ah Sook had.

With a bitter heart she handed the sum to the Benevolent Society brother and made her mark in his ledger. In her mind, she adjusted the balance she still needed to free her father. It felt like a kick in the face. She wished there was something she could kick back.

She stormed aimlessly through the maze of tents, past people hanging their laundry to dry. Others sat mending clothing with thread and needle, or patching shoes or tents. Without thinking about it, Ling Fan found herself back in the main cooking area.

Tan Din stood beside a covered wagon, talking to Wong Wei. He didn't seem to be enjoying the conversation, but Wong Wei was the one who looked truly miserable. Somehow he was even thinner than he'd been a few days ago. He was wearing his long blue coat again—he must've won it back—but it hung from his shoulders like a scarecrow's costume.

Their eyes met briefly. For a second, Wong Wei looked surprised, then angry, but just as quickly, his face became a mask of indifference. His gaze slid past her as though she were a stranger. He climbed onto the seat at the front of the wagon and took up the donkey's reins.

Ling Fan chewed her lip. Part of her wanted to take Wong Wei's cue and walk away, but part of her still wanted to salvage their old camaraderie. She felt vaguely guilty that she'd beaten him at the chance to go to Cape Horn. But now, their fortunes were more or less even again. Surely Wong Wei would see it that way if he knew the whole story. When Tan Din caught sight of her and beckoned, she headed over to the wagon.

He waved a piece of thin blue paper at Ling Fan. "From the sisters at the orphanage in Guangzhou. It says my daughter wants a real American bak gui doll. A doll with yellow hair, red lips, and blue eyes that can open and close." He shook his head. "For days I wonder where I'm supposed to find such a bak gui doll, then Wong Wei tells me that he's seen one in Illinoistown. He says it's in the general store that he passes on his way to Sully's Saloon. We're going there now. I have a coin or two saved and"—he shot a distasteful look at Wong Wei—"he has some trading of his own to do. You have good American English, Tam Jing Fan—why don't you come too?"

She was keenly aware that Wong Wei had heard every word from his perch, but he gave no indication of how he felt. This, more than Tan Din's hopeful face, prodded her to jump onto the back of the wagon.

The wagon was empty except for a few small bags stuffed beneath the front seat. They were Wong Wei's, Tan Din explained with a dark look. Ling Fan thought it best not to pry further. She settled in, enjoying the breeze that blew through the wagon's front opening.

In the weeks since her last trip, the rough path that led to

Illinoistown had become a road wide enough for two wagons. The donkeys made good time on the smoothed surface. Wong Wei spoke a few words to Tan Din from time to time, but he paid no attention to Ling Fan.

Ling Fan tried to ignore his snub, though she made sure her voice was loud enough to carry as she told Tan Din about her paltry bonus. Tan Din threw his hat on the floor of the wagon in disgust.

"After everything you went through, the railroad should give you triple hazard pay!"

Ling Fan could hardly disagree. "It's strange that the baskets caught on fire right before they could be used," she said. "It's strange the device jammed when it did."

"Bad luck, that's all," said Wong Wei.

But Ling Fan was thinking of the boy at the edge of Cape Horn telling her about the "man-shaped" ghost he'd seen before the fire broke out. The idea that someone could've deliberately tampered with the baskets made her sick. Working on the railroad was dangerous enough. Who would cause more destruction and mayhem on purpose?

"Bad luck for some means good luck for others," Ling Fan mused. "Who stands to gain?"

"Union Pacific, damn them," Tan Din growled.

"Could someone from Union Pacific sneak around our work sites unnoticed, though?"

Wong Wei cleared his throat. "I don't see why you're giving this so much thought. It's the bak gui bosses' problem, not ours. As long as we get paid, who cares about the Americans' rivalries?"

Ling Fan thought of pointing out that they couldn't get paid if they died in one of these strange "accidents," but she decided there was no point in bickering with Wong Wei and changed the subject.

"How is your daughter?" she asked Tan Din.

"The sisters write that she's a sweet, mindful little girl but that she spends most of her free time standing at the eastern gate, the one that faces the harbor." He smoothed the thin pages of his letter before carefully refolding them and tucked them into an inner pocket of his tunic.

"Do you really think you can find a doll in Illinoistown?"

"You can get anything in Illinoistown these days," Tan Din replied, "if you have the money or a little something to barter for it." He nodded at Wong Wei with his chin. "That one plans to get himself a proper bak gui hat to go with his bak gui coat."

Tan Din stretched out, pushed his hat over his face and began to snore. Ling Fan must have dozed off too, because the next thing she knew, the even sway of the wagon changed to jolting stops and starts, and voices filtered through the stiff canvas covering. She crawled to the narrow opening at the back of the wagon and stared out. The town had transformed since her last visit: more buildings, more streets, more people. They passed farmers, cattle handlers, teamsters, carpenters, and painted ladies, all within the span of three buildings.

Ling Fan felt eyes following their progress through the town. She heard mutters of "Chinamen," "coolie," and "railroad." Twice, someone spat a stream of tobacco juice onto the dirt in their wake.

The wagon rolled toward the end of the main street where sawdust and wood chips still lay like freshly fallen snow around the skeleton frames of new structures. At the end of the row stood an especially large building. A long painted sign that read CHATE & LIPPTON GENERAL GOODS stretched across the entrance. "This is it," said Wong Wei. "You'll spot the doll right away. Meet me at the supply depot when you're done." Ling Fan and Tan Din climbed out of the wagon and mounted the steps to the wooden porch. Wong Wei clucked to the mule and the wagon continued down the road.

Ling Fan crossed the porch and peered into one of the store's windows. Open sacks of grain, flour, rice, salt, sugar, and coffee slouched against the front counter, which was a wide wooden plank balanced on top of two sawhorses. Barrels and crates were crammed against the walls and under tables full of wares, and more items hung from the rafters. Never had she seen so much household wealth in one space.

Tan Din stood beside her, squinting to see all the way to the back of the store. Suddenly, he clapped her on the shoulder and pointed toward a shelf. On it was a doll dressed in a gown made of blue satin and lace. Little white gloves covered its hands, and tiny patent leather shoes peeped out from under a layer of snowy cotton petticoats. Long golden ringlets framed a porcelain face with rosebud lips and plump pink cheeks. Its blue glass eyes were framed by a thick fringe of dark eyelashes.

Ling Fan thought the bak gui doll was hideous, but she knew that Tan Din had set his heart on it.

"You! Chinaman! Get away from my store!" snapped a tall, white-haired woman as she mounted the steps. Like the doll, she wore a long blue dress that covered everything below the loose, ropy flesh of her chin all the way down to the tops of her black-buttoned boots. Her white hair was pulled into a tight knot beneath her bonnet, and her thin mouth was like a gash across her face.

"I want . . ." Tan Din began in his halting English, pointing into the store. He reached inside his tunic and pulled out a bag. The woman stepped back with a squeak. "I want . . ." He shook the bag, and the universal sound of metal coins clanking against one another rang out. Her eyes flashed understanding, but her face became a mask.

"If you want to buy something, Mr. Chinaman, you'll have to come back tomorrow. I don't do business on the Lord's day."

Then why are you here? Ling Fan wanted to ask. *Why come to your store today, if not to open it?* She had seen it often enough since she'd arrived in America, and still she could never fully understand it. The bak gui seemed to have one set of rules for themselves, and another for anybody who looked different.

"He wants to buy your doll," Ling Fan said. Perhaps the promise of a specific purchase would change the woman's mind.

"How many?" Tan Din shook all the coins into his palm and held them out. "How many?"

The woman peered through her round gold wire-rimmed glasses at the coins in his hand. "That doll costs considerably more than what you've got there," she said. "It was made in Belmont. It's a high-class doll for little ladies."

Out on the street, a bak gui in dusty red suspenders and a patched hat called out, "Aww, go on, Dinah Chate. Sell the Chinaman one of your dollies. That's as close as he's ever gonna get to a fancy lady!" He slapped his knee and bent almost double, laughing at his own joke.

Two spots of red spread across the woman's cheeks. "If the Chinaman has the money, of course the doll is his to buy," she said coldly. She named a price that almost made Ling Fan gasp aloud. That was enough to feed a family in China for a week.

The man in suspenders whistled. "Raising your prices, are you, Mrs. Chate? Could swear the one I bought for my girl cost half that."

"Is that true?" Ling Fan demanded. "Why do you ask for a different price if a Chinese person wants one?"

The shopkeeper stared at her as though a frog at her feet had just learned to speak. "I can price my wares however I see fit. Your friend can take it or leave it."

Angry heat rose along the back of Ling Fan's neck. She wanted to reach up and slap the glasses off the woman's haughty face. It was obvious she wanted nothing to do with them, not even to make an honest sale, and all because they were Chinese.

"Let's just go," she muttered to Tan Din, not having the heart to look at his hopeful face. At least they could have the satisfaction of refusing to give this woman any of Tan Din's hard-earned money.

But Tan Din seemed not to hear her. He was twisting, stretching, and bending to untie and unbutton various pieces of his clothing. He looked as though he were trying to reach an impossible itch that traveled the length of his body. "Nah, nah, nah," Tan Din said triumphantly as he added two more gold coins and a crumpled piece of American paper money to his handful. "I take now?"

The shopkeeper looked at what was in Tan Din's hand and her nostrils flared as though she smelled something unpleasant. "That's still not enough. You need twenty more cents."

Ling Fan glared at the shopkeeper. "Here." She thrust a few of her own coins into the shopkeeper's hand and stared at her, unblinking, until the woman silently unlocked the door and slipped inside. She reemerged a minute later with a box in her hand.

Ling Fan took it, opened the box to make sure the doll was there, and then pulled Tan Din down into the street by the elbow.

"But I was just getting ready to bargain," Tan Din protested. "I've bargained down a merchant or two in my time."

"Trust me," Ling Fan said grimly, "there was no bargaining with that shopkeeper." It was enough that Tan Din had what he'd come for, even if it cost twice what it should have.

They hadn't walked far when the sound of a crowd reached their ears. Just by the tone, Ling Fan knew it was angry.

The new street ended at a long, low building. At each end was a set of swinging doors that gaped open, and the cool scent of alcohol drifted from within and hung like a cloud over the assembled group. A dozen men stood around what looked like a bundle of dusty blue cloth in the middle of the road. As Ling Fan and Tan Din drew closer, one of the men rushed forward and kicked the bundle, flipping it over to reveal Wong Wei, pale and bloody.

"We told you coolies to keep away from here with your poison," he said as he drew back to take another running kick. "If you don't understand the words, you can at least understand this!" His thick-soled boot caught Wong Wei's chin. Wong Wei's head snapped back.

Ling Fan surged forward, but more people were gathering to watch the spectacle, blocking her path to Wong Wei. It was like trying to claw her way through the mountains with her bare hands. When she dared to push past someone, she was shoved violently backward.

Wong Wei was trying to get to his feet, pulling himself onto his hands and knees just before another kick knocked his arms out from under him. The kicker stepped back and mopped his face with a checkered cloth he pulled out of his back pocket. Another man, dressed in a black coat and shiny boots, stepped forward. He held a cane that had a carved bird's head at one end. The others looked at him expectantly as he knelt beside Wong Wei.

"Look here. Just you give Georgie his money back, and we'll let you crawl back to your sneaky-eyed friends on the railroad," he said softly, reasonably.

After what seemed like an eternity, Wong Wei spoke. "I give back," he said through thick, swollen lips.

"Yes, that's right. Give it back." The well-dressed bak gui held out his hand.

Slowly, Wong Wei raised his head and looked the man in the eye. "I gived back. I gived back! I no more give back." Wong Wei spat into the hand thrust at his face.

The bak gui leaped away and lashed out wildly with his cane. The curved bird beak drew a heavy red gash across Wong Wei's face. Over his screams, the bak gui turned to the crowd, shouting, "You heard him. He refuses to give back the money he stole from Georgie. These coolies do nothing but steal our work and feed our youngsters poison. Give him what he deserves!"

Horrified, Ling Fan tried again to push her way through the crowd to get to Wong Wei. It was no use. She leaped up onto a nearby horse trough.

"Listen to him! You're twisting his words!" she cried. "He gave it back! He gave the money back!"

Even those closest to her only stared at her as though she were gibbering nonsense. Before she could say more, strong arms lifted her off the trough and carried her into the shadows of a nearby building. Ling Fan struggled furiously.

"Let go of me!"

"Stop fighting me, boy. I'm not your enemy." Her captor set her down, and she whirled around and found herself staring into the scarred face of Jonathan O'Brien.

"He said he gave the money back! He doesn't have the money anymore! They have to know the truth!"

"Do you think this crowd really *wants* to know the truth?"

Ling Fan looked at the sea of angry faces surrounding Wong Wei. "We have to do something."

O'Brien turned to Thomas, who was standing nearby. "Go get Lars Randall." Thomas took off at a run.

Ling Fan kept her eyes on the bak gui, who now seemed to be quarreling amongst themselves. "Who is Lars Randall?"

"Closest thing this town has to a sheriff," Jonathan O'Brien said. "He hates the idea of you Celestials working on the railroad, but he hates rabble-rousers even more."

The crowd had split into different groups. One faction began shouting, "String 'im up to the big oak!" while another called for tar and feathers. Still another suggested that Wong Wei's queue be cut off, a mark of disgrace that would make any Chinese man shudder. Finally, the man with the cane held up his hands.

"Friends, why be particular? This moment is as good as any to teach the Chinaman a lesson. Why not teach it so he learns? Be patient and you can each have a piece of him." Shouts of agreement were suddenly silenced by the sound of horse hooves galloping closer. Several bak gui looked around nervously before slipping down the alleyways between nearby buildings. The man with the cane looked up, irritated, as a chestnut stallion carrying two riders rounded the corner.

Thomas O'Brien clung to the saddle behind a man dressed from head to toe in black. His hat was pulled low over his eyes, and Ling Fan could only make out a long, thin mustache that outlined his mouth. He swung down from the saddle easily and approached the crowd at a casual pace, but every movement spoke of a powerful man. Ling Fan saw a coiled leather whip on one hip and a revolver on the other. A few more men turned and walked away.

Thumbs hooked into his belt, he stopped a few feet from Wong Wei's bloody, crumpled body. "H'lo there, Dick Chate. Folks. Heard a ruckus out here. What's the problem?"

"Just settling an argument, Lars," the man with the cane said. Ling Fan couldn't help wondering if he was the husband or brother of the hateful shopkeeper. "No need for you to step in. We're just about done explaining to this here Chinaman that we don't want his particular brand of smoking tobacco around here." Someone in the crowd snickered.

"Glad to hear it, Mr. Chate," Lars Randall said, scanning the crowd. "'Cause it seems to me that a Chinaman can't sell that poison if there ain't no buyers wanting it to begin with." What was left of the crowd looked like they wished they'd left earlier with the others.

"True, very true, Lars," Dick Chate said with a sigh. "I myself have tried time and again to get these good men to understand that. Today, I got as far as getting Georgie here to swear off the stuff. We were in the middle of getting his money back when you arrived."

Ling Fan couldn't stand this anymore. She took a breath, ready to launch herself at them all.

"Mr. Randall, if I may interrupt," Jonathan O'Brien said suddenly, limping forward. Some of the people in the crowd caught sight of his face and looked away. "I saw with my own eyes when the Celestial gave the money back in the saloon. He gave it to that fellow over there." Jonathan O'Brien pointed at a bearded man dressed in patched overalls. "He has it in his pocket along with a bag or two you might find interesting."

"Hand it over, Georgie," Randall said.

"It's all lies, Lars." Georgie's jaw tightened.

For one terrible moment, Ling Fan wondered if Wong Wei had been lying. She herself had caught him in so many half-truths and schemes . . . But no, here was Jonathan O'Brien vouching for Wong Wei, saying he'd seen the transaction himself.

Randall took a step toward Georgie. Georgie spat in the dust before he reached into a pocket and tossed the contents to the ground.

"Wong Wei said he already gave the money back," Ling Fan burst out. "And those men beat him anyway!"

Lars Randall glanced at her, a look as cool as the tongue of a snake flicking into the air. He bent over and scooped up the bags and coins from the dust.

"Who can understand what Chinamen are saying with that talk they do?" Dick Chate shrugged. "Are we done here, Lars?" He stepped around Wong Wei and entered the saloon, swinging his cane.

Something in the crowd seemed to unravel. One by one, people turned away. Randall and O'Brien huddled together, deep in conversation. O'Brien's limp was so heavy that he looked as though he himself was staggering drunk.

Ling Fan and Thomas helped Wong Wei to his feet. "Help me get him to our wagon," Ling Fan said. Between the two of them, they were able to half carry, half drag Wong Wei to the wagon, which sat in the shade of the depot. "It seems that every time I see you or your uncle, I'm thanking you for your help," Ling Fan remarked.

Thomas's ears turned red, but he said steadily, "Uncle hates bullies more than anything. He believes it's important to understand others, especially if they live differently than you. I guess that's partly why he married a Cheyenne woman."

"Cheyenne? An Indian woman?" Ling Fan heard occasional mentions of American Indians. Her fellow sojourners knew very little about these people—who seemed, in fact, to be many different cultures spread throughout the vast country.

"It was a few years back. Uncle doesn't say much about it. He lived with the Cheyenne for a while—out on the Plains, far to the east of here. But then something happened. Something terrible." Thomas frowned, the red flowing from his ears down his neck. "That's how he got his limp and the scar on his face. He won't talk about it, but Pa says whatever happened out there changed him. He's so much angrier than he used to be."

"What do you think happened?"

Thomas shook his head. "All I know is that the other railroad company, Union Pacific, had a lot of trouble with Indians. They wanted the Indians out of the way—wanted them gone. So the army stepped in—drove people out of their homes. Even massacred whole villages."

Whole villages? Ling Fan stared at him, then looked away. After everything that had happened today, she hadn't thought she could feel more horrified.

"*Bak gui.*" The syllables felt gritty on her tongue, full of dangerous, sharp edges.

Thomas flinched as though the word had struck him across the face. "Not all of us are like that," he said softly. He turned and walked back toward the center of town. As Ling Fan watched him go, Ah Sook's voice whispered in her ear: *They are not our friends.*

She didn't know what to think. Bak gui acting like friends,

friends turning into strangers. The past few days had been a whirlwind of contradictions.

"There you are! I lost track of you in that mess!" Tan Din appeared, out of breath, still clutching the box with the precious doll. "Let's get out of here."

Wong Wei rolled over with a groan and vomited over the side of the wagon.

"That's what you get when you deal opium to bak gui," Tan Din told him, stowing his precious box beneath the wagon seat.

Ling Fan climbed up beside Tan Din on the wagon seat after making sure that Wong Wei was as comfortable as possible. As they followed their shadows up the trail, something wet blew against her face. She brushed it away impatiently, pulling her tunic collar tight against the rain. Ice-cold water slid down the back of her neck. Only then did she notice the lacy white dust that clung to her sleeves.

It was snowing.

CHAPTER
17

Snow!

Before she came to America, Ling Fan had imagined snow as a kind of cold, magical dust that fell from the sky and blew into piles. On the day she saw her first snowflake, she was transfixed by its delicate complexity.

That winter, she discovered that snow came in many varieties. The large gossamer puffs of spun sugar that drifted from the heavens were replaced by tiny gray pellets driven by furious wind. They lashed against Ling Fan's face like hundreds of tiny daggers. Snow on the ground churned with the mud to form puddles of gritty gray-brown stew during the day, but at night it froze into slick sheets that were hard as rock. One morning, Ling Fan opened the flap of her tent to see a world covered in a thick layer of crusty, sparkling cream—yet another type of snow.

She wished she could talk to someone about it. But the workers around her only cursed the cold wet stuff and wished it out of their way. They had no time for or interest in her whimsy, and she didn't want to draw unnecessary attention to herself by bringing it up.

The work crews had finally reached Donner Pass and begun work on Tunnel Six—Summit Tunnel, the hardest stretch of the mountains to get through. Or so the bak gui said. Ling Fan wasn't sure if she believed them. For all she knew, Tunnels Seven, Eight, Nine, and Ten would be just as challenging.

Now that her arm was fully healed, Ling Fan had been assigned to work on Summit Tunnel. Wong Wei was on the team too, but his shift was opposite hers. Tan Din and his pots and pans were stationed at the base camp, which had moved near Tunnel Five, half a mile away. She only saw him once a week when he came by with his ragged donkey train to restock her work crew's food supplies. As the days brought more snow, she saw even less of him. Workers made do with flavorless meals cobbled together from their personal stashes of rations and warmed over tiny fires.

The snow was so high at the Summit Tunnel work site that sojourners had to dig passages beneath and through the drifts, connecting the living areas to the main work area. Within this warren of snow tunnels, sojourners slept in wooden sheds, digging chimneys and airshafts through the snow to let in fresh air.

Ling Fan had been in America for almost six months. She missed her brother. She missed her father. She missed Ming. She missed Aunt Fei. She even missed Momo the cat. She missed having someone to tell any thought that popped into her head. Jing Fan had always stopped whatever he was in the middle of doing and listened to her, asking her questions, considering her thoughts as carefully as his own. Jing Fan would've understood about snow.

Perhaps that was why she started writing more letters to him. She looked forward to the time when she could put ink to paper and quiet her mind with the familiar strokes of her pen.

After dinner, she went back to work with the night shift.

Strobridge promised bonus money for those who worked around the clock. Ling Fan slept in snatches. It didn't matter whether it was night or day, whether she was working or resting. It was always night inside the work site's snowy tunnels. She hadn't seen the open sky in weeks. Ling Fan felt herself start to lose track of time.

Jing: It feels like an entire mountain of snow fell on us overnight. We'll have to dig our way out the same way we're digging our way into the mountain!

Before she lit a match to burn the note, she looked over what she'd written and sighed at the state of her handwriting. The characters sprawled across the page like a drunken sailor. These days, her fingers could barely bend to hold the pen properly to form the elegant sweeps and arcs that her father had taken such pains to teach her. A child could do better. Well, Jing Fan would understand.

Ah Sook began to drive Ling Fan's crew harder, demanding that they work faster and longer. Ling Fan counted herself lucky when she found a moment to relieve herself in a dark corner of a snow tunnel between shifts. At least her bleeding still hadn't started. Was it because of the heavy labor she'd done these past months? Aunt Fei used to gossip about women who took on too much farmwork. Whatever the reason, she was glad.

She had just finished retying her trousers when cries of pain echoed through the work site, sounding like the wails of a hundred ghouls. Rushing back to Summit Tunnel's entrance, she found workers from the other shift emerging early, dragging limp bodies along the ground.

"What happened?" she asked Fei Gei. He pulled a flask out his pocket and gulped before sitting on a nearby bedroll. Low lantern light reflected off the patches of burned skin on his face. He'd survived the terrible fire at Cape Horn, but it had left him with hands that shook even when he rested.

"The nitroglycerin"—his mouth worked bitterly around the bak gui word—"exploded too early. My brother . . ."

Ling Fan hadn't even known he had a brother working with him on the railroad. She thought of Jing Fan. "I'm sorry," she said instinctively.

Fei Gei sounded numb. "So many killed. Many more injured."

Ling Fan didn't wait to hear the rest. She was already running to the spot where the injured had been carried.

One of them was Wong Wei.

∧ ∧ ∧

As it turned out, Wong Wei's luck had again covered him with its twisted humor. He had tripped in the darkness and fallen. Had he stayed on his feet, the flying chunk of granite would surely have hit him square in the head instead of landing on his outstretched hand.

Now he lay on the ground, moaning and clutching the bleeding, broken hand. "Where's the doctor?" Ling Fan demanded.

"Back at base camp," Chin Lin Sou said, his face grim. "Snowdrifts have closed the mountain paths, so there's no chance of fetching anyone. For now it'll be up to us to take care of the injured as best we can."

Ling Fan bit back a furious retort. This wasn't Chin Lin Sou's fault—he always tried to do right by his workers. And he was facing the same impossible conditions they were. Even so, she couldn't stop the anger building up inside her. The sojourners deserved better than this. Even Wong Wei.

"Fine," she said. "I'll do what I can for this one." She knelt down by Wong Wei and managed to wrap his hand in rags just before he passed out.

Chin Lin Sou and Ah Sook went around to each of the injured with a bucket of black tea mixed with morphine.

"We're lucky no more were hurt," Chin Lin Sou muttered to Ah Sook. "If Strobridge and Crocker insist that we work with that demon liquid again, they should at least give us enough medicine for the injured."

"The bak gui are desperate," Ah Sook said, kneeling over another bloody body. "They're *behind schedule*." He used the American phrase that Ling Fan heard the bak gui foremen shout whenever they wanted workers to move faster or work longer. "If we continue at this pace, Union Pacific will reach Promontory Point long before us and claim the bonus money for finishing first."

"At this rate of death and injury, there won't be any sojourners left to enjoy that bonus money."

Privately, Ling Fan agreed as she looked at the dozen wounded men scattered on the ground.

By the time her next work shift started, three of the wounded had been taken someplace else. Ling Fan didn't ask where.

∧ ∧ ∧

Ling Fan couldn't tell anymore whether it was morning or night. Her days began with her work shift; her evenings ended after she'd tended to Wong Wei. Fei Gei had helped her move him to the shed in the snow tunnels where she slept between shifts. Wong Wei was delirious with fever. He kept trying to fling off his blankets and get up, asking what day it was, then crying out "I missed the drop-off!" or "They're after me!" A foul odor was starting to come from his injured hand, and he screamed and fought when Ling Fan changed his bandages.

I just know he's mixed up with trouble again, she wrote to her brother. **Some days, I'm so tired I'm tempted to just walk away. But I know Baba would be so disappointed that I was turning my back on a person in need. I would be no better than Widow Chang! I hope you don't think your little sister is a fool.**

Between tending Wong Wei and working her own shifts, she hadn't had a single free moment to burn her notes to Jing Fan. She'd taken to keeping them in a bundle that she thrust under her bedroll before falling dead asleep. In the mornings she rolled them up inside the bedding before racing off to join her crew. Jing Fan would have to wait to read them. Often, though, just the thought of writing to her brother was the only thing that calmed her nerves.

Chin Lin Sou tells us there has been a thaw, and one of the paths from base camp has been cleared enough to bring in fresh supplies.

With the supplies came a bak gui doctor and medicine. Ling Fan was sure she hadn't imagined the warm breeze blowing through the maze of snow tunnels. "Spring at last!" she cried, happy enough to say it in English to the doctor.

He looked at her pityingly. "It's still February, boy. Spring ain't exactly around the corner yet. Last winter was pretty bad, but nothing compared to this one." He told her how even with great shovels attached to the steam engines, the company was still unable to keep the railroad tracks clear.

That night she wrote, **Snow again.**

At least with the help of the bak gui doctor, many of the injured recovered enough to rest comfortably. Some even went back to work. Wong Wei's fever broke, and he could sit up and talk for a few minutes before falling into a fitful sleep. He fretted over getting back to "the job."

"Rest," Ling Fan urged. "You'll be no help to anyone if you reinjure yourself from trying to work in your condition!"

"Men who don't work don't get paid," he moaned. "With this injury I've already lost two weeks' pay. I'll never make enough to pay back my debts."

She patted him clumsily on the shoulder. "Don't think about it now. Just try to get some rest. We'll figure something out."

Wong Wei would not be soothed. He clutched at Ling Fan's jacket collar and pulled her close. "Jing Fan, you have to do something for me."

Wariness descended on her like an old tattered shawl as she looked at Wong Wei's pale face, shiny with perspiration. She wondered if his fever had returned. "What?"

"There's a job I have to make good on by tomorrow. I've already missed one delivery. I can't miss another." Wong Wei lowered his voice. "Get me my bag." Reluctantly, she pulled it close to him. He rummaged inside and pulled out a thin packet wrapped in paper.

"Put this beneath the third slop bucket in the latrine by morning. Then, at the end of the first shift, go to the storehouse at the southern edge of the work site. You'll find a pile of rocks and an old rusted bucket full of sand. There will be a package hidden there. Bring it to me. Whatever happens, don't tell anyone what you're doing."

A hundred questions swelled up at once. "Oh, Wong Wei,

what have you gotten yourself into now?"

"I'm just doing what I have to do to take care of myself." His sweaty face glistened in the lantern light. "You'd do the same if you were in my place."

She bit back a sharp retort. Here she was, disguised as a boy in the middle of a snow-packed mountain thousands of miles away from home. What right did she have to judge Wong Wei's desperate decisions when her own had brought her to this very spot?

"Will you help me?" he pleaded. Ling Fan stared at the packet as if it were a cobra. "Please!" His voice was high and frightened when she hesitated. "It has to be done. Promises were made—!"

"All right," she finally said, moved mostly by the fear in his voice.

Only then did Wong Wei let himself lie back and close his eyes.

∧ ∧ ∧

The next morning, Ling Fan raced to the latrine. The knot in the pit of her stomach twisted while she waited for two workers to finish their business. Finally she was able to slip the packet in place without being noticed. At the end of her shift she wound her way through the snow tunnels to the southernmost storehouse.

Sure enough, there was a package hidden behind a rusted bucket. It was no bigger than her hand and wrapped in brown paper. A soft rattling sound like sand in a corn husk came from it. She was surprised: she'd expected coins. She weighed it in her hand, resisting the urge to open it, before thrusting it into an inner pocket of her padded jacket as she made her way back to Wong Wei.

He sat up eagerly, took the packet, and examined it. His relief was palpable. "I knew I could count on you," he whispered. He pushed the packet into his canvas sack and pulled out another like the one he'd given her yesterday. "Now you know how it's done."

Ling Fan spent the rest of the week delivering Wong Wei's packages. The packets from him were all the same, but the ones that she found at the end of her shift varied. Some were like the first, while others were oddly shaped; once she could've sworn from the heft and bulk that one was a length of coiled fuse. She fought the urge to look. Whatever scheme Wong Wei was involved in, she was better off knowing as little as possible.

She had just dropped a package off one day when she heard voices behind her in the latrine. The voices were muffled by the sound of iron buckets dragged across the icy ground and crashing against the wall. She paused to listen.

"Have you checked the other privies?" Chin Lin Sou demanded. As usual he spoke quietly, but she heard the fury in his voice.

"Of course. I didn't find any other packages," Ah Sook said. "What should we do?"

Ling Fan's blood ran cold. They'd discovered her drop-off. She edged closer.

"Keep watch. Somebody will be by to leave another one. And when I catch the person trading or selling this poison, I'll gladly strip him and drive him into the freezing snow myself."

Poison. That had to mean opium. Wong Wei had already been caught dealing opium once, back in Illinoistown.

Apparently the beating he'd gotten there hadn't stopped him; he'd simply found other customers.

Mind churning, Ling Fan hurried back to the sleeping shed she shared with Wong Wei.

She found him sitting up in his nest of blankets, more agitated than usual. Eyes bright, face flushed, he refused to eat when Ling Fan brought him a bowl of rice from the common pot. He swatted her hand away when she felt his forehead. It was cool and clammy. "Chin Lin Sou found the last package I left," she told him. "He's not happy."

"You'll have to find a way to make another delivery tomorrow," he said.

Ling Fan gaped. "Your fever must have scrambled your brains. How am I supposed to do that now that Chin Lin Sou has caught on?"

"We don't have a choice. Promises were made. You don't want to know what'll happen if the deal's broken."

"We? It's your deal. Your promises. I said I'd help you if I could, I didn't say I'd lose my place on the railroad for you. I need this job. I need this money."

"You're not the only one who needs money," Wong Wei said, resting his head in his hands. His posture reminded Ling Fan of that day on the *Cormorant* when he told her he'd gambled all his money away. So much had happened since then, but through it all Wong Wei had been her link to home. Lantern light glinted against the coin that hung at his throat. She thought of his intended bride, Mei, waiting for him, just as Baba was waiting for her.

Ling Fan watched the little flame in the kerosene lamp lift and flutter in the invisible drafts that haunted the snow tunnels. Finally, she took a deep breath. "I'll do the run for you tomorrow. But it will be the last one." She leaned over and turned the knob on the lamp to lower the flame. "I'm sorry."

Wong Wei's shoulders slumped. "If that's how it'll be," he said softly, "don't be surprised if I do what has to be done." His bedding rustled as he turned to face the wall. Ling Fan stared at his huddled form. That had sounded like a threat.

In the darkness, she was certain she heard the *taptaptap* of pickaxes bouncing off distant walls.

CHAPTER 18

A h Sook was already through his second flask of whiskey by the time Ling Fan walked over to the latrine the next morning. She found him seated on an upturned bucket at the entrance to the privy, scrutinizing each arrival, with the empty first flask at his feet. Soon, the foot traffic slowed to a trickle as work crews settled into their labor. Ah Sook's chin sank on his chest and snores bounced off the walls.

Ling Fan slipped the packet under the slop bucket. She walked swiftly to Summit Tunnel, expecting to hear footsteps running after her or feel a hand fall on her shoulder. All day she kept an ear out, waiting for Chin Lin Sou to come and drag her out into the snow. Would they catch the recipient of Wong Wei's opium? Would there still be a package with his payment waiting at the rusted sand bucket?

At the end of the shift she ran to the southern storehouse. To her relief she caught sight of a small paper-wrapped bundle tucked in its usual spot.

Walking back through the snow tunnels to her sleeping shed, Ling Fan imagined she could feel the weight of the snow above her head, could feel it pressing in from all sides.

The light from the tiny kerosene lamp in the shed offered no warmth, and she longed to bundle herself up in her bedroll.

First, though, she stopped to check on Wang Wei. He stirred, and the faint odor of fetid flesh wafted up to mingle with the incense that Ah Sook kept burning day and night throughout the work site. It kept the worst of the spirits away, he insisted.

"It's done." Ling Fan knelt down and held the packet out to him. Wong Wei's eyes were bright in the dim light. He didn't move. Ling Fan laid the packet by his side and went back to her bedding. Any relief she felt from fulfilling her last obligation was erased by the weight of Wong Wei's eyes on her. She felt them following every movement as she slid into her bedroll and reached for her bundle of letters.

It wasn't there.

She groped deeper, but with the flutter of dread in her chest came the truth.

"Is this what you're looking for?" Wong Wei had thrown back his blankets and pulled himself upright so that he sat with his back against the wall. His face glistened with sweat from the effort. In his lap was her bundle of letters.

Ling Fan's blood thundered in her head even as she fought to keep her voice under control, hoping the situation could still be salvaged. "Ah, thank you, friend. It must have dropped out of my bedroll this morning."

"You should be more careful with your things," he said, dangling the bundle of letters by its string. "People around here will take any little thing you leave lying around. Did I tell you the time Bing Lai tried to steal Li Bo's socks? Li Bo proved they were his because he said they smelled like the insides of *his* boots and not Bing Lai's."

"You're right. I should be more careful." Ling Fan tried to chuckle but it sounded more like the bleat of a sheep. She reached for the bundle.

"So many letters. What did you have so much to write about?" A sly smile twitched at the corner of his mouth. "Are they love letters? Ah, Tam Jing Fan, you devil. I knew you were hiding something from me!"

Relief swept over Ling Fan like a cold wave. Of course, she should've guessed that Wong Wei couldn't read. Few of the workers could. The letters would be a jumble of nonsense to him. "Yes, you're right. They're nothing but foolish tripe. I should just burn them."

"No, no! Read one to me. You wouldn't believe how boring it is lying around waiting to die." He pulled one loose. "Read this one."

Ling Fan took the letter and spread it open on her lap. She licked her lips as she looked down at her own handwriting sprawled across the page. The words blurred together. "Sweet Ting, we've been working on this tunnel for weeks and . . . and . . ." Her mind stumbled over what else would be in a love letter. "I miss you . . . more than . . . more than . . . I miss the sun and stars above my head."

Wong Wei was listening with his eyes closed, his face so still and pale it looked like an opera mask. He sighed. "I miss you more than the sun and stars," he repeated. "You should be a poet." Ling Fan felt lightheaded and absurdly pleased.

"Give them here, I can find a better one," she offered. She felt as though she'd just faced down a dragon and won.

But Wong Wei tapped the bundle against his chin, frowning. "I miss you more than the sun and stars," he murmured. Then he smiled his hawkish smile, eyes never leaving her face. She felt pinned under his eyes. And she felt the blood drain from her face as she realized that he knew.

"That does sound much better than *Sometimes I'm tempted*

to just walk away . . ." His eyes flashed. "Signed *Little Sister.*"

Ling Fan tried to swallow, but her mouth was so dry that she could feel her throat muscles rub against themselves. "Wong Wei, there's been a terrible misunderstanding," she said, trying to think fast. "Some of those letters are just notes for a tale I'm planning to write when I return home. Just foolish invented fancies. Give them here."

She tried to grab the letters, but despite his weakened condition Wong Wei was surprisingly fast. From under his blankets, he pulled out a long-bladed knife and aimed it at her as he pulled himself up into a standing position. The motion made him gasp but his grip on the knife was steady. "I have to applaud you. You had us all fooled."

Ling Fan licked her lips. "Let me explain. I wanted to tell you the truth, Wong Wei. You've been my friend, you've been like a brother to me. But I couldn't take the risk!"

"You can explain till these mountains fall down around your ears," Wong Wei said. "I'm really not interested. But I can think of a few men who might find your situation fascinating. Shall I go fetch them?"

"Wait." Such a little word. Why was it so hard to push the air out of her mouth to say it? "I'll do your jobs for you. Isn't that what you want?"

"What I want?" Wong Wei didn't look at her as he considered the question. "I want to go home as the rich man I promised Mei I would become. I want to march into her family compound and pour a satchel of gold coins onto her father's table. I want to order the outer doors opened so that a dozen roasted pigs can be carried in on the shoulders of the villagers, followed by twenty freshly steamed chickens and thirty trays of fish from the river. I want the entire village to feast for a week in that house. And when we're done I want to take my bride to the compound I will have built so we will live out our days there."

He winced as he shifted his injured hand. Thick shadows flickered grotesquely on the stone walls.

"You're going to help me get what's owed to me."

"How am I supposed to do that?" Ling Fan said, trying to slow things down so that she could think of a way out.

She should fight him and try to take the knife away.

She should run, lose him in the maze of snow tunnels and flee the mountain.

She should find Chin Lin Sou and Ah Sook and expose Wong Wei as the opium dealer.

But for each desperate plan, she could see an equally desperate end.

She could fight him and wind up dead, her blood drained by the long-bladed knife.

She could run away only to freeze halfway down the snow-blocked mountain paths.

She could expose Wong Wei to Chin Lin Sou, but Wong Wei in turn would still expose her own secret.

Wong Wei looked at her through narrowed eyes. "I should've seen it all along. There always was something wrong about you, starting with those lovely scholar's hands of yours."

Ling Fan kept her eyes locked on Wong Wei. If she moved fast enough, maybe she could pin his knife hand against the stone wall. But before she could make a move, he started sidling toward the door.

"I'll tell you what. I'll keep your secret, but it'll cost you. Every payday, you'll turn over half your earnings to me."

"What?" Her voice bounced off the walls and rolled down the tunnel. She took a step toward him, fists clenched, but he raised the knife higher. "You're out of your mind if you think I'm going to do that!"

Wong Wei smiled. "I wonder what the others will do when they find out you're a girl. Run you out? Drop you off at the nearest whorehouse? Certainly not before they've had their fun."

Ling Fan blanched but pushed the image from her thoughts. "Why are you doing this? I've never done anything to you. I've always helped you! I thought we were friends!"

"Friends?" Wong Wei sneered. "There are no friends on this railroad! Everybody is here for one thing only, and that's to make as much money as they can, as quickly as they can, any way they can."

Ling Fan sprang at him, slamming him hard against the wall. She felt his knife whip against her side, and then pain shot upward from her stomach. The shock of it loosened her grip on Wong Wei, and he twisted free. She doubled over, biting back a moan. Blood formed around a long gash that went through her heavy jacket, through her tunic underneath . . .

With a sudden strength that must've come from desperation, Wong Wei delivered a savage kick to her abdomen, just below the knife wound. She screamed and crumpled to the ground.

Through a haze of sweat and blood, Ling Fan saw Wong Wei slip the bundle of letters into his coat pocket. Then he picked up the kerosene lamp from the floor along with the brick-shaped package Ling Fan had carried back from the latrines. He knelt beside her long enough to check her injury. "You'll live," he declared, staggering back to his feet. "You're more useful to me alive than dead. I'll put the letters in a safe place where they'll be found if anything happens to me."

The world faded into a haze of grotesque shadows that flared on the wall and followed Wong Wei as he left the shed, turning down the passageway that led to Summit Tunnel. The shed grew dimmer with each of his departing steps, until it was dark.

Ling Fan lay on the ground, her body curled around the pain that blazed in her stomach. Everything was ruined. Her earnings cut in half. Her father in prison. Her family humiliated and shamed. She had nothing to show for her scandalous, impulsive act but the tiny morsel of railroad she'd helped carve out of the mountainside.

She wasn't sure how long she lay there, pinned in place by the darkness and her pain. It felt like an eternity, but couldn't have been more than half an hour. Eventually, she became aware of distant voices and the faint sound of hammers and picks against granite walls. How strange that the world continued on as usual as her life crumbled around her.

TapTapTapTapTapTap

Getupgetupgetup

The words ran through her brain, following the rhythm of the picks as they cut into the mountain rock.

She had to stop him. She would stop him.

Ling Fan hauled herself to her feet. The pain in her stomach was like a burning fire. She groped around in the darkness until her hand found the spare lantern. Nearby were matches. Her hands were slick with her own blood, and they shook, but after several tries, she was able to light the lantern. She found a strip of cloth and tightly bound her wound. Fortunately, Wong Wei was right; the gash was long but shallow. She spent a few more precious moments casting about the shed for any kind of weapon, but could only find a short-handled iron pick. She hefted it in one hand, picked up the lantern in the other, and set off through the snow tunnel that Wong Wei had taken.

As she neared Summit Tunnel's entrance, the snow tunnel became lighter, and the air colder. She stumbled through the fresh snowdrifts that blew in with the wind. They grew deeper the closer she came to the end of the passageway. Then finally she was out in the open air.

Light blasted her from every direction. Snow clutched at her legs as she tried to stagger forward. Icy air sliced through her lungs, and tears that streamed from her eyes froze as she tried to blink the glare from her vision. It was snowing again, and the wind whipped the tiny pellets into a frenzy.

He wouldn't have gone into Summit Tunnel. He wasn't strong enough to work yet. So where had he headed?

Along one edge of the mountainside, a small work crew was clearing the path that led toward the base camp. Almost as soon as they had shoveled down to brown earth, the path was covered again by a thick lacy film. Here and there, spurs of bare rock seemed to float above the sea of white, like islands.

Otherwise, the mountainside, the trees, the path, the entire world had disappeared under a massive white blanket. There was no sign of the campsite's labyrinth beneath. And no sign of Wong Wei.

A swath of freshly churned snow was Ling Fan's first clue. Following it and squinting through the swirling fakes, she thought she could make out a dark speck in the distance, moving south. She started toward it—and sank into snow that came up to her chest. The cold made her gasp, and the heaviness of the snow stopped her in her tracks. She flailed wildly, trying to push her way forward, but instead she lost her balance entirely. She fell.

Snow closed over her head, filling her nostrils. She thrashed out, trying to get to her feet, but the snow was like quicksand. Finally, she came up against something hard and unmoving, managed to brace herself against it, and pushed her head up for air. She clung to the rock panting, like a swimmer who had finally made it to shore. She'd lost her lantern and her pick, but at least she could breathe.

Looking over her shoulder, she could barely make out the dark speck before it disappeared around a white mound. A moment later a wisp of black smoke drifted into the sky, and she thought longingly of a fire. She started to shiver violently.

It wasn't until she felt the vibrations through the soles of her boots that she realized she wasn't the only thing shaking. She looked up and over her shoulder.

A scream froze in her throat. Great slabs of snow and ice were sliding down the mountainside—a gigantic wave, sweeping trees and boulders along under its weight.

The crew at the path threw down their shovels and tried to flee, but the river of snow churned around their legs, making them flounder like fish caught in a whirlpool. Ling Fan ran, pushing through the snow toward a high rocky spur. Just as she reached it, she felt something seize her ankle, and she was tossed high into the air. She saw the bare rock rushing up to meet her. Noise swelled around her. Pain that felt like a spike ground up her shoulder.

Then nothing.

CHAPTER 19

The smell woke her.

Once, Ling Fan had walked through the lane behind the butchers' stalls in the village market, and the smell then had been nothing compared to this.

And the sound: like a thousand rocks clattering down a mountain chasm. It took her a moment to recognize it as groans coming from men. Injured men.

Ling Fan started to sit up, but her body felt like granite. Turning her head brought on a wave of nausea and pain that left her gasping until the world dissolved into darkness once more.

She didn't know how long she slept, but the light around her was different when she opened her eyes again. She was on a cot in a room she didn't recognize. Her head ached, and after probing gingerly, she discovered that it was wrapped in bandages. Terror crashed over her like a bucket of icy water. Somebody had touched her while she was unconscious. Somebody had handled her body.

Someone knew.

She had to run. Had to hide.

Ling Fan sat up and ripped off the blanket, expecting to find herself stripped naked. But no, she was still wearing her tunic and loose trousers. They were cold and soaking wet, but she'd never felt happier to be clothed in such misery. Her secret might still be safe after all.

The walls of the room began to sway, and Ling Fan's stomach twisted. She barely had enough sense to lean over the side of the cot to retch into the chamber pot sitting next to her. She lay back down just as the wall in front of her parted and a little girl with a mop of golden curls stepped through, her arms piled high with towels.

The girl took one look at her and let out a shout. "Ma! Chinaman's awake!"

Ling Fan started to sit up, but the room spun. The walls seemed to be moving as if blown by a breeze. She sank back against the pillows, feeling as though lead weights were tied to her head, shoulders, and arms.

A yellow-haired woman entered the room carrying a pitcher, a basin, and a roll of fresh bandages. "You know English, don't you." It was a statement rather than a question. There was something familiar about her direct gaze.

"We could hear you yelling in your sleep," the little girl added.

The woman filled a glass with water from the pitcher and gave it to Ling Fan.

"Thank you." Ling Fan hesitated before accepting the glass, making a show of drinking while swallowing as little as possible. She needed a moment to collect her thoughts. Where was she? How long had she been unconscious?

She could see now that she was in a tent with half a dozen other cots. The people on them were so still and quiet that she hadn't noticed them before. So still and quiet that . . . Ling Fan swallowed. She was sharing this space with corpses.

"I never thought it would be like this," the woman murmured. "When my husband sent the message to come tend the wounded, I thought I'd be helping with a few broken arms and legs, not . . ." She stopped and shook her head. "The things James gets me into."

James must be James Strobridge. And that was why this woman seemed so familiar. She was Mrs. Strobridge, the woman Ling Fan had seen in Illinoistown a few months ago. But what was she doing here?

Mrs. Strobridge seemed to read her mind. She said, "My husband brought us up to this camp in the fall—it was supposed to be temporary, but then the snow began. Now we're as stuck as everyone else!"

She sat down on a stool beside Ling Fan's bed and, after arranging fresh bandages beside the basin of water, began to unwind the linen wrapped around Ling Fan's head. Bloody swaths of cloth fell to the floor. Ling Fan's head felt light and cold without them. The dull ache began to throb.

"What happened?" she asked.

"You were caught in the avalanche up by Summit Tunnel," Mrs. Strobridge replied.

"Avalanche." Ling Fan rolled the strange English word in her mouth. She remembered the snow rushing toward her like a wave, remembered the screams of the nearby workers and the deep-throated roar that shook the ground.

But now she was at the base camp, in this closed-off section of the medical tent.

"Lucky for you that Clara and I spotted you as soon as you were brought here." Mrs. Strobridge's fingers were light but firm.

"Ma told them to put you in this section so you could have peace and quiet," Clara declared as she gathered up the soiled bandages. "Ma said your head would get better away from all that groaning and moaning out there." She tilted her own curly head toward whatever lay beyond the tent flap.

"You have quite a gash in your head," Mrs. Strobridge said briskly. "The doctor had to put in ten stitches."

A bolt of white-hot lightning surged through Ling Fan. Her hands went to her side where Wong Wei's knife blade had sliced through her tunic. Under the torn fabric, she felt the swell of a fresh bandage wrapped across her rib cage.

"Don't worry," Mrs. Strobridge said. "No stiches for that. And I bandaged you up myself after I had you moved in here."

Ling Fan's throat tightened. Mrs. Strobridge would've had to take off the tunic to get at the knife wound . . . She felt along her chest and could tell that her usual bindings were still in place. So the woman had put her in this secluded area, bandaged her, reclothed her—and decided to keep her secret.

Mrs. Strobridge only said, "I remember you from Illinois-town, but we can't keep calling you Mr. Chinaman, now can we? What's your name?"

Ling Fan hesitated. She wanted to trust this strange bak gui woman who seemed as much out of place here on the rail-road as she herself felt. "Tam Jing Fan." Best to stick with her brother's name. A bak gui wouldn't know the difference, but if a Chinese person heard Mrs. Strobridge call a worker Ling, they'd be suspicious.

"Well, Tam Jing Fan, I think you should lie back and try to get some rest. You're safe here. You're a very lucky . . . sojourner."

The walls swayed gently as Mrs. Strobridge passed through. Ling Fan caught a glimpse of the rest of the medical tent, crowded with wounded men.

Ling Fan lay back, suddenly weak with relief. She squeezed her eyes shut against the spinning room. She must have slept because the next thing she knew, the room was in shadows.

Somebody sat beside her cot.

It was difficult to turn her head. "Tan Din, is that you?"

"You're finally awake!" Not Tan Din's voice, but one she recognized.

"Thomas O'Brien. What are you doing here?" Ling Fan sat up gingerly, expecting the room to tilt and twirl. But the ache had receded to a corner of her skull, and the world stayed put. For the moment, at least.

"I looked everywhere for you after I heard about the avalanche near your work site. I was about to give you up for dead when I overheard the Strobridge kid say something about the Chinaman who talks American. I knew it had to be you. I didn't think you'd be in here!" He broke off, glancing at the unmoving bodies that surrounded them.

Hazy memories of rushing snow, noise, and being tossed around roared through her head, nauseating her. She tried to focus. "How far did the snow slide? What about the workers at the other tunnels? My friend Tan Din? He wasn't that far away."

Thomas's face darkened. "Tan Din, you say?"

"Yes! Is he hurt? Is he . . .?"

The tips of Thomas's ears reddened, as they so often did when he was uncomfortable. "He's been locked up by Strobridge."

"What?" Ling Fan was sure she'd misheard. But Thomas looked so solemn it had to be the truth. "Why?"

"They say he set off an explosion to start the avalanche on purpose. They say all these accidents we've been having on the railroad were done on purpose, by someone in the pay of

Union Pacific. They say your friend Tan Din is a traitor."

"That's impossible!" Ling Fan didn't know whether to laugh or scream. "Tan Din wouldn't do that. He wouldn't even know how to do something like that."

"All I've heard is that lots of people saw a puff of black smoke right before the avalanche started. Strobridge sent a crew up there to check it out, and they found three workers buried in the snow near a whole mess of gunpowder and fuses. One of them was Tan Din."

Ling Fan clenched her teeth. "What do they say happened?"

Thomas stared at his feet. "Two of them aren't saying anything, since they died before Strobridge could talk to them. And your friend Tan Din won't talk to anyone."

"They have the wrong man. Tan Din would never be part of such a dishonorable act," Ling Fan said fiercely. Her stomach roiled as she spoke. She'd said almost those exact words about her father. *This can't be happening! Not again!*

"You have to admit the whole thing looks suspicious," said Thomas. "What were those men doing up there with all that gunpowder?"

Ling Fan gritted her teeth. "Wrong place at the wrong time. He could've been making a food delivery to or from Summit Tunnel, or running an errand for someone else. He had no reason to try to disrupt our work!"

"Well, the money. From Union Pacific. Probably a lot more than what he earns in honest wages."

She wanted to slap him. "Tan Din wouldn't risk people's lives just for more money." But she could see that no one would be convinced by that argument. For most people, it was easier to believe someone was guilty than to make any effort to find the truth.

The same thing had happened to Baba when he was arrested. Not one person in the village had a reason to think ill of him, yet none had raised a voice to help when he was dragged to prison.

Ling Fan ignored the flash of pain that sliced through her side as she threw back the blanket and groped around on the floor for her boots. Her head spun, and she choked back the gorge that rose in her throat. The boots were still damp and stiff from the snow, but she jammed her feet into them and surged upright.

"What are you doing?" Thomas sounded alarmed.

"I'm going to get to the bottom of this. I'm going to talk to Tan Din."

"Didn't you hear me? He's not talking."

She wondered how hard anybody had tried. "He's my friend. I have to help him somehow. Where have they put him?"

"In one of the storage sheds. But they've got a fellow guarding it. You won't be allowed near him."

"We'll see about that." She found her quilted jacket folded neatly at the bottom of the cot. It was soaking wet too. She shoved her arms into the sleeves and struggled to close the damp clasps.

"Look, it's not like you can just go up to Strobridge and demand that Tan Din be released."

Her hands curled into fists. Baba had been condemned to prison without anyone to defend him. She wasn't going to let it happen again. "I am not going to lie around and do nothing." She pushed through the tent's door flap, with Thomas at her heels.

Outside, light reflecting off the snow blazed around them. Ling Fan paused to stare up at the distant entrance to Summit

Tunnel and the slope beyond it. Thomas followed her gaze, shading his eyes against the glare of the snow. Ling Fan could just make out two dark specks moving around on the higher ground, close to the spot where she had seen the smoke right before the avalanche. Something caught the light, and she squinted against the sudden glint.

"What's that?" she murmured.

"Probably Strobridge's men going through the blast site again before Crocker comes."

"No, I mean what's *that*?" Ling Fan pointed as again, something caught the lowering rays of the sun and flashed like a tiny flame.

Thomas cupped his hands over his eyes too. "Dunno. Probably just the light on something stuck in the snow up there."

"Has anyone besides Strobridge's people been up there since the avalanche?" Ling Fan asked, a suspicion beginning to take shape in her mind.

Thomas shrugged. "Probably not. What's there to see?"

"Maybe nothing." Ling Fan started to wade through the snow, up the path that led from the base camp to Summit Tunnel. "Maybe something to prove that Tan Din had nothing to do with this mess."

They went up the path silently, saving their breath for the snowy climb. Once they reached the area the avalanche had passed through, they sometimes had to resort to hands and knees. Ling Fan wondered how Strobridge's men had been able to get out here as quickly as Thomas said. Of course, the climb would probably be easier without a bashed head and a knife wound.

The darkened entrance of Summit Tunnel yawned wide. They continued past it, onto higher ground.

From several hundred yards away, they could smell the familiar odor of burnt gunpowder still in the air. At last, they climbed over a crusted mound of melted snow that had refrozen and suddenly found themselves standing at the edge of a blackened crater. It was as though a giant had scooped out a fistful of the mountain and tossed the rubble and snow aside.

Ling Fan walked carefully around the blast site, eyes fastened on the ground. Just as she was about to give up, something flashed in the snow and ash. She dropped to her knees.

Her fingers closed on something smooth and thin. It was a round disk with a square hole in the center. A tattered fragment of leather string ran through it.

"Isn't that a Chinese coin?" Thomas asked. He took the coin and held it up to the light, turning it over and over. "I'm sorry, Jing Fan, but this coin will only make things worse. A Chinese coin found at the scene of a Chinese crime. Just the thing to hang your friend."

Ling Fan could barely keep from snatching it out of his hand. "This isn't just any Chinese coin! I know who it belongs to. Oh, I should've realized sooner! It was Wong Wei up here setting off the blast!"

Wong Wei had never felt any loyalty toward the railroad or his fellow workers—his only priority was the money he could get. And this explained the sudden bursts of extra cash, the long disappearances, the periods of extreme anxiety. Wong Wei had been behind the accidents all along.

Ling Fan kicked at the charred ground. She remembered the soft rattle of powder in the packets she'd delivered for Wong Wei. She remembered placing the last one by Wong Wei's side, remembered him scooping it up before he fled into the darkness. So that was the deal he'd made: opium powder for gunpowder.

She shuddered. At least it had only been gunpowder, not the volatile nitroglycerin that had killed even more people. Nitroglycerin would've taken off the top of the whole mountain, not just caused an avalanche. Still, she hated knowing that she had been an unwitting tool of this destruction.

"Wong Wei? Isn't he your friend too?" Thomas stared at her.

"Not anymore," she said.

"How can you be so sure it was him, though? Is he the only Celestial who wears a Chinese coin on a string?"

"Wong Wei is definitely involved in this. He's always trying to find a way to make easy money. And I know he was up here because—" She closed her mouth just in time and finished weakly, "I just know that's the kind of thing he does." Not convincing, but at least she hadn't said, *I chased him up here myself after he discovered that I'm a girl.* "We have to tell someone about this."

Thomas looked doubtful. "I can't imagine that Strobridge would hear you out. He's already made up his mind."

"Not Strobridge," Ling Fan said. "We have to find Chin Lin Sou. If we can convince *him*, Strobridge might listen to him."

"You're brilliant!" Thomas said as he shuffled through the snow to keep up with her.

Or just desperate, Ling Fan thought.

All the way back down to the base camp, Ling Fan's mind whirled. She had always known that Wong Wei was a desperate man. His reckless gambling had forced him into all manner of dangerous undertakings. And she knew firsthand how ruthless he could be. If he could turn on her, after all they'd gone through together, for the sake of more coins in his pocket, it wasn't hard to imagine that he would accept Union Pacific's money in exchange for damaging the railroad.

"Penny for your thoughts," Thomas said, dropping into step beside her as the ground leveled off.

"Why do you want to give me a penny?" Ling Fan asked.

Thomas chuckled. "It's just a saying that means you've been quiet for so long, I'm wondering what you're thinking about."

Ling Fan glanced at Thomas's round, freckled face and felt a wave of weariness. Thomas had been kind to her. She wished she could tell him the whole truth. It would be such a relief to finally be able to talk to somebody about her worries instead of having them constantly thrash around inside her own head.

But no. She was in deep trouble as it was. She couldn't take any more risks. Instead, she replied, "Just worried about Tan Din. Will Chin Lin Sou believe us? Will Strobridge believe Chin Lin Sou?"

Thomas made a rueful face. "Strobridge likes to keep his own council about things. Still, if there's a Celestial around who has his ear, that would be your Chin Lin Sou. Strobridge trusts him. That has to count for something. But . . . where is everyone?"

The base camp's tangled pathways had been churned brown and trampled into a mash of frozen grit. Clothing swung from ropes like flattened, frozen scarecrows. Fire pits sputtered as snowflakes blew into the flames. Everywhere, Ling Fan saw signs of the sojourners—but not a single person seemed to be in the camp.

As she and Thomas drew closer to Chin Lin Sou's tent, though, a buzz of voices filled the air. Dozens of workers were crowded around the wooden sheds used for storage and for housing pack animals. They'd been built and taken apart many times as the base camp edged farther east, so they always looked on the verge of collapsing: the walls buckled, and the roofs bowed beneath the weight of the snow.

One of them had been hastily emptied, its contents piled around the door. A bak gui sat on one of the lidded barrels, a rifle resting in the crook of his arm. This must be the shed where Tan Din was being held.

And there was Chin Lin Sou, standing on top of an over-turned wooden crate and facing the crowd. Ah Sook stood at his elbow, a scowl deepening the furrows in his craggy face. In contrast, Chin Lin Sou looked like a benevolent schoolteacher, trying to placate a group of rowdy children.

Some of the sojourners caught sight of Thomas, and the tension in the air twisted tighter. "They sound angry," Thomas said uncomfortably. "I should probably leave."

Ling Fan's impulse was to tell him he had nothing to fear. But she realized with a jolt that Thomas wasn't fearful for his life—not the way Wong Wei had been back in Illinoistown. Could Thomas ever truly understand the helpless terror she, Wong Wei, and Tan Din had felt that day?

"Right. I'll talk to you later," she said stiffly.

"If you need us, you can find our tent next to the double oaks by the stream." He pointed to two tall oak trees that looked like a pair of giant crossed fingers. "Anything we can do to help, call on us. Good luck." He turned and left.

"Tan Din has not been arrested by the bak gui authorities," Chin Lin Sou was saying. "Strobridge wants to talk to him first before making a decision."

"He didn't do anything!" somebody in the crowd shouted. "The bak gui are just looking for an excuse to blame us for all these accidents!" Grumbles of agreement rippled through the crowd.

"It's not right that Tan Din's locked up like an animal!" yelled someone else.

Ling Fan's heart leapt as she took in the size of the crowd. She'd feared this situation would be a repetition of what had happened to her father, when no one had dared defend him after his arrest. But the sojourners were banding together in support of Tan Din.

"We'll know more once Strobridge has talked to him," Chin Lin Sou said. "Until then, the best thing you men can do is continue with your jobs."

Chin Lin Sou stepped down from his crate and headed off toward his tent, with Ah Sook at his heels. The crowd turned away, rubbing their heads, their chests, their stomachs. Some were still grumbling about Tan Din's treatment, while others talked of swapping shifts, of blisters and bunions, of herbal remedies and half-remembered poultices.

Ling Fan hurried after Chin Lin Sou. "Wait. Please."

"What do you want, boy?" Ah Sook growled.

Her fingers curled around the flat, round coin in her pocket. It helped steady her. "A moment of Chin Lin Sou's time. Please. It's a matter of life and death."

Ah Sook snorted, but Chin Lin Sou regarded her coolly. "Yes?"

"It's about Tan Din," she said in a rush. "He didn't do it. I know because . . ." Just then, beyond Chin Lin Sou's shoulder, she caught sight of a familiar figure.

He was watching her with the intensity of a carrion bird about to strike, and when he caught her eye, he shook his head deliberately, once, twice, then smiled. He reached into his coat and pulled out a sheaf of papers.

Ling Fan felt as though the coin in her pocket had turned

to ice. Cold tendrils wound around her hand, traveled up her arm and encircled her entire body, rooting her to the spot.

"Because why? Out with it, boy, we haven't got all day," Ah Sook growled.

At the same time, Chin Lin Sou demanded, "What is it? What do you know?" He followed her gaze over his shoulder, but Wong Wei, of course, had disappeared into the maze of tents.

"I'm sorry," Ling Fan said, the coin gripped so tightly in her fist that the edge of it felt like a blade. "I was mistaken." She hurried away, hoping that Wong Wei was watching, but feeling Chin Lin Sou's eyes following her too.

CHAPTER 20

Rumors rippled through the camp all night. Some said Tan Din would be strung up by his queue like a scarecrow in Illinoistown, others said he'd be stripped naked and covered in tar and feathers and made to dance for the bak gui like a chicken, while still others insisted he'd be hanged at dawn.

The rumors spread and doubled back, becoming steadily more gruesome. Ling Fan tried to stop listening after she learned what "drawn and quartered" meant. She wanted to put her fingers in her ears but worried the gesture would seem girlish. So she resorted to keeping to the edges of any crowd, never staying in one spot long enough to hear a full conversation. Nobody truly knew anything, so why listen to the speculation?

In her jacket pocket was the coin she had found near the blast site. Wong Wei's lucky coin. There had to be a way to get to Chin Lin Sou without Wong Wei seeing her. But even if she did, surely Wong Wei would reveal her secret as soon as Chin Lin Sou questioned him. She paced, chewing her lip.

By midnight, most workers had gone back to their own tents. Lanterns and fires were damped down. Ling Fan perched on a snow-crusted log, unable to stand the thought of crawling into bed in the tent she'd shared with Tan Din, while Tan Din sat awaiting the judgment of the bak gui bosses. She looked over the embers of the little fire, toward the darkened supply shed the bak gui had turned into a temporary prison for her friend.

Memories from the past six months crowded into her mind. Tan Din hauling hundred-pound sacks of rice. Tan Din wielding a cleaver in each hand, chopping meat to a pulp while he shouted directions to her on how to prepare bean sprouts. Tan Din's smile, wide enough to split his face, as he carefully packed his daughter's new yellow-haired doll into a package to be shipped home.

Her thoughts were interrupted by loud braying, coming from the shed next to Tan Din's makeshift cell. A worker was struggling to drag a team of donkeys in for the night. Even after the door was closed, Ling Fan could hear the animals kicking at the thin walls like children in the thrall of a temper tantrum.

The idea came to her all at once. A moment later she was on her feet and racing through the camp to the double oaks Thomas had pointed out.

∧ ∧ ∧

Early the next morning, Ling Fan crouched behind a tree near the sheds, gripping the sack she'd slung over her shoulder. The first rays of sunlight were just starting to trickle into the sky when Jonathan O'Brien came up the path leading two donkeys on a rope. Thomas was astride one and was clearly having a difficult time keeping his seat. His donkey bucked and kicked and snapped irritably at the other.

"Hullo, friend!" Jonathan O'Brien called to the guard stationed outside Tan Din's shed. "Can you lend us a hand here? These beasties are worse than Satan."

"I ain't supposed to leave the prisoner," the guard said, looking warily at the animals.

"Seeing as they're only going round back here, you're hardly leaving your post now, are you? All you have to do is hold this one while we settle the other, there's a good lad."

Before the guard could protest further, Jonathan O'Brien had looped the reins loosely around the other man's hand and pulled Thomas's resisting donkey around to the back of the shed. Flummoxed, the guard waited as sounds of thrashing and braying filled the morning air.

"Look out, uncle! He's loose!" Thomas's voice rang out from behind the shed, followed by a tremendous crash. The donkey charged out from behind the shed and dashed into the brush.

"JesusMaryandJoseph!" Jonathan O'Brien roared. "After it!" He ran around to the front of the shed, Thomas at his heels, and caught the guard by the arm. "We can cut it off down there!" he cried, pushing the guard ahead of him. "Quick, or Strobridge will have our heads!" The confused guard stumbled along with the O'Briens, leaving the second donkey blinking in the morning sun.

As soon as the shouting faded into the distance, Ling Fan dashed out of her hiding place, grabbed the donkey who'd been left behind, and led it to the back of the shed. "Tan Din!" she called softly.

She heard movement from inside. "Aiya! Tam Jing Fan, is that you?"

"Keep away from the wall!" From her bag, she dragged out one of the iron-headed hammers used to drive chisels into the granite walls of the tunnels. She hefted it in both hands and swung it low against the back wall. Splinters of wood flew in all directions as she took another swing. Ling Fan dropped the hammer and began tugging on the broken boards. She could see inside now.

"What are you doing?" Tan Din cried from his spot in the corner, where he struggled to stand up. He was hampered by a length of rope that was tied to his hands and feet.

"What do you think?" Ling Fan snapped back, exasperated. "Getting you out of here!" She pushed through the rest of the broken wood and climbed inside the shed. "We have to hurry." With the knife she'd brought, she sawed through his rope, and they crawled back through the hole in the wall.

Once outside, Ling Fan tied the sack across the donkey's back. "There's enough provisions in there to last you a few days," she said and handed the reins to Tan Din. "The O'Briens think you should head due south."

Tan Din remained standing in the morning sun looking stunned.

"Hurry! The guard will be back soon. He'll think the walls were damaged by the kicking donkey, so nobody will be blamed for your escape. But you have to leave now."

Tan Din climbed onto the donkey's back, and Ling Fan led it by the bridle down a southerly path. She was relieved to find that the frozen mud and ice along the trail made it difficult to spot any tracks. Still, she kept looking over her shoulder, expecting a gang of furious bak gui to come tearing after them any moment. Once they were out of sight of the camp, she stopped.

"This is as far as I should go. You're on your own from here."

Tan Din squinted into the rising sun, then pushed his hat back and massaged his face. Ling Fan caught a glimpse of thick, spikey black hair where his long smooth queue had once hung down his back. Lin Fan felt a stab of anxiety. Chinese men were forbidden to cut off their queues. It was considered an act of defiance, an insult to the emperor. She wondered which bak gui had cut Tan Din's hair yesterday. Had his guard done it in a moment of malice? Had Strobridge ordered it as part of Tan Din's punishment, knowing the distress it would cause? Tan Din would never be allowed back into China without his queue—he'd have to wait for it to grow back. How many more years would his daughter have to wait for him?

For that matter, how many more years would it be before she saw her own father? The thought of Wong Wei's threat swept through her like a cold wave. She had to come up with a plan to deal with him, or else all her sacrifices would add up to nothing.

Tan Din was still looking thoughtfully into the distance, apparently in no hurry. A feeling of desolation washed over Ling Fan as she realized this was probably the last time she would ever talk to him. She suddenly felt awkward and unsure of what else to say.

"Jonathan O'Brien says there's farmland to the south where you might find work, or you can try to get back to San Francisco."

"There are plenty of tin mines in the hills farther south too," Tan Din mused. "Easy work, compared to what we have to do in these mountains."

Ling Fan felt as though a piece of herself was being torn away. "But you won't earn nearly as much money as what you could be getting from the railroad. Not nearly what you should get for the sweat and blood you put into your work."

"I'm grateful that I'm still alive to do any work at all."

"But you shouldn't have to be the one to leave! You didn't start that avalanche. Why should you be punished because the bak gui can't find the true culprit?" Ling Fan was almost shouting. "It's not right. How much longer will you have to work now before you can see your daughter?"

The heat of her words refueled the fury that seemed to burn in her all the time these days. Strangely, though, they had the opposite effect on Tan Din. The raw, wild energy he used to throw into preparing meals for the workers was gone, and the man who sat astride the donkey was as still as a mountain boulder. For the first time since she'd met him, Tan Din seemed completely at peace.

"I hope they find the true culprit before he gets even more people killed." He looked back at the mountain range that lay low on the horizon to the northwest. "Either way, my time on the railroad is done. There's no point bashing our heads over things that can't be changed. Don't fret over me. This is a small bump in my sojourn. Fate's way of telling me that it's time to move on."

She wanted to scream that fate had had nothing to do with it. Wong Wei and the bak gui bosses were to blame, plain and simple. Her nails dug into her palms inside her clenched fists.

Tan Din looked into Ling Fan's eyes. "Don't turn bitter on me. There's so much more to this country than the work on this railroad. And so much more to life than grabbing as much money as you can."

Before Ling Fan could absorb his words, Tan Din had pulled his hat back down low over his eyes. "I can't thank you enough, Tam Jing Fan, for what you've done today. I hope that one day I can find a way to repay you."

She tried to think of a way to sum up everything she felt but only managed to choke out "It's I who should thank you."

Tan Din waved her words away. "I just hope my own daughter grows up to be as brave as you." The meaning of his words sank in and her jaw fell open. Before she could even think to stammer a denial, Tan Din was clucking to the donkey and urging it down the path.

How long had he known? Ling Fan tried to think back to a moment when she might've given herself away, tried to recall a shift in his attitude toward her. She couldn't. From the day she first met him on the SS *California*, he had been an unswerving friend. As she watched him disappear from view, a new kind of grief threatened to overwhelm her. It wasn't the breath-stopping, jagged agony she felt for her brother and father, nor the gut wrench of leaving China. This felt like the slow cooling of a blissfully warm summer day.

With the sun creeping higher into the sky, and a full day's work ahead of her, she made her way back up the path.

∧ ∧ ∧

Search parties were sent out as soon as Tan Din's escape was discovered. Thanks to her injuries, Ling Fan wasn't allowed to join the crews clearing up the Summit Tunnel work site, so she had to cool her heels at the base camp, helping with odd jobs and waiting to see if Tan Din would be recaptured.

By the end of the day the search parties had returned empty-handed, lifting an invisible weight off Ling Fan's shoulders.

In the evening, she met up with the O'Briens at their tent. "The poor fellow who was guarding the shed is missing too," Jonathan O'Brien reported. "Most likely he realized the trouble he'd be in for letting his prisoner give him the slip, and beat his own hasty retreat."

"Just as well for us," said Thomas. "Now there's nobody around who knows we were over by the sheds."

"Just make sure you come up with a good yarn to explain how you got so battered up," added his uncle.

Thomas was nursing a black eye and a split lip he'd gotten from the bucking donkey that morning. "It serves me right for putting so many burrs under its saddle," he said ruefully. "But how else were we going to get that beast to jump around? I'm just glad I didn't break my neck!"

"The important thing is that our friend is safely away," Jonathan O'Brien said. "All's well that ends well."

Ling Fan frowned. "Wong Wei could still cause more trouble."

"Weren't you going to talk to your foreman, Chin Lin Sou?" Thomas asked.

"There hasn't been time," Ling Fan muttered. "And I'm not sure he'd believe me anyway."

"It's worth a try at least."

Ling Fan had a hard time meeting Thomas's gaze. The O'Briens had proven themselves to be loyal friends, but Wong Wei's blackmail was one problem she couldn't bring herself to tell them about.

"Our Celestial friend is right to be cautious," Jonathan O'Brien said. "Best not to stir the pot until you have firm evidence in hand."

"But what about the coin?" Thomas protested.

"Can you prove it's Wong Wei's?"

Thomas's ears began to redden. O'Brien spoke more gently.

"Look, lads, things will come out all in good time. Best just let it be for now." O'Brien clapped Ling Fan on the back. "Let us know if you'll be needing help to bust any more people out of prison." He winked before pulling his battered hat low. Only a patch of his scarred cheek showed under the brim. He turned and limped back into his tent, whistling.

"Seriously, Jing Fan," Thomas said, a frown still playing across his freckled face. "Anything we can do for you, say the word. Or even if you'd just like company—stop by and sit with us a spell." He bade her good night before she could think of a response.

As she pushed her way through the thick blanket of snow back toward her own tent, Ling Fan mused over the irony: she'd lost the two friends who'd started the sojourn with her, only to find two new ones here on the Gold Mountain.

The familiar evening sounds of male laughter and shouts were at a comfortable distance. It was still cold, but the stars were like a million jewels scattered across a black silk cloth. Somewhere out there, Tan Din might be staring up at the same stars, breathing the same crisp air, alive and safe.

∧ ∧ ∧

The next day was the last Sunday of the month—payday.

Usually Ling Fan lingered to watch a game or two after she collected her wages from the paymaster. Today, however, she stuffed the coins into the silk pouch that hung around her neck and hurried back to Tan Din's old tent. She had almost reached it when she heard the footsteps behind her. She spun around, one hand clutching the bag at her throat.

Wong Wei was steadier on his feet now—no sign of fever in his face. He was smiling, arms folded.

How had she ever thought he resembled her brother? The edges of the coins in her bag bit into her fingers as she finally admitted to herself that she'd only seen what she wanted to see.

"Ah, payday." He sighed. Something glittered in his hand. A knife.

Ling Fan swallowed. "Please, Wong Wei," she whispered. "Don't be cruel. My father needs this money."

Wong Wei's smile sharpened. "Cruel? If I was really cruel, I'd take all your money, shout your secret to the whole camp, and leave you to the dozens of lonely men here. I still can, you know."

He stepped forward until he was only a few inches away from Ling Fan, his knife tip at her throat. His breath, heavy with whiskey, blew against her face. She edged backward until her back came up against a tree. The knife tip moved slowly from her throat, down the side of her neck, then to her chest. She felt it trace against the hidden shallow curves of her breasts.

"If I was really cruel, there are so many other things I could do." His voice was thick.

Ling Fan was frozen in terror. This was worse than she had imagined. If she made any noise, called for help, what would stop Wong Wei from revealing her secret? But if she did nothing . . . Her mind cast wildly around for some plan of action even as her body was as still as stone.

Voices singing drunkenly drew closer to them. Wong Wei blinked as though he were coming out of a dream. He held out his free hand. "The money. Now."

Shaking, Ling Fan pulled the bag out and counted half the coins into his waiting palm. Wong Wei's eyes never left her face as he caressed the coins and dropped them into a coat pocket. He bowed mockingly before he withdrew.

When he was gone, Ling Fan fell to her knees, anger and relief churning inside her until it all spilled out in hot, bitter tears. She didn't even care if anyone saw or heard her.

215

Failure. She was a failure. She had been a fool to think she could carry through such a wild scheme. She should've never left China, never tried to take her brother's place. She wasn't Jing Fan. She was just a foolhardy girl who was in over her head, and now her father would continue to languish in prison because of her.

Finally, her tears spent, Ling Fan moved to sit on a log outside her tent, thinking. She felt like an insect caught in a spider's web. As long as Wong Wei had the power to expose her, she would be at his mercy. The only way to free herself was to destroy the web and crush the spider.

But how? She wasn't strong enough to fight him. She had to beat him at his own game.

Ling Fan was sure he was involved in the damage that plagued the railroad. He must be in contact with the rival railroad company, Union Pacific, doing their bidding. If she could find a way to make certain Wong Wei was caught in the middle of some mischief, Wong Wei would be dismissed from his job on the railroad, and her problems would be solved. She just needed proof.

She would have to keep as close an eye on Wong Wei as he seemed to be keeping on her.

CHAPTER
21

Meals were haphazard affairs without Tan Din. For the past two days, his cooking crew had shuffled about like newly made gui.

"Aiya!" Ling Fan cried on Sunday evening when she spied a boy tossing bok choy into the vat reserved for washing dishes. Tan Din would be apoplectic if he saw his kitchen in such disarray. She could stand it no longer.

Ling Fan seized the meat cleaver somebody had been using on watercress. She pointed it at each worker in turn. "You, keep the fires stoked. You, stir the vegetables. And you"—she pointed at the man she'd taken the cleaver from—"will learn how to properly cut a chicken apart."

The men swore and grumbled at first, but they remembered her as being one of their own and soon fell into a smoother rhythm. For the rest of the evening Ling Fan directed and harangued until supper for the workers started to wind down. Only then did she spot Chin Lin Sou leaning against a nearby barrel, sucking on a bone. Her cheeks warmed as she wondered how long he'd been there, watching the cooking crew, watching her.

He nodded in approval as his gaze swept over the cooking area, at the men damping down the fires and cleaning up.

"Well done, Tam Jing Fan. Tan Din couldn't have done better. It looks like the men have a new head cook."

"I—I . . ." she stammered. This was the last thing she had expected.

A smile flickered across Chin Lin Sou's face as he tossed the bone onto the midden heap. He licked his fingers. "And now we can once again have meals that don't taste like over-boiled slippers."

After that, her days were filled with chopping, tossing, stir-ring, washing pots, stoking fires, and hauling water. She wasn't Tan Din, but the cooking crew followed her orders just as quickly.

With the job taking up all her attention and energy, keeping track of Wong Wei turned out to be much harder than she'd expected. She only saw him in passing when he turned up for meals—and once a month, when he collected his share of her pay. Each time he did, she spent the remaining night counting and recounting the precious sum of money that was still hers and wracking her brains about how to take him down.

∧ ∧ ∧

Late winter turned to spring and then summer. Summit Tunnel was nearly complete, and the smaller tunnels that followed it had brought the railroad out of the mountains and into Nevada. Thousands of workers were packing up their tents and heading out to lay down more railroad track through the blistering desert. The base camp felt empty. **Now I know what the bak gui mean by "ghost town,"** she wrote her brother.

In August, Fei Gei persuaded Ling Fan to join him on a trip into Grass Valley, a small nearby town. The Chinese locals there had organized ceremonies for Gui Jie, the Hungry Ghost

Festival. The summer before, Ling Fan had been aboard the *Cormorant*, out of her head with seasickness, during this important festival. Now, although she barely knew Fei Gei, she felt she couldn't refuse his invitation.

Fei Gei's older brother had been blown to bits by the premature blast in Summit Tunnel a few months ago. Since then Fei Gei had been tormented with the thought that his brother's spirit was doomed to wander the Gold Mountain as a guhun yegui—an abandoned soul, a wild ghost—because he hadn't had a proper burial. Gui Jie was the festival to soothe all lost, hungry spirits, especially those who'd suffered sudden violent deaths or couldn't be buried in their ancestral homes. Ling Fan thought with a shudder of all the sojourners who'd died since the railroad began. She didn't hesitate to pay her twenty-five cents to join the festival in Grass Valley's Chinese quarter.

Sunday was their only free time, so they made sure to arrive early. Lanterns were lit and the air was heady with burning incense and joss paper. Altars were laden with food for the dead, but vendors had plenty of food for the living. Music from Chinese instruments flowed out of the local temples along with the murmured chants of priests.

At the end of the day, Ling Fan helped Fei Gei fold joss paper money into little boats. Each boat was set on fire before being launched down a stream that led out of town. She watched the flotilla of tiny vessels blaze like hundreds of stars in the dark water.

∧ ∧ ∧

In the early fall, Ling Fan took the donkey carts into Illinoistown for one last supply run before she would join the other workers out in the Nevada desert. From now on, Chin Lin Sou would arrange for supplies to be sent out on a train along the finished railroad line.

The End o' Line had pushed beyond Illinoistown long ago, but the town had kept growing. There were more bak gui, but even more sojourners milling about as well, and Ling Fan overheard talk of the town's name being changed to Colfax. The saloon was twice as big now, as was the general store where Tan Din had purchased the doll for his daughter all those months ago. Ling Fan picked up her pace as she walked past its new pinewood veranda.

"Yoo-hoo! Mr. Chinaman! You there, Mr. Chinaman!"

Ling Fan turned to see Clara Strobridge waving to her with all her might from across the street. Before she could even lift a hand to wave back, Clara was dashing headlong toward her, dodging donkey carts and being roundly cursed by horseback riders.

"Hello, Miss Strobridge," Ling Fan said, but Clara Strobridge wrinkled her nose.

"Clara. Or you can call me Miss Clara if you must."

"And I am Tam Jing Fan," Ling Fan replied, amused. "What a pleasant surprise to see you in town." The pretty little caboose that the Strobridges had used as their home was nowhere in sight, having gone with the Pioneer up the newly laid tracks. "I trust your mother is well?"

"Mother's here to take care of some business," Clara said. "She's as busy as a bee, and mad as a hornet at that nasty Mr. Liston, but she'll like seeing you. Come say hello!" She gestured toward one of the newer buildings at the end of the street. A sign that read CENTRAL PACIFIC RAILROAD OFFICES hung over the door. A swaybacked mule was tied to a nearby hitching post.

"Mr. Liston is Mr. Crocker's clerk," Clara explained. "He brings papers and mail and such from Mr. Crocker." She paused to draw breath and added, "I don't like him. Mama doesn't much like him either."

Mr. Liston, according to Clara, was always showing up to bother them with this or that. He always had something to say about how Mrs. Strobridge did the paperwork for her husband and seemed annoyed when she didn't change her ways to suit him. Mrs. Strobridge did not work for Mr. Liston and wasn't afraid to tell him as much, but a day or two later, a note would arrive from Charles Crocker, and that would be that.

"Mama thinks Mr. Liston should mind his own business. Or better, mind the business of a different railroad."

Just then, the door to the office building opened and a barrel-chested man with a tangled beard stepped out, followed by Mrs. Strobridge. The man had a pile of papers tucked under one arm, and he was red-faced and talking rapidly. Mrs. Strobridge, on the other hand, was impassive, standing with hands clasped behind her back as the man railed on. He clapped a round derby hat on his head and took his leave, walking down the stairs with stiff dignity just as Clara and Ling Fan approached.

"Well hello, Tam Jing Fan." Mrs. Strobridge smiled and held out both hands in welcome. "It's so good to see you up on your feet! I've thought about you often since the avalanche."

Ling Fan was unsure if she should take Mrs. Strobridge's hands, remove her hat, or bow. She compromised by whipping off her hat and bowing low. "I am very well, thanks to you. I never had the chance to thank you properly."

"Tam Jing Fan, have tea with us!" Clara shouted. Again, Ling Fan felt flustered. How strange that here in America she had become used to gruffness and curses. She longed to accept

Clara's artless friendliness, but out of the corner of her eye, she saw Mr. Liston staring at them as he mounted his donkey.

"You are very kind, Miss Clara, but I must bring food supplies back to base camp," Ling Fan replied. "I hope to see you again." She touched her hat and bowed to mother and daughter before turning to go. As she made her way back to the depot, Ling Fan felt eyes on the back of her neck. She turned and caught sight of Mr. Liston still staring at her from across the street.

Later that afternoon, Ling Fan guided the donkey team past the last of the buildings on the outskirts of Illinoistown and onto the path that led back to the camp. The sunshine felt good on her back. All around her was the faint echo of trickling water running together to form tiny streams. Ling Fan breathed deeply, savoring the crisp air that ran through the valley. The days were warm, but the nights were starting to bite. She looked forward to being out of the mountains and in the desert before winter came again.

She caught the rancid, smoky odor before she saw the donkey-mounted figure pull away from the shade of a tree and stop on the path ahead of her.

Mr. Liston was not a particularly short man, but his trousers bunched around his knees and ankles in a manner that made him appear too small for his clothes. He lit a new cigar from the stub of his old one and tossed it off to the side.

"You know English pretty well," he remarked without preamble. "For a Chinaman."

She bristled but said nothing. She was fully aware of the rifle slung across Liston's saddle. She eyed the sparse land around them and wondered if it would be better to run for cover or try to turn her wagon train around and race back to town. As if sensing her tension, her donkeys stamped their feet impatiently and shook their heads, making their tackle jangle.

"It's brutal, tough work," Liston continued, gesturing vaguely over his shoulder in the direction of the base camp. "Nobody ever believed you coolies would get this far, this fast. Nobody but Crocker himself. Said if Chinamen could build that big fancy wall of yours, you could sure as hell build a railroad."

Ling Fan wondered what her brother would've said to this strange mixture of compliment and insult. All she knew was that Liston's words had the taste of mud, and she wished she could thrust them back down his throat.

Liston wasn't done. "Too bad Charlie Crocker doesn't take better care of his pets. Real shame. You Chinamen haven't been here long enough to know that not all bosses are the same."

"What do you mean?"

"Only that you should remember there are two railroad lines headed toward Utah, and only one is run by Central Pacific and the Big Four. There's some what knows how to make and keep a deal fair and square."

"Why should you care? You work for Central Pacific yourself."

"Actually, I prefer to say that I work for myself, and I know how to find the deals that suit me best." Liston rubbed the side of his nose and winked.

"What do you want?" Ling Fan demanded.

"Well, as you may know, the Big Four and the Union Pacific bosses like to keep things lively. They're all in a lather about which company's going to be the first to reach Promontory Point in Utah. And of course, any accidents can slow down the work, give the other side an advantage. My friends with Union Pacific would be willing to provide a lot of money to make sure accidents happen on the Central Pacific line."

Ling Fan felt the thud of her heart against her rib cage. Her mind snagged on those words: *a lot of money*. More money than Wong Wei had taken from her over the past several months? Enough money to get home and finally free Baba?

But she couldn't trust a man like Liston. She had to be careful.

She swallowed and said, "Perhaps I would make just as much money turning you in to Crocker and Strobridge. They're offering a great deal for information about trouble-making scoundrels, I hear."

To Ling Fan's surprise, a grin spread slowly from around Liston's cigar. "You really think they'll take a Chinaman's word against mine? Besides, what do you care which railroad wins the race to the finish, so long as you get your gold? Help us out and there'll be a sweet bonus for you too."

Ling Fan chewed her lip. She knew what her father would say about causing damage—perhaps putting people's lives in danger—in exchange for money. She knew what she herself had said about it a few months ago. *Dishonorable*. And yet . . . everything about the way the bak gui treated the sojourners was unfair, from the lower pay to the constant casual insults to the truly deadly threats Wong Wei and Tan Din had endured.

Did she really care what happened to the bak gui and their railroad? A cold, angry part of her didn't.

"How do I know that if I do this work for you, the reward will be as you say? How do I know you won't just turn *me* in?"

Liston shrugged. "You're right to be suspicious. Let's start with a small job, very simple, very quick, for a small fee. How does three dollars sound?"

Ling Fan tried not to gape. Half a week's pay for something simple and quick—surely that was too good to be true.

She thought again of the money Wong Wei had stolen from her. Someone had paid Wong Wei to cause trouble for Central Pacific. It could very well be Liston—or else it was probably another bak gui working for Union Pacific.

If she did a job for Liston, kept her eyes and ears open, learned more about what the troublemakers were up to, she might finally be able to turn the tables on Wong Wei. All she needed was solid evidence that he was working against Central Pacific.

And if she had to work against Central Pacific in the process—well, three dollars a job was good money.

Liston watched Ling Fan narrowly from behind the smoke rising from his cigar. "Well? What do you say?"

CHAPTER 22

I t was easy.

The first job was just a matter of breaking enough essential tools to cause a few days' delay. The second job was no more complicated: hobbling a dozen mules. Soon, she was causing minor mayhem all over the camp. Days turned to weeks, then months, while the sack of money she kept well hidden in her tent grew with each job. She'd thought she'd be suffused with guilt, but she discovered a certain satisfaction in sowing chaos. It felt like payback for all the slights she'd endured since coming to America.

Even so, her dreams were filled with Baba's disapproving frown.

The days of tunneling and blasting through granite were over. After punching their way out of the mountains, the Central Pacific workers were now racing across the Nevada desert. Instead of snow and ice, Ling Fan's days were filled with grueling heat and thoughts of water—though at night the temperature dropped enough to make her shiver in her tent.

As winter gave way to spring, Crocker urged everyone on with promises of bonus money for enduring the heat. And in March, Liston offered Ling Fan four dollars instead of the usual three for her next job.

It was as though she were watching somebody else move her body. Feet took her from spot to spot along the fresh graded plane that was cleared for new rail. Gloved hands buried gunpowder beneath the sandy Utah soil close by the marked junctures. *Fuse needs to be cut and laid,* a voice in her head reminded her. *Best do it later,* it whispered, *as close to detonation time as possible.*

Everybody from bak gui bosses to Chinese graders saw her, but nobody saw what she did. She was just another sojourner moving along the track. They would never be able to say anything more precise than that a Chinese worker of slight build and wearing a woven hat had come by, added a bit of this or that to the ties, and moved on.

That night, under a wide, moonless sky, a gold-red ball of light burst into the air over the tracks two miles to the west. Seconds later, a sound like thunder echoed off the low hills surrounding the camp. This was quickly followed by shouts, running feet, mules being kicked awake and hitched to carts carrying barrels of water. They rattled through the dark toward the fire chewing rapidly through the temporary supply sheds that lined the tracks.

Ling Fan watched the shadowy movements through the walls of her tent as they stretched and lurched in a grotesque dance. She rolled over and squeezed her eyes shut, but the shadows refused to leave, flitting across her closed eyelids.

In her dreams, she was back at Cape Horn, hanging in a basket off the cliff. The basket spun, faster and faster, as she tried to strike a flame to ignite the fuse, but all she could get was a tiny spark. The sparks started to collect at the bottom of her basket like orange snow. They turned into red flames that crept up her legs, past her hips, licking at her like a dozen ruby tongues.

She woke with a gasp. Her bedding beneath her was damp, and she felt a strange band of heaviness across her lower back that was almost painful. With dread she reached down, and even before her fingers encountered the sticky mess, she knew that her bleeding had finally started.

She cleaned up as best she could in the semidarkness—at least the bathing area was deserted since everyone's attention was focused on the disaster she herself had started. She ripped her oldest tunic into strips and fashioned a crude version of the padding Ming had shown her once. When she finally returned to her bedroll, she closed her eyes tight against the world, feeling as though a mountain of weariness had settled across her shoulders. One more thing to be careful of.

In the morning, the scent of wet, burnt wood clung to many of the workers as they squatted here and there around the camp, chewing through a cold breakfast. Fresh crews hopped onto mule carts headed back to repair the break in the tracks.

While her cooking crew finished washing up from the morning meal, Ling Fan followed an overgrown path through a thicket of nettles and new trees and found the cluster of four white rocks Liston had assured her would be there. Beneath the largest one were the promised pieces of gold and a folded note detailing her next job. She thrust everything deep into her tunic and nearly jumped right out of it at the sound of a twig snapping behind her.

She ducked behind the trunk of a wind-stunted juniper tree just as a tall figure, clad in a long dusty-blue jacket and a battered brown hat, came into view. He had his back to her as he approached the four white rocks just as she had. Her chest clenched. Wong Wei!

As she crept forward to get a closer look at what he was up to, the figure spun around, fist cocked. Ling Fan stumbled to a halt. "Jonathan O'Brien!"

O'Brien's scarred face twisted. Ling Fan had never seen such a malevolent look on him before. For the first time since she'd known him, she felt frightened. But a second later, he was smiling so warmly that she was sure it must've been a trick of the shadows.

"Tam Jing Fan, boyo, you startled me!" He clapped her on the shoulder. "I almost knocked your Celestial block right off!"

"That would've been hard to do since I was about to flatten you," she replied, almost giggling from the gush of relief that washed over her. O'Brien carried a burlap sack, which he dropped to the ground with a metallic clatter.

"What's that for?" she asked, nodding at his bag.

"Nothing that concerns you," O'Brien snapped. Ling Fan flinched, wondering if she'd somehow offended him.

O'Brien took a red handkerchief from his pocket. "I'm sorry," he muttered as he mopped his face. "Everyone's on edge because of these damn *accidents*. Tommy's been out all night with one of the cleanup crews. He hasn't been back yet." He stuffed the handkerchief back in his pocket. "What brings you up here?"

Knowing that Thomas had been out all night repairing the damage she was responsible for felt like a knife twist in her gut. "Just getting some fresh air before I have to start cooking lunch for my work crew," she answered. The lie felt like poison in her mouth. The coins hung heavily in the inner pocket of her tunic. She couldn't look at O'Brien but turned and pretended to scan the western horizon.

A smoky haze still hung in the sky. In the distance, a broken line of weary workmen trudged back from the track, their faces smudged with soot. Ling Fan spotted a donkey cart galloping into the camp, driven by Thomas. He pulled to a stop in front of the medical tent and leapt out of the seat. Even from this distance, Ling Fan could hear him shouting for help.

She broke into a run, her heart beating in her throat. She didn't stop until she reached Thomas's cart. By now a bak gui doctor and a few other workers were lifting two bloodied men out of the cart.

"What happened?" Ling Fan cried.

"The wall of a shed collapsed on us while we were trying to put out the fire," Thomas gasped, leaning against the side of the cart. The two injured men were whisked into the medical tent. Ling Fan stared helplessly after them.

Thomas started to take a step toward her but crumpled to the ground with a moan. Instantly, O'Brien was by his side. Ling Fan hadn't even realized he'd followed her back into the camp. Together, they settled Thomas against the wheel of the donkey cart. Only then did Ling Fan see the growing dark stain on the right side of his coat.

O'Brien nudged the coat open and hissed at the sight. A thick splinter of lumber, oozing blood, was embedded in Thomas's side.

"Oh, Thomas!" Ling Fan gasped. He must've been injured when the shed wall collapsed on his cleanup crew. Of course he'd helped everyone else first. Ling Fan felt her eyes burn.

O'Brien shook off his own coat, wadded it into a ball, and pressed it against the wound.

"Hold this here," O'Brien said, pressing Ling Fan's hands down on the cloth. "Don't try to pull that splinter out. He'll bleed out for sure. I have to . . . I'll go get . . ." He was up and running into the medical tent before he'd finished his sentence.

Ling Fan knelt by Thomas's side, watching the wadded jacket slowly turn red and sticky beneath her hands. "Thomas, hang on," she whispered. His eyes were closed, and his face was so pale that his freckles seemed to float across his skin. "I'm sorry."

People, donkeys, carts continued to rush around them in every direction, but she heard and saw them as though from the bottom of a deep well. From very far away, a voice said to her, "It's all right, Jing Fan. Let go."

She felt a hand shaking her shoulder firmly but gently. She looked up into Jonathan O'Brien's tired face. "Let go, lad. These men can help Tommy now." Over his shoulder, she saw the doctor and his helpers. Numbly, she stood up and let them take her place.

"He's in good hands now," O'Brien assured her as Thomas was carried into the medical tent. "Best go get yourself cleaned up, lad."

Only then did she notice the dark patches of blood smeared across her palms. Thomas's blood. She instinctively wiped her hands on her tunic, then realized she'd stained it red as well.

"Go on," said O'Brien. "He'll be up and about by the end of the week, mark my word." But his voice shook.

She nodded and stumbled away, still wanting to say or do something, but feeling more deeply with each step that she'd already done enough.

She fetched a bucket of water from the casks in the cooking area and headed back to her tent, where she changed into a fresh tunic and scrubbed at the stained one for what felt like hours. But despite her best effort, a large, rusty shadow remained. She buried her face in the tunic and sobbed, glad for once that Tan Din no longer shared this space with her. What would he say if he knew how much destruction she'd caused? She had never meant to hurt anyone, least of all Thomas.

A ball of burning shame seemed to be lodged in her throat. It grew bigger and hotter with every breath she took. She wished it was hot enough to burn her into a pile of ash.

Well, if that happens, don't expect me to clean up your mess, boy. Out here on the Gold Mountain you have to clean up your own mess. Tan Din's imagined voice was so clear in her mind that Ling Fan sat bolt upright, almost expecting to see him glaring down at her. The tent was empty. The light from the setting sun glowed through the tent wall.

She knew what she had to do.

∧ ∧ ∧

In the morning she left a note under the stone where she had picked up her last set of instructions. Shortly after lunchtime, when the workers had returned to their jobs and Ling Fan was dumping scraps into the midden heap, she heard her name called.

Liston was lurking a few yards away.

In panic, Ling Fan looked around, but her assistants were busy with their own tasks. From this distance, if they saw her they'd simply think she was taking orders from a bak gui boss. She hurried over to Liston.

"Just what do you mean by this?" he demanded, shaking her note.

"Exactly what it says. I am no longer interested in helping you and your associates. You are an American businessman, Mr. Liston. Isn't this how things are done in your country?"

Liston's eyes narrowed. "Ah, I see. All you Chinamen are alike, aren't you? Thick as thieves. You've talked to that other one, Wong Wei, no doubt. It's more money you want, is that it? You want the same as him, five dollars a job. I'll have to contact my associates, but I might be able to arrange it."

Ling Fan braced herself, trying not to think of her father. "That's not it," she started to say, but Liston spoke over her.

"Of course, the work would have to be more significant than what you've done so far. Wong Wei's set to do some pretty risky stuff."

This was the chance she'd been hoping for. If she could somehow be included in whatever Wong Wei was involved in, she could get proof of what he was up to—proof that she could take to Chin Lin Sou and the bosses. Or better yet, she could find a way to get him caught in the act. "Anything he can do, I can do too," she said, her heart and mind racing. "I could do it even better."

Liston guffawed. "Charlie Crocker did get himself some scrappy pets all right. Well then, here's the thing. Seems the Big Four have a little bet going with the Union Pacific folks. They're saying Central Pacific can lay more track in a day than Union Pacific can in a week. They've settled on April twenty-eighth as the day to put it to the test. Lots of money riding on this. Lots of pressure on the workers. With all the extra rushing around, I wouldn't be surprised if an accident or two might not occur on such a hectic day. Suppose you manage to create enough mayhem on April twenty-eighth that your bosses lose out. Of course, Union Pacific will reward you for your help in their victory."

Ling Fan nodded. "What will Wong Wei be doing?"

"That's his own affair. Talk to him yourself if you want to team up with him. Otherwise, it's every coolie for himself."

Ling Fan pushed down her frustration. She would need to find out more about this bet and figure out what Wong Wei was planning.

After the dinner shift, Ling Fan stopped by the medical tent where Thomas was resting. The doctors, though not unkind, wouldn't let her in to see him. Ling Fan hung about and fretted, unable to shake the memory of Thomas's pale face staring up at her. She could only bring herself to leave when Jonathan O'Brien walked by and invited her to sit with him at his tent.

"He's lost a good deal of blood, but he's a fighter," O'Brien assured her over his small cook fire. He filled a bowl from the pot over the fire and gave it to Ling Fan. She spooned a chunk of greasy rabbit meat floating in brown water and made the showy slurping noises that Aunt Fei had taught her as a sign of good manners, all the while swallowing as little as possible. "He'll be up and about before you know it."

Ling Fan blew lightly at the rising steam, thinking, as the fragrant gray wisps fluttered and reformed, that Aunt Fei had said something similar when Jing Fan was dying. She sighed.

"Don't fret, lad," O'Brien said. "All's well that ends well, as my old granny used to say."

"But *how* will it end?" She was thinking about her own hopelessly tangled predicament and hadn't meant to speak aloud, but O'Brien answered with his usual practicality.

"The railroad companies will keep trying to outdo each other. Each pushing across the land as fast and hard as it can, by hook or by crook, until one of them finally reaches Promontory Point."

"Hook or by crook?" Ling Fan repeated blankly. She usually enjoyed puzzling out American idioms, but tonight she was too sick with worry to even try.

"Fairly or not, depending on which method gets the best results."

"Like this . . . intentional damage we've been seeing."

"Yes, exactly like that. There's been more of it because we're getting close to the end. Another hundred miles, I hear. Crocker's laying bets with the Union Pacific bosses."

Ling Fan stiffened. "What kinds of bets?"

"The way I hear it, Union Pacific laid six miles of track in one day, and now Crocker is going about saying we can do ten."

"Ten miles of track in one day! He can't be serious!" Ling Fan shook her head. Even now that they'd crossed into the flat desert of Utah, Central Pacific's workers had been averaging four miles a day.

But O'Brien looked strangely thoughtful. "With Crocker's ambition and Stro's organization, we might be able to pull it off. Besides, with all that's riding on the bet, you can bet Strobridge'll offer a handsome bonus to the crew that leads the work that day!"

Ling Fan turned everything over in her mind. A part of her balked at the sheer audacity of it. But another yearned to be on that lead work crew. She knew the sojourners could outpace the Union Pacific workers. They'd come so far, through the Sierra Nevada, through the Donner Pass, through the winter of '67. Watching ten miles of track flow across the land in one day would be quite a sight.

And of course there would be bonus money. Not to mention an extra payment from Liston if something went wrong for the Central Pacific team. There was no doubt in Ling Fan's mind that Wong Wei would find a way to be on this job.

And if Wong Wei were caught making trouble on a day when the stakes were so high, not a single person, bak gui or

Chinese, would lend an ear to anything he'd try to say about her. Especially if it sounded the least bit outlandish. He would be removed from the railroad, and she would be safe, still employed, with her full wages left to herself. With Wong Wei out of the way, she would soon be able to secure the rest of the money she needed—a few months' worth of wages, by her rough reckoning. She imagined the tears of joy and amazement Ming and Aunt Fei would shed as she led Baba through the courtyard, a free man at last.

Ling Fan kept that image in her mind as she headed for Chin Lin Sou's tent. This next step would be difficult to pull off. Ever since Tan Din's escape, Chin Lin Sou had become far less open to listening to the workers, spending most of his time alone in his tent. Recently he'd even stopped taking his meals with the other workers, relying on Ah Sook to bring him food from the cooking area. Ah Sook was the only one who came and went freely from his tent, and even he seemed to have limited access these days.

It was that stage of dusk when colors took on a richer hue. The long spikey leaves of yucca plants stood out like slender chips of emeralds. Indian paintbrush pulsed vibrantly red amidst the sagebrush by the sides of the path. Up ahead was Chin Lin Sou's tent. In the gloaming light, Ling Fan could clearly make out the ragged patches sewed inexpertly to one side. Weather stains peppered the stiff canvas. She saw the faint glow of a kerosene lamp through the seams of the tent.

Ling Fan took a deep breath before ducking through the flap. Once inside the tent, away from the little spring breeze that cooled the evenings, she was enveloped by the warm breath of a pipe resting on the low table beside Chin Lin Sou's straw pallet. The table also held a pile of papers, a bowl of half-eaten rice, and an open pen and ink set. The kerosene lamp was perched on top of a box at the foot of his bedding. The tent, though far larger than any Ling Fan herself had slept in, was still not high enough for her to stand erect, and she had to half crouch, half crawl forward to reach him.

Chin Lin Sou sat cross-legged on the ground, surrounded by maps and charts. He glanced up at her, his face neutral. "You don't have an appointment."

"No," said Ling Fan, "but I need to talk to you about something very important."

Instead of bristling at her insolence, he sighed. "About the bet, I take it."

She nodded. "I want to be on the lead work crew for the twenty-eighth."

His expression stayed neutral, unreadable. "Strobridge wants people at the front who can set a fast pace. They're key to this whole thing."

"I'm fast."

"Go back to your cooking crew, Tam Jing Fan." Chin Lin Sou started to shuffle through the maps he held.

Ling Fan leaned forward and slapped a hand over them. She'd gone through too much to be dismissed like this!

"Do you remember Cape Horn? I would've died there if I'd been a little slower or a little weaker. I've survived cave-ins, an avalanche. I've proven that I belong on that frontline crew."

His face darkened, and she wondered if she'd crossed the line and was now about to be thrown off the railroad entirely. Even so, she made herself stare back without flinching.

She counted her breaths, waiting. He studied her face as though he had never fully seen her.

After a moment he nodded and picked up his pipe.

"All right. I don't have to tell you how important this day will be. It could be an enormous turning point for all Chinese workers here in America, not just us sojourners. Everyone, from silver miners to California farmers."

Ling Fan lifted a shoulder, unsure what he meant.

Chin Lin Sou continued speaking softly, more to himself than to her, as he stared into the haze of pipe smoke that swirled around his head. "We live each day in the moment, feeling as though our toil has no end, as though our bosses will continue to drive us like cattle until we drop or until we finally feel that we've earned enough to bring home. But I believe that this work we do is like the first strikes a miner makes in a granite wall. We hammer away and at the end of the day, all that's done is a dent. And yet, in time, that dent becomes a small hole, which becomes a bigger hole, then a tunnel that eventually finds its way through an entire mountain chain. So too are we sojourners making the first tiny dents into a country that is still so new, people still don't know its true contours. Surely we can find a place in a country still trying to decide what it is."

Ling Fan tried to imagine the miles of track behind them, the great peaks of the snowy Sierra Nevada, the taste of dust and gunpowder as Chin Lin Sou did. Not wasted sweat and blood scattered carelessly about by bak gui bosses, but the mortar and mud building roads that future Chinese would walk on freely.

It was an appealing vision. But was it just another way of distracting the sojourners from the realities of true day-to-day living? Another false promise to keep them hopeful, so that the bak gui could keep taking advantage of them?

On her way back through the camp, she paused to stare up at the brilliant swath of night sky arching overhead. She thought again how the night sky was the same in China. Was there a window in Peng Lu Prison that Baba could look out from?

Alone in her tent, she wrote to her brother. **I don't know the answer to any of it, but I do know that I'll keep my promise and finish what I've started.**

CHAPTER 23

April 28 dawned warm and hazy. Hundreds of men marched in ragged lines to the end of the track laid the previous day. Ling Fan's work group was about a hundred sojourners in total. Ling Fan knew most of their faces if not their names. She spotted Wong Wei immediately. Of course he'd gotten himself assigned to the lead crew as well. He shot her a smirk just before she looked away.

Five supply trains stood nose to caboose along the existing track. Ironmen, fishmongers, nugget people all stood at attention like soldiers in an army. Charles Crocker, on his black stallion, cantered up and down the lines like a general, not doing anything in particular but making certain he was noticed. Strobridge was calmer. When the whistle blew, he began the day with a simple sentence: "All right, men, let's get to work." And they did.

With the efficiency of a machine, workers unloaded supplies from the trains. Ling Fan's group rolled ahead on a flatbed. Every hundred feet or so they scrambled off the little tram and shook buckets' worth of iron nails and bolts along the flattened length of dirt. Behind them, others threw down the iron rails and wooden ties, and still others did the work of pounding the rails onto the path. The process began to take on a rhythm that was almost musical. There was no room for distraction or mistakes. Everyone knew his place.

All morning, Ling Fan heard the steady metallic bark of hammer against iron, felt the ground vibrate as iron rails dropped to the ground and were hammered into place.

She kept Wong Wei within sight. She knew he was doing the same because several times their eyes met across an expanse of track and he flashed the old mocking sneer that she yearned to slap off his face. So far he hadn't done a single suspicious thing. The moment he made his move, she would alert Ah Sook and Chin Lin Sou.

When the lunchtime whistle blew, they had measured more than six miles. As usual, the bak gui workers ate apart from the sojourners. Ling Fan couldn't help feeling a surge of pride when she saw her assistant cooks arrive with the meal train to serve rice, dried fish, boiled vegetables, and tea.

As they stood or squatted over their food, some sojourners complained of time wasted on the meal. "Time enough to eat at the end of the day after we've reached our goal."

Ah Sook waved these comments aside. "The bak gui are like women and small children—they have to eat to keep up their strength. We might as well enjoy the little break." He passed around a familiar flask.

At the edge of the group, Ling Fan finished her food quickly and got up, wiping her hands on her trousers. She looked around for Wong Wei.

No sign of him. Ling Fan cursed herself. Where had he gone?

Ling Fan made her way back to the work site, trying not to look frantic. He couldn't have gone very far.

That morning, they had been laying straight track along the flat desert ground. But by noon, the ground had begun to rise, and the hills on either side of them had slowly grown. In fact, to the east, about a hundred yards ahead, was a large bluff that the workers had been directed to skirt around rather than to try to go over. Ling Fan headed toward it, thinking she'd get a better view from higher ground.

As she climbed, the sparse, dry grass gave way to rockier ground, and what had seemed like a gentle swell from a distance turned out to be a fairly steep incline. The surveyors had been right to suggest angling the tracks around this jut of land. Ling Fan was panting by the time she reached the top.

From where she stood, she could see the rail lines stretching toward her from the western horizon. Shading her eyes against the sun's glare, she could make out Ah Sook as he directed people to get back to work. The swing of a familiar gait caught her eye. Could that be Wong Wei, helping another worker roll a heavy wooden barrel of ties farther up the grade in preparation for the ironmen? She had to get closer to be sure. She was about to head back down to the work site when she heard a sound on the other side of the incline.

She froze. Having hammered countless iron spikes into rock herself, Ling Fan recognized the sound with every fiber of her being. Somebody was driving a spike into the rocky wall on the other side of the little cliff she was standing on.

She turned and crept back up the bluff, staying low. What work could anyone possibly be doing out here? She heard no voices, but the sound of steady hammering grew louder. Once she reached the top, she crawled to the edge of the bluff and peered over. About halfway down, a narrow ledge jutted outward from the rock wall like a pouting lip.

A man in a long, dusty blue coat and a broad-brimmed brown hat was harnessed into a leather sling. He was balanced along the ledge, swaying slightly as he pounded a stake into the stone wall in front of him.

The anchor attached to his sling was near the top of the bluff—easy for her to reach. She could've knocked it out with a stone. She could've turned and raced to the get Ah Sook. But something made her call out.

"Wong Wei."

He looked up, his eyes widening in panic but then narrowing when he saw Ling Fan.

"You don't have to do this," Ling Fan said in a rush. "I won't tell anyone what you've done, so long as you stop the damage and stop taking my money . . ."

Wong Wei went back to his hammering. His thin lips pulled back in a rictus of contempt. "You'd better leave now while you can, *girl*. When I'm done with this, I'll put the word out. What do you think will happen to you once the men find out who's been walking amongst them all this time? When they're done with you, not even the cheapest brothel would take you in."

Ling Fan looked down into his thin, pale face. "I'm not afraid of you anymore, Wong Wei." She hadn't realized this until she said it aloud, but it was true. After all she'd been through, she knew she would find a way around any threat he put before her.

She backed away from the ledge and raced back down the bluff toward the work site.

She never knew how Wong Wei managed to get to the ground and catch up to her so quickly. She didn't even hear him coming until he tackled her.

They both tumbled through the tall grass. Ling Fan kicked out and felt a bone crack against the bottom of her boot. Wong Wei's grip didn't loosen. If anything, the blow seemed to give him the surge of strength he needed to twist around and pin her to the ground.

Ling Fan looked up into his furious, muddy, bloodied face just as he lifted a large rock above his head. She couldn't even free her arms to ward off the blow. The old Ling Fan would have flinched, turned her head aside and screwed her eyes shut, but the Ling Fan who had lived on the Gold Mountain for the past year and a half locked eyes with Wong Wei, daring him to watch her die.

So when a figure appeared behind him and brought a rock down on the back of his head, Ling Fan wasn't surprised that he pitched forward on top of her. It took a minute to wriggle out from under his weight, even with the help of his assailant. Free at last, she could only blink up at the familiar figure before her. It took another minute to get her breathing under control enough for her to gasp out, "Tan Din! What are you doing here?"

Tan Din pushed his hat to the back of his head and ran a hand over his face as he contemplated the bloody heap at his feet. The old familiar gesture seemed at once oddly casual and perfectly appropriate.

Ling Fan stood there shaking. "Is he dead?"

Tan Din knelt down and put his ear to Wong Wei's chest. "No. The snake always did have a thick skull. I should've hit him harder."

"He'll wish you had too." Ling Fan told him everything as they walked back around to the bluff's rocky face and looked up at the spot where Wong Wei had been working. The harness still dangled from the ropes. On the ground was a canvas bag filled with picks, hammers, and fuses.

Tan Din shook his head. "I never trusted that boy. I can't say I'm surprised that he was behind all the accidents."

"Or some of them, at least." Ling Fan hid her face by bending down to rummage through Wong Wei's pack. She wasn't ready to admit her own dealings with Liston. "How did you know we were out here?"

"I didn't! Just heard the news about that big bet between the two companies and was curious to see how it would play out. The mine where I've been working is only a day's journey away, so I came to take a look. Saw this high point and thought it'd make a good place to watch." Tan Din squinted up at the ledge. "Looks like he wanted to blow the whole bluff down to block the path of the oncoming tracks. It would've taken hours to clear everything or even go around the mess."

Ling Fan looked up from Wong Wei's pack. "Tan Din . . ."

"Can't see why he started to drill the blast hole so low," Tan Din muttered, craning to get a better look. "It'd take half as much gunpowder if he went a little higher. And there's something else up there, I can't quite make it out—"

"Tan Din!"

Tan Din looked down at what Ling Fan had found in the pack and leapt back as though she were holding a cobra. Ling Fan herself stared disbelieving at the bottle of yellow liquid in her hand.

Nitroglycerin.

CHAPTER
24

"**W**here did that come from?" Tan Din demanded, staring wide-eyed at the bottle.

"It was in the bag. I didn't know what it was until I took it out." Ling Fan held the neck of the bottle gingerly, at arm's length.

"Put it back. No, put it on the ground. No, don't move." Tan Din pushed his hat back and scrubbed his face. "Give it to me." Without waiting for argument, he gently plucked it out of her hand.

"At least it doesn't have the fuse yet." Ling Fan tried to swallow.

"With this stuff, it doesn't really matter. I've heard even a really sharp jolt can set it off. You'd better find Ah Sook, quick as you can."

"I can't just leave you here!" Ling Fan cried.

With painstakingly slow movements, Tan Din lowered himself onto a boulder, keeping his hand level. "Tell him everything's that happened. He'll send people who know how to take care of this stuff. Go on. Hurry."

Ling Fan turned and fled, feeling cowardly and disloyal for leaving him alone with the deadly yellow liquid. She raced along the uneven ground, heading toward the group of sojourners who had resumed spreading nuts and bolts between the plates. Ah Sook must be somewhere nearby. She dodged past a group of bak gui who were tugging the wooden ties into position. One of the men looked up, startled.

"Tam Jing Fan!"

Relief washing over her. Never had she been so happy to hear a bak gui's voice. "Jonathan O'Brien!" She changed course to run up to him, ignoring the stares from the other bak gui. "We need your help!"

"What is it? What's wrong?" O'Brien allowed her to pull him away. Immediately, two other bak gui workers moved in to take O'Brien's place, and the work continued.

"You have to help me find Ah Sook. We found nitroglycerin. He'll know what to do." She knew she was babbling, but O'Brien's eyebrows shot up when he heard *nitroglycerin*. His expression was strangely unreadable as she gasped out the rest.

"I'll be damned if I didn't see him go off that way a few minutes ago. Probably looking to relieve himself. Come on."

He led her to the line of supply trains parked farther back on the track. The area was deserted now—Strobridge had all the workers focused on pushing the rails forward, and the trains wouldn't be edged along to catch up until their contents were needed again.

Ling Fan struggled to keep up with O'Brien's long legs. She lost sight of him when he ducked around a railcar.

"Are you sure he went this way?" she called. O'Brien didn't answer. When she rounded the car, he was nowhere in sight. Neither was Ah Sook.

"Hello? Ah Sook? Mr. O'Brien?" Silence. She stared wildly around, then ran the length of the supply train twice before she forced herself to stop. She tried to listen for the sound of nearby movement. All she heard were the distant crash of hammer on metal, the low thud of iron dropped into place and the incessant buzz of hundreds of voices talking at once.

"Mr. O'Brien?"

Something heavy landed across her shoulders. The ground rushed up at her as her knees buckled. Numbness spread up her spine, across her shoulders, to her neck. A veil of tiny black stars drifted across her vision just as a pair of worn, dusty boots shuffled into view from behind her. They were so close to her face that she could hear them creak as the owner squatted down.

"I'm sorry, lad," O'Brien said. He tossed aside the branch he had just whacked her with and pulled out a coil of rope from his coat pocket. "It wasn't supposed to happen like this." He rested his knee on her back and pulled her arms behind her.

Her head still swam from the blow. She could barely lift it high enough to spit the red Utah soil out of her mouth, let alone form words. She thought of yelling for help but realized no one would hear her over the sounds of the day's work. "Why are you doing this? I thought you were our friend."

O'Brien was tying her wrists together with one end of the rope. "Please believe me—this has nothing to do with any of you Celestials," he said. "You've all been used by powerful men whose only goal is to haul in as much money as they possibly can, no matter who gets hurt in the process. I will not stand by and let this monstrosity be finished. Too many innocent lives have been ruined by it."

Pinned down as she was, Ling Fan couldn't even turn her head to look at him. She tried to make sense of his words. "What are you talking about?" She thought of Tan Din, holding the jar of deadly gold liquid, and tried to move, but the rope seemed to pull tighter the more she struggled. "What did you do?"

"What I had to. What any decent person would do to keep this railroad from chewing up any more lives." He shifted position and wound the other end of the rope around her ankles.

"You caused the accidents!"

"Not all of them. I'm not the only one who wants to see this ended, to see innocent people spared."

"You're worried about innocent people getting hurt? What about the people who were hurt by your own actions? Were you the one who tampered with the equipment at Cape Horn? You almost killed me! And what about Tan Din?"

O'Brien gave the rope a tug to test the knots. "I'm not saying my hands are clean. But whose hands are when it comes to war? You Celestials came here for the promise of gold, never bothering to look further than your own gain, never looking up from the work to ask where any of this would lead. You would take your gold and go back to your homes far away, congratulating yourselves. You never stop to look over the top of the Gold Mountain, into the valleys where the people live. Lived."

"You mean the Indians."

"The Cheyenne, the Lakota, the Arapaho. This was their home before anyone else claimed it, Tam Jing Fan. They've lived here for countless generations, at peace with the land. Then the American government set out to destroy them. Wiped out whole communities to make way for a stinking metal track. My wife! Our daughter! Gone! What's there now? Miles upon miles of empty grassland and the long gray snake that carries a monstrous iron horse, dragging along more people who'll throw up their shops and cheap saloons to fill the space."

O'Brien was breathing hard as he stood up.

"But why all this sneaking around? Why not just come forward and air your grievance?" Ling Fan gasped. If she could keep him talking, distract him enough, perhaps she'd find an opening to escape.

"This railroad is too damn big to stop with honest effort! I never meant to hurt you, or any of the workers for that matter. But I couldn't just stand by and let the work continue." He stuffed a balled-up handkerchief into her mouth and tied another cloth around it to hold it in place as a gag. As he stepped back, he looked like he was about to say more, then thought better of it and turned away. He slipped between two of the supply train cars and was gone.

Ling Fan immediately began to twist around until she rolled up against the track between the railcars. She rubbed the rope binding her wrists against a spike jutting out of one of the rails, sawing frantically, half the time catching her own flesh against the metal. After what felt like an eternity, the rope frayed enough for her to free her hands. She tore the gag from her mouth, then had to scrabble wildly at the ropes around her ankles before she could get up and stagger out from behind the supply train.

She felt nauseous and dizzy. Her vision was blurry. She squeezed her eyes shut, trying to clear her head. She had to find Ah Sook and get help for Tan Din.

Opening her eyes, she sighted the gray iron line of rail curving through the desert and, farther on, the rocky spur where she'd left Tan Din. The work crew was laboring on the track up ahead, still nowhere near the bluff. But under her shading hand, Ling Fan caught sight of O'Brien's familiar limping stride. He was headed straight toward Tan Din and Wong Wei.

O'Brien meant to finish the job that she and Tan Din had just prevented. There was no time to get Ah Sook. Ling Fan tore after O'Brien, flying through the scrubby brush.

She had almost reached the bluff when the ground seemed to ripple like a wave beneath her feet. A moment later a roar filled the air. Ling Fan threw herself down and covered her head with her arms as rocks and dirt spewed outward as though blown by a typhoon.

When she looked up, she saw a plume of thick black smoke hanging in the air like a great finger from heaven, pointing at the spot where she had stood with Tan Din less than half an hour ago.

CHAPTER
25

Ling Fan scrambled to her feet and ran to the base of what had been the bluff. All that was left was a mass of broken boulders.

Had O'Brien and Tan Din fought over the nitroglycerin? Or had O'Brien snuck up and struck Tan Din down from behind? And what about Wong Wei? Were they all buried beneath the rubble?

She had worked too long on the railroad to hope anyone might still be alive beneath the rock.

Still, she searched frantically for signs of a body—*any* body, but it was Tan Din she desperately wanted to find. She didn't want people coming to the wrong conclusion about who had caused the destruction. Already she could see workers approaching on donkey-drawn carts—a cleanup crew sent to clear the wreckage. If they caught her here, she'd surely be blamed for the explosion, just as Tan Din had been blamed for last winter's avalanche. She didn't have much time . . .

As she skirted the eastern edge of the rubble something seized her ankle. She struggled, her panicked mind thinking only: *Gui! Gui! Gui!* She pulled back with her other foot and kicked out as hard as she could, expecting her foot to plunge through ephemeral mist, and was shocked to feel solid flesh.

"Aiya!" the gui moaned with Tan Din's voice and let go of her.

"Tan Din?" Ling Fan whispered. "Is that really you?"

"Who else, you little fool!"

Anything else he said was muffled as Ling Fan laughed and cried and clawed at the rubble and dirt until she had freed him. Amazingly, he wasn't hurt aside from a great many bruises. "You need to hide. You shouldn't be seen!"

She half dragged him to the shelter of a patch of scrub bushes a dozen yards away. The cleanup crew was arriving. Reluctantly she left him with her canteen of tea and the promise to return later. Then she slipped in amongst the workers who had begun hauling rubble aside.

The blast had gone off close to the base of the bluff, causing it to collapse mostly upon itself instead of fully blockading the path of the oncoming tracks. Wong Wei and O'Brien would've been disappointed, had they survived.

Ling Fan assumed they were buried somewhere in the debris, but their bodies didn't surface while she and the rest of the cleanup crew worked. Crocker himself rode back and forth shouting orders. To the west he urged the workers to continue laying rail, never mind the mess ahead. To the east, he roared at the cleanup crew to haul rocks aside as though their lives depended on it. By the time the track reached the blasted bluff, the path was completely clear.

The race went on.

Ling Fan was swept back up with her original crew, pouring nails onto the ground for other workers to hammer in. Before she knew it, the sun was nearing the end of its arc, drifting inexorably closer to the horizon just to the right of the gleaming rails. At last, time was called and the final distance tallied up. Ten miles and fifty-six feet!

Cheers erupted. Men threw their hats into the air, stamped their feet, and thumped each other on the back. Some took out rags and mopped their eyes and faces. Crocker and Strobridge climbed down from their horses and shook hands all around. Ling Fan was glad, but not just for the sake of the bonus money. Tan Din was alive. That fact felt so much more miraculous than the ten miles of finished track.

The sun was well below the horizon and darkness had soaked into the surrounding countryside by the time she made her way back down the newly laid tracks. Tan Din was waiting for her by the wreckage of the explosion.

They sat facing each other across a tiny fire Tan Din had built a short distance away from the train tracks.

"When you didn't come back with Ah Sook this afternoon, I thought something must've happened to you," Tan Din explained. "I realized that snake Wong Wei could never plan that whole operation on his own. Somebody else had to be out there keeping an eye on things, and you must've run into him. I couldn't sit there any longer waiting for the crew to come along and find me with that explosive in my hand, so I put it into the deepest crevice I could find and headed back the way you'd gone. I hadn't gone but a hundred yards when I met up with the real snake devil."

"Jonathan O'Brien."

"I thought: *Ah, here's a bak gui we can trust!* So I try to tell him about the explosive. He grabs me, shakes me, says: *Where is it?* I think: *He doesn't understand my bad American words.* But now I see he only wanted to finish Wong Wei's job."

Ling Fan imagined the scene as Tan Din continued: O'Brien trying to force Tan Din to reveal where he'd hidden the explosive. Tan Din confused, resisting, until Tan Din sees a movement out of the corner of his eye. Wong Wei, running straight for the hidden liquid.

"Aiya! I should've remembered a snake can slide out of any knot. He just reached into that hole like a greedy child and . . ."

The explosion had knocked Tan Din and O'Brien off their feet. Fortunately, they'd been at the far edge of the blast radius and were only stunned. Tan Din had seen O'Brien stumbling away from the scene. Wong Wei, of course, had not been so lucky.

"Good riddance to both," Tan Din declared.

Ling Fan shuddered. She wouldn't wish such a death on anyone. But she wasn't sure how to feel about O'Brien's escape. Her earlier shock over his treachery was replaced by a riot of conflicting emotions.

He hadn't simply lied to her. He had put her life, and other workers' lives, in jeopardy again and again through his destructive acts. And what about Thomas? Was he part of O'Brien's plot to undermine the railroad, or had he been duped as well? Had their friendship these past months all been a sham?

She scoured her memory: the first encounter in Illinoistown, the terrible near-lynching of Wong Wei, breaking Tan Din out of his prison. No, all those acts of decency had been genuine, she was sure. As she struggled to reconcile the kind Irishman with the ruthless one, his anguished words came back to her.

Whole communities . . . My wife! Our daughter! Gone! A rush of guilt swept through Ling Fan. She'd given no more than a passing thought to what might be happening to the people who'd been living in the railroad's path. She had been too absorbed by her own troubles.

As echoes from the raucous celebration at the new End o' Line drifted back to her, she thought of all the people who'd been hurt because of this railroad: hundreds of workers dead or maimed, countless Indian communities and families destroyed. And for what? Greed, ambition? Had selfishness been the engine that drove it all?

Perhaps, in many ways. But looking down at her own hands, shadowy in the night, she supposed that all the workers had their own reasons for doing this work, their own stories to tell.

"We have to tell Chin Lin Sou." Ling Fan paced around the fire. "He can tell the bosses . . ."

"Tell them what?"

"That Jonathan O'Brien is behind today's explosion, and other problems too—and that he's still out there somewhere, plotting against the railroad."

Tan Din made a noise in the dark. "And what, exactly, would be the point of that? You've got no proof that O'Brien was involved in any of this."

"I know who he and Wong Wei were working for. I met the man myself!"

"If the bosses hear *that*, they'll have you in a jail cell before you can blink."

Ling Fan sighed. "All right. I won't mention that, or O'Brien. But I have to at least tell Chin Lin Sou about Wong Wei. Perhaps he can spare some workers to come back here and dig for his body."

"And what will that accomplish?"

"For starters, if word of his fate spreads, that might make others think twice before trying to cause more trouble." She pictured Liston chomping on his cigar as he invited yet another sojourner to do the Union Pacific bosses' bidding. "And if nothing else, Wong Wei will get a decent burial."

Tan Din shook his head. "Still looking out for that snake after all he's done."

Ling Fan sat back down and stared into the fire, thinking of O'Brien again. If her father had to suffer for crimes he had never committed, why should a man be allowed to walk away from the damage he had truly caused? He ought to be held accountable. Ironically, she once might've sought out Jonathan O'Brien to talk through a dilemma like this.

As though he could hear her thoughts, Tan Din said, "Let it go."

"I wish I could. It's like gristle. I keep chewing on it."

"Then chew on this: he lost."

"How can you say that?" Ling Fan demanded. "Think of all the men who've been killed or injured because of him!"

"You say that O'Brien told you he wanted to keep the railroad from being completed."

"So?"

"So, how far away from Promontory Point do you think we are? How long will it take for Central Pacific to reach it? A week? Two weeks? And Union Pacific will be there right before or right after you. The railroad will be finished despite everything he and his associates have done."

"He can still try something. Even when it's finished he can still cause a lot of damage."

"Maybe. But once trains start going along those tracks, with people and goods, there'll be plenty of interest in protecting them. That means more people looking for outlaws like O'Brien."

She wondered what her father would think of all this. In some ways, Jonathan O'Brien reminded her of him. She suspected that he would disapprove of O'Brien's methods but have a great deal of sympathy for his motives. O'Brien had been wrong to take matters into his own hands the way that he had, but what had he been up against? A fearfully powerful group of people who rode roughshod over anyone who stood in their way!

"It's back to the tin mines for me the morning," said Tan Din. "Try to get some sleep, Tam Jing Fan."

Ling Fan shivered in the cold desert air and drew her knees up to her chin. "It's Ling," she heard herself say. "My name is Tam Ling Fan."

She held her breath.

There was only the slightest pause before Tan Din replied, "Ah." His voice was gentle and unsurprised. "Good night then, Tam Ling Fan." In the darkness, his breathing slowed, deepened, and turned into a low rumble.

Ling Fan felt as though a sack of granite had lifted off her shoulders. Sleepless, she watched the last embers of their fire fade and listened to the whistle of Tan Din's breath. Eventually she stood up and made her way to the tracks a dozen feet away.

The rails glinted dully in the moonlight. A faint glow to the east was the only hint that workers were still up and celebrating today's achievement. *Bak gui.* The Chinese workers were probably ensconced in their tents, exhausted. Their time for celebrations would come only when they returned to their home villages in China. There they would hold feasts that went on for days.

That reminded her of Wong Wei. Her instinctive relief that he was dead gave way to more complicated feelings. What would his fiancée think when Wong Wei never returned? Usually friends of workers took it upon themselves to notify families in China of a death. Who among Wong Wei's cronies would take that responsibility? For that matter, who but Ling Fan and Tan Din even knew what had happened to him? Would his fiancée believe Wong Wei had forgotten her? Abandoned her to pursue his own whims? She would never know the lengths he'd gone to in the hope of getting back to her.

Ling Fan's head throbbed. Emotions whirled through her mind in an endless loop, leaving her exhausted but restless. She wished she could blow them away like the flame of a candle.

The rails stretched across the dark desert ground like a silver bracelet. Lightly, gingerly, like a traveling acrobat she had once seen back home, she placed first one foot, then the other along a single rail and began to walk. She paid no heed to which direction she went, only concentrating on keeping her balance. She wondered what she would look like to somebody watching from the heavens. She wondered what her brother would make of everything that had happened to her since he'd died.

Had she done the right thing? Had there been another way? Ling Fan stopped, turned, and retraced her steps. Right or wrong, what was done was done. Tan Din was right. The railroad would be completed in a matter of weeks. Soon, everyone would scatter in a thousand different directions, following their own paths. And with a full month's wages plus the bonus from working today, she would finally have enough money to return home.

She didn't feel triumphant as she'd always imagined she would. Wasn't this exactly what she had hoped to achieve? The reason she'd suffered so much, taken such risks?

Her father safely back home.

And then? What would happen after the first wave of celebration died down? Would life go back to how it had been before Baba was arrested? Ling Fan stared down at her hands. Scarred, rough, callused, filthy, and swollen. Nobody at home would recognize them now. She could imagine her aunt's expression when she saw them.

She remembered when Wong Wei had remarked on her soft "scholar's hands." Not anymore. Now she held them up, spreading the fingers wide. She could feel every callus and crack, every tendon, it seemed. These were strong hands. Strong enough to carve a tunnel through Sierra Nevada granite, strong enough to haul hundreds of pounds of rock, strong enough to hold on for dear life from a sheer cliff over the American River.

Hands that could do anything she put her mind to.

∧ ∧ ∧

Weeks later, the two trains met. A massive ceremony was planned for the driving of the last spike. A wire was wound around it so that the telegraph operator on the other end would receive some kind of signal the moment it was hammered in. The vibrations never made it through, so a telegrapher had to type in the message: DONE.

Ling Fan would learn about this much later, on the trip back to San Francisco. Strobridge ordered a series of trains just for the sojourners wishing to head home. On the day of the ceremony—May 10, 1869—Ling Fan was kneeling in her tent, rolling her few possessions into squares of silk and tucking them tightly into her pack for the long journey. In the distance she could hear the roar of the crowd at the ceremony like the breaking of waves on a rocky shore. She also heard the sound of feet stopping outside her tent, and then a cough. Ling Fan backed out slowly, already knowing who it was.

"Chin Lin Sou wants to see you," Ah Sook told her, and Ling Fan followed him past the few remaining tents. Most were empty. A small work crew was going around, folding up the canvas sheets and stacking them neatly. Sojourners had rolled up their belongings almost as soon as they had received their final pay and headed off, north, south, east, and west. Many, like Ling Fan, were bound for San Francisco to catch the next ship home. Others were looking for more work in America: on farms, in tin mines, even on other railroads.

Everywhere the signs of people packing up and leaving were evident: broken stools, shredded bedding, dented pots, or broken crockery. A few workers were poking through the debris with sticks, looking for anything worth keeping.

Inside Chin Lin Sou's tent, the papers that used to sprawl across his table now sat in a box along with his few personal items. She found him writing at his desk, smoke rising from the pipe that sat in a bowl next to his pen set. He finished a phrase and looked up.

Ling Fan had told him as much about the events of April 28 as she thought would be believable. She'd included the return of Tan Din but left out the involvement of Jonathan O'Brien. Chin Lin Sou had questioned her closely and repeatedly, but she stuck to her version. Tan Din had been right—no good would come of accusing O'Brien, and she didn't want Thomas to fall under any undue suspicion.

In the end, Chin Lin Sou had fixed her with an even stare and simply said, "Very well. We'll leave it as you say." She knew he suspected she was withholding something and was grateful that he trusted her enough not to pursue it.

Chin Lin Sou had sent a team to dig in the rubble by the bluff, but all they'd been able to unearth was a fragment of a bloodied blue coat.

"I had Ah Sook fetch you here so I could ask you to do one last job for me," he said now. He gestured to a crumpled sack beside him. Ling Fan recognized it as Wong Wei's. "I realize

I'm asking a lot from you, considering your last encounter with him, but I thought it best to ask somebody who lived near his village. You needn't feel obliged to actually deliver it to his family. Entrusting it to the Benevolent Society in your district will be more than enough. I've written a letter expressing the railroad's regrets for his death as well as details on how to collect the remaining salary owed him. I'm sure his family will have no trouble getting what's due."

Part of her was tempted to toss Wong Wei's possessions into the nearest fire. Let his family suffer and wonder, as he would've had hers suffer. But that bitter impulse faded, like an unpleasant taste that lingered after food had been swallowed. She felt more pity for him than anything else. She bowed her head and accepted the bag.

"The second thing is this." Chin Lin Sou slid an oilskin sack across the table. Ling Fan picked it up. Her eyes widened at the metallic clinking within. Chin Lin Sou added, "Mr. Strobridge did promise to pay for any help in apprehending the culprits."

Slowly, regretfully, she replaced the sack on the table. "I didn't tell you about Wong Wei for the money." She swallowed. *Some things matter more than money* felt like the right answer to say aloud, though it wasn't the entire truth either.

Two years ago, she would've grabbed the bag without hesitation, not caring how she came by it, so long as the money helped pay for Baba's release. Now, thinking about everything that had happened with Wong Wei, Tan Din, and the O'Briens, she wished there could've been another way.

Chin Lin Sou nodded as though he were finishing a conversation with himself. "Nevertheless, it is yours to do with as you will." He pushed the sack back across the table. Ling Fan picked it up again, then shouldered Wong Wei's bag.

"Safe journey, Tam Jing Fan."

Outside, Ah Sook was nowhere to be seen, and Ling Fan was glad. She wasn't sure what she could've said to him without starting a fight. She wondered briefly if he too would be staying in America or if he would make the journey home.

"So, it's back to the Celestial Land, is it?"

Thomas O'Brien's voice behind her stopped her in her tracks. She turned and was relieved to find him smiling at her. He was fully recovered from his injury now, but Ling Fan knew his uncle's disappearance had left him lonely and confused. She'd never told him what had really happened on April 28. As far as Thomas knew, his uncle had simply vanished. Ling Fan hated seeing him brood over it—knowing any answers she held would only raise more questions and cause him more pain—so she'd been avoiding him lately. At the moment, though, his expression was untroubled.

She nodded to him. "And you?"

Thomas grinned. "I'm off to Boston. My cousin says there's loads of work there. I'm going to get to ride the rails east and see what kind of workmanship the Union Pacific boys put into the thing!" They walked together through what remained of the camp. "And what will you do when you return home? Will there be a line of fine ladies awaiting your offer of marriage?"

Ling Fan was staring across the valley that lay south of the campsite. The train tracks flowed along the bottom like a silver ribbon. "I haven't really thought about it." It was true. She'd been so focused on the moment when she would bring her father home. If she could bring him home. If he was still alive after all this time in prison.

Cautiously she allowed herself to imagine Baba safe in the house she grew up in. She would fix all his favorite foods, and they would stay up all night talking. She imagined telling him everything, starting with the moment she left home. And then . . . she wondered if she would still be expected to marry. The thought of marriage appealed to her less than ever. If she agreed to marry anyone at all, it would only be someone who would treat her as an equal.

She put the thought aside for now. There would be plenty of time to argue the point with her family when she got home. She had no doubt, after all she'd done, that she would be able to stand her ground.

"Well, come find me here in America if you get bored," said Thomas.

They came to a fork in the path. Ling Fan held out her hand. Thomas took it.

"God be with you," he said.

Ling Fan smiled. "Goodbye for now, Thomas O'Brien. Who knows, I might show up again when you least expect me."

Back at her tent, Ling Fan opened Wong Wei's bag. Wrapped inside an extra shirt was a bundle of folded papers knotted together with a piece of twine. She took it out and set it aside. Then she counted out coins from the oilskin sack and slipped them into the silk pouch she wore around her neck. When she finished, at least half as many coins remained. She pulled Wong Wei's lucky coin out of her pocket and wound its string tightly around the oilskin sack before pushing it back into his bag.

Ling Fan finished her own packing. The last things she placed in her canvas bag were a chunk of black rock—heavier than one might think for its size—and an iron spike as long as her hand. Then she picked up the bundle of letters along with the bags, lifted the flap of the tent, and stepped out. The late spring sun felt hot on her face.

She followed the faint path that led to the cooking area, which was deserted. She knelt down in front of one of the smoldering fire pits and stirred the embers back up with a stick until tiny flames started to dance. She tossed the bundle into their midst.

Ling Fan suddenly felt as light as the ashes circling into the sky like dozens of black moths. She smiled, imagining her brother dusting the crumbs from a spirit pastry off his fingers as he turned over the pages one by one, finally able to finish reading her story. She hoped he would like it.

Ling Fan joined the line of men headed to the waiting train that would take them to Sacramento. The huge metal engine gleamed, great clouds of steam rising out of its smokestack like a dragon huffing impatiently.

Ling Fan paused before climbing aboard, taking one final glance around her. The tracks flowed out in both directions, disappearing at the horizon. Beyond that horizon lay an infinite number of stories and an infinite number of possibilities—some horrifying, some wonderful, some a mixture. All of them, good and bad and in between, had been helped along by her hand. If she could not be wholly proud of that, if she could not be wholly at peace with it—well, perhaps this was as it should be. She was her father's daughter, after all. But she was also a sojourner in her own right, who had been to the Gold Mountain and survived.

With a full heart, Ling Fan boarded the train.

CHAPTER 26

Home!

Well, not quite, not yet, but Ling Fan's heart swelled as her ship steamed into the port of Guangzhou. Her countrymen bustled along the docks, shouting, cursing, haggling in Cantonese and half a dozen other Chinese dialects. The signs in flowing calligraphy, rather than angular blocky English print, felt strangely liberating. It felt as though she had shrugged off a bulky, overly warm coat and could now finally feel the sun's warm rays against her skin.

Before she boarded the *Cormorant* for the final leg of her return trip, she stopped at the Guangzhou branch of the Benevolent Society, where she arranged for Wong Wei's effects to be forwarded to his family. Then she completed the remittance paperwork for her wages from the railroad. The sack hidden deep inside her bag weighed heavily—it held nearly two years' worth of blood, sweat, and tears after all—but she herself felt as light as air.

She didn't sleep at all on board the *Cormorant* as it slowly toiled up the Pearl River. Some of her giddiness was replaced by a gnawing anxiety. She imagined a hundred different ways she could be greeted when she finally stepped over the high threshold of her home. She might be treated like a triumphant warrior. Like a hero back from a wild journey. Like a lost soul. Like a vagabond.

What she didn't imagine were the two small figures sprawled in the front courtyard of her aunt's compound. One was a thin little girl wearing a dusty blue tunic and loose black trousers. The other was a fat little boy with bright eyes and round red cheeks. They were both absorbed in a picture the girl was scratching in the dirt with a stick and only looked up when Ling Fan stopped in front of them.

"Go away," the little girl commanded. "My popo isn't here. She's gone to get herbs from Widow Chang."

Popo? Ling Fan stared down at the girl. Her pointed chin and thick eyebrows looked eerily familiar. She looked to be about two years old. The boy, perhaps a year younger, stared at her silently.

"If you don't go away," said the girl, "you'll be in big trouble when my popo comes back!"

"But I live here," Ling Fan said, pushing her hat back and smiling. "I'm Tam Ling Fan. And you must be my cousin Ming's little girl."

The girl glared up at her, unimpressed. "You're not Tam Ling Fan. You look like a boy. And anyway, Tam Ling Fan was stolen away by mountain bandits! Everyone knows that!"

"That!" the little boy echoed, standing unsteadily beside his sister. "That!"

"Everyone knows . . . what exactly?" Ling Fan prompted as delicately as she could.

"My mama told me that a long time ago, before I was born, mountain bandits came to this house in the middle of the night and stole a very important piece of paper. She said her cousin Ling Fan probably woke up and tried to stop them, but she was so beautiful the bandits fell in love with her and stole her too." The little girl paused and wrinkled her nose as she looked Ling

Fan up and down. "You're not her. You don't look like a beautiful lady. You don't smell like one either."

Ling Fan didn't know whether to laugh or cry. Of course, Aunt Fei would never allow the family to be shamed by Ling Fan's act of scandalous disobedience. She would've had to concoct a way for the family to save face. But *mountain bandits*?

Ling Fan lifted her sack from her shoulder and set it carefully on the ground. She knelt down until her eyes were level with the girl's. "What's your name?"

"Fa Mei Ling, but everyone calls me Mei Mei," the girl answered.

"Do you like stories, Mei Mei?"

Mei Mei sat back on her heels. "Only if it's a good story."

"What if I told you that it wasn't mountain bandits who stole your popo's important paper, and it wasn't mountain bandits who ran off with Tam Ling Fan?"

Mei Mei's eyes widened. "Then what happened to her?"

"Well, she decided to take that paper herself and—"

"Jing! Aiya!"

Ling Fan turned in time to see an old woman sink to her knees in the dusty road just beyond the outer doors. A bundle of herbs dropped from her hand. "Jing! Jing!" she gasped. Ling Fan rushed over in time to catch her before she collapsed completely. Her aunt felt like a tiny bird in Ling Fan's arms.

"No, Aunt Fei, it's me. Ling Fan. I'm home."

∧ ∧ ∧

Aunt Fei looked as though she had aged far more than the two years Ling Fan had been gone. Her hair, once glossy black streaked with silver, was now dull gray. It looked brittle against her pillow. Her face was gaunt and lined like an apricot left out in the sun for too long. Her hands, folded on top of the quilt that Ling Fan had drawn over her, were gnarled. Blue veins stood out beneath spotted, parchment-thin skin. Still, it was Aunt Fei. Her eyes were still piercing and bright.

"You're back," Aunt Fei whispered. She raised a quivering hand and touched the tip of Ling Fan's queue as though still unsure if she was real. "I was so sure I'd lost you too."

Ling Fan ducked her head, trying but failing to blink back tears. They fell onto the silk quilt where they mingled with Aunt Fei's tears. Then the two of them were hugging and laughing and crying all at the same time until they were out of breath.

"Are you well?" Ling Fan retreated behind formality, suddenly feeling shy.

"Well enough, well enough." Fei smiled, her eyes never leaving Ling Fan's face.

"And Baba?" she asked, half afraid of the answer.

Aunt Fei closed her eyes. "Still in prison, of course. Weaker and more hopeless every time I visit."

But alive. Ling Fan let out a long breath. Just then, she heard voices in the hallway.

"What do you mean she 'fainted because of a strange boy'?" a woman's voice demanded sharply. "And why is your brother covered in mud? Aiya, Mei Mei, can't I rely on you to do anything right?"

Ling Fan straightened up just as they reached the doorway. The woman standing there was stout, swollen with another pregnancy. She had hold of Mei Mei by the elbow with her left hand; the little boy clung to his mother's leg.

"Hello, cousin!" Ling Fan moved toward her to embrace

her, but Ming stepped back quickly, pushing the children behind her. Ling Fan's arms dropped back to her side.

"Take your brother back to the house," Ming commanded.

"Why?" Mei Mei whined. "You said we could play here today!"

"Do what I tell you or I'll show you again what happens when you don't!" Ming snapped. Mei Mei grabbed her brother's plump hand and stomped away. Ming turned back to Ling Fan.

"You're back," Ming said coolly. Except for the slightest tremor in her voice, she might as well have been commenting on the freshness of melons in the market. Ling Fan hadn't expected this reaction. She had always believed that Ming, of all people, understood her heart and mind. But now here she was, staring at Ling Fan as though she were a snake that had slithered in from the garden.

"It's so good to see you, Ming," Ling Fan said. "I've missed you."

"And have you done everything you said you would in your letter? Sailed to the Gold Mountain and brought back a fortune?" Ming still spoke in her strangely dull, cool tone, but two red spots blossomed on her cheeks and spread down her neck.

"I did." Ling Fan held out her sack. "Here it is. Now Baba can come home!"

Ming stared at the sack. For a moment, Ling Fan thought Ming would break into a smile or weep in relief, but she did neither. Instead she bowed her head slightly, turned, and left without another word. Ling Fan started after her, but Aunt Fei called her back.

"I don't understand." Ling Fan felt as though she had been slapped in the face. "Why is she being like this? This money will bring Baba back home to the family. Isn't that what we all want?"

"Two years is a long time," Aunt Fei sighed. "Things have been very difficult, especially for Ming. She was the one who thought up the tale of mountain bandits abducting you. The Bao clan would've been furious if they'd learned the truth, and we would've been shamed in the eyes of the whole village. People seemed to believe our story, but still, the uproar over your disappearance was tremendous. People couldn't stop gossiping about it, especially since we were already under the cloud of your father's arrest. Ming's mother-in-law still takes every opportunity to torment Ming over our family's troubles."

Ling Fan remembered Lao Fa Seem as a mean-spirited, sour woman. It was easy to imagine her taking pleasure in making Ming miserable. Ling Fan chewed her lip. She hadn't allowed herself to dwell on what was happening back home during her sojourn in America. She had been too focused on reaching her goal. Meanwhile her aunt and cousin had been forced to face suspicion and unjust speculation every day. The enormity of the mess she'd left behind pressed down on her. She wished she could make up for the pain she had caused.

"Is it true what you told Ming?" Aunt Fei whispered. "Have you made a fortune?"

"Yes," Ling Fan said. "It's time to bring Baba home."

∧ ∧ ∧

It took more time than Ling Fan liked to make the arrangements. Negotiations, exact amounts, timetables, all eked out in painstaking detail. But Aunt Fei was relentless and, in the end, successful. Three months after Ling Fan set foot back in China, Baba was released from Peng Lu.

They waited for him at the prison entrance, and Ling Fan was secretly relieved not to be allowed in. Her memories of the decrepit hallways were still vivid enough to give her nightmares.

As she stood with Aunt Fei, she wondered what Baba would think of her weatherworn, sunburned face and rough hands. She now wore her hair in a plaited bun instead of the queue she'd grown used to, and she was dressed like Aunt Fei in a loose tunic and soft-fitting pants, but even in women's clothing she knew she stood out. It was something about how she held herself, how she walked and talked. People stared when she passed them in the road.

The sun had just touched the tip of the mountain behind the estate when a man stepped hesitantly outside.

His hair had gone snowy white, and he seemed unable to stand erect without the use of a cheap bamboo cane. He blinked as though the sunlight hurt his eyes. Ling Fan was afraid even to breathe lest a careless sigh shatter the fragile scene.

"Ba . . ."

Baba lowered his arm, and his eyes focused on Ling Fan and Aunt Fei. His chalky-gray face melted into an expression of joy as he stumbled over to them. A fierce, cold little wind blew around them, tearing at their clothes and hair, but Ling Fan wrapped her arms around her father and aunt, holding them firmly against it.

"Ling." Baba's voice was thick. "You look . . ." He lifted a hand and ran it wonderingly over the hair growing patchily on her forehead, where she'd stopped shaving it. He took in her tanned and toughened skin, her muscular arms. "Strong."

Ling Fan smiled as she dashed away the tears that ran down her chin. "I have so much to tell you."

AUTHOR'S NOTE

In 1863, construction began on the Transcontinental Railroad, a US government project that would eventually connect Sacramento, California, to Omaha, Nebraska. (Preexisting tracks ran from the East Coast to Nebraska, so the project would make it possible to travel between the East and West Coasts by train.) Two rival railroad companies, the Central Pacific Railroad Company and the Union Pacific Railroad Company, were in charge of the job.

In 1864, Central Pacific hired the first Chinese laborers to work on the western portion of the railroad. By 1865, thousands of Chinese migrant workers—known as sojourners—made up a majority of the workforce. Approximately 10,000–15,000 Chinese from the Guangdong Province of southern China worked on the railroad at any given time. By May 10, 1869, workers had laid 690 miles of track from Sacramento—through the Sierra Nevada mountain range and the deserts of Nevada and Utah—to Promontory Point, Utah, where their track met up with Union Pacific's track. The work was grueling, backbreaking, and sometimes deadly.

Despite the undeniable fact that thousands of Chinese laborers were indispensable to the creation of the greatest engineering feat of the nineteenth century, very little is known about how they lived and who they were. Primary source documentation such as letters, journals, and even employment information are largely nonexistent. Most of their names remain unknown.

I began writing *Gold Mountain* because I was in search of a face and a story for these amazing unknown workers. Who were they? What brought them halfway around the world to endure not just the brutal labor, but the derision of so many Americans? Tam Ling Fan's story is only one possibility in a sea of thousands.

The novel is first and foremost a work of fiction, but many elements of the plot are based in fact. For instance, while I've imagined the acts of sabotage that Ling Fan and other characters carry out, members of the Cheyenne and Lakota Nations did engage in deliberate disruptions of the railroad. The US government targeted numerous Indigenous nations for intimidation, forced removal, and other violence during this period, and they resisted in many ways. At the same time, members of the Pawnee Nation acted as scouts for Union Pacific, guarding the railroad from Lakota attacks. The stories of Indigenous nations' involvement with the Transcontinental Railroad, while not mine to tell, are as varied and complex as any others. More information is available in sources such as *An Indigenous Peoples' History of the United States* by Roxanne Dunbar-Ortiz.

Railroad workers also did face mishaps with gunpowder and nitroglycerin, avalanches, and cave-ins. I relied on historical accounts for details of the work at Cape Horn, Summit Tunnel, and the Ten-Mile Day on April 28, 1869, as well as the life of Hannah Strobridge. Many other details and events simply couldn't fit into the book, including the historic although unsuccessful strike for better wages organized by Chinese workers during the summer of 1867 (before Ling Fan leaves China in the novel). These stories are riveting in and of themselves, and I encourage interested readers to learn more about them through sources such as Stanford University's Chinese Railroad Workers in North America Project: http://web.stanford.edu/group/chineserailroad/cgi-bin/website/.

QUESTIONS FOR DISCUSSION

1. Why does Ling Fan feel that disguising herself as a boy and taking a railroad job in America is her best chance of earning the money to free her father? What are the alternatives and why does she reject them?

2. Ling Fan, Tan Din, and Wong Wei each have personal reasons for wanting to earn as much money in America as possible. What are the similarities and differences in how they pursue this goal?

3. What are some of the ways that Chinese workers on the railroad are treated differently than white workers?

4. How do Ah Sook and Chin Lin Sou differ as leaders? Why does Ling Fan respect Chin Lin Sou more?

5. Why do you think Ling Fan gives Wong Wei the benefit of the doubt and goes out of her way to help him so many times? Have you ever had a "friend" who behaved in ways that remind you of Wong Wei?

6. Tan Din tells Ling Fan that there is "so much more to this country than the work on this railroad." Do you agree or disagree? In what ways do Ling Fan's experiences on the railroad reflect broader American values and power structures? What aspects of America has Ling Fan *not* seen as a railroad worker?

7. Ling Fan realizes she hasn't given much thought to the impact the railroad's construction has had on Indigenous nations. Have you ever realized you were benefiting in some way from a system or a situation that harms other people? What did you do?

8. Jonathan O'Brien takes it upon himself to undermine the railroad. Do you agree or disagree with his justification for his actions? Do you think a different approach would've been more effective? Why or why not?

9. Chin Lin Sou believes that Chinese railroad workers are "making the first tiny dents into a country that is still so new, people still don't know its true contours. Surely we can find a place in a country still trying to decide what it is." In what ways has this prediction come true? In what ways has it not?

10. How has Ling Fan changed since she began her sojourn? In what ways does she remain the person she has always been?

ACKNOWLEDGMENTS

This book owes its existence to the support and encouragement of so many wonderful people. Shelley Berg, Karen Winn, Ted Robitaille, Theresea Barrett, and Jane Dion are amazing writers and invaluable critique partners. I could never have found my voice without them.

I am forever grateful for my wonderful agent, Emily Keyes, for believing in me, and for my amazing editor, Amy Fitzgerald, who has made this book so much better.

I am grateful for the 2011 SCBWI Multi-Cultural Works-In-Progress Grant. Proceeds from the grant helped fund a portion of my research.

A myriad of readers from Grub Street talked me through my early drafts: fantastic classmates as well as wonderful instructors and mentors Michelle Hoover, Karen Day, and Kate Racculia.

I could never have finished this book without the care and support of all my friends and family. Many thanks to Matt Lehman for giving his complete support to all my projects, no matter how big or small.

Special thanks go to the staff of Bristol Lounge, especially host Mehmet Ozturk for always welcoming us with a smile and a glass of delicious chardonnay. I look forward to the day we can return in person and raise a glass to you.

ABOUT THE AUTHOR

Betty G. Yee was born and raised in Massachusetts. She spent much of her early life reimagining stories or writing sequels to them. Betty has taught elementary school for over twenty years. When she's not teaching, reading, or writing, she enjoys traveling, biking, and eating french fries. She lives with her two bossy cats, Zara and Piper.